It's Always Been You

Elin Williams Dastrup

ISBN: 9781611661507
Copyright © 2020

Y Mountain Press, all rights reserved

Cover design by Brooke Larson

byustore.com and amazon.com

Follow at:

Facebook: www.facebook.com/noblesonofgod

Instagram: @elindastrup

Reviews for "It's Always Been You"

"Powerful. Courageous. A real page turner. Inspiring. Real. Gritty. Occasionally mind-blowing. This book left me thinking long and hard about the process of betrayal and finding one's self, finding peace, and finding hope. For someone who is going through the middle of painful infidelity, or anyone who wants to understand the process of one's family's journey, this book provides an empathetic, sincere and hopeful perspective on healing painful wounds."— Emma McAdam, LMFT, creator of Therapy in a Nutshell

"'It's Always Been You' resonates with vulnerability and sincerity. A powerful reminder as the characters share their messy and metamorphic journey to find the healing power of love and the Atonement. Their determination to hold onto each other, instead of pride and pain, is breathtaking. Is it possible that the privilege of being soulmates might come with the power to save a soul?"—Barb Smith, life coach, community advocate

"It was refreshing to read how one couple worked through trauma and poor decisions. It gives hope to others who might be struggling with some of the same issues of sexual trauma and addiction. I will recommend this book to others with the idea of it giving them hope and some guidelines for recovery and a healthier relationship." — Mary Jane Nelson, MSW, LCSW

"'It's Always Been You' is one of the most daring and sincere books we have read. The story weaves the despair and the hope, the light and the dark together in such a way that allows us to see who we each really are as beloved children of Heavenly Parents, regardless of our choices or situation. Life is not an easy road, and this book offers a real view into one of the very painful wedges that often destroys a marriage and a soul and shows the journey in a way that can bring tremendous hope."—David and Tamara Gilliand, marriage educators, entrepreneurs, and parents of eight daughters

"This is a story that is true to life. Having worked with hundreds of couples over the years suffering with betrayal trauma and different forms of sexual addiction, I found this book really hitting a sore button that needed to be told. Sex addiction, especially porn addiction, is like a terrible tsunami plaguing the world and destroying individuals and families. There is nothing more profound than hope. I highly recommend this book."—James B. Lewis, LCSW, CLC, author of "Guide to Recovery From Addictive Arousal & Sexually Compulsive Behaviors" and "6 Principles for Achieving Personal Balance"

"A beautifully written story of infidelity, forgiveness and love that surprised the intellect and captured my soul. I can't wait to read it a third time."—Gina Hemingway, mother and teacher

"I took a quick look just to see what the book was all about. Hours later, and well past my bedtime, I finally put it down. I liked the Q & A at the end, because I did have those questions and they were all covered. The book was raw and emotional, and the intricacies of relationships were wonderfully written. To read your story of love of our Heavenly Father begs the question, 'Do you believe in repentance? Really, do you?' An amazing read!"—Kelly Graham, counselor and life coach

"This book is a good reminder that we always have a choice, even when it seems like all of our choices have been taken from us. How we choose to react can make an impossible situation evolve into something more deep and meaningful than what we started with. This story could have gone so many different ways and by the end, I even surprised myself for what I was rooting for."—Jon and Lindsey Geertsen, parents

For our daughters, Kayla and Courtney.

Thank you for loving wholeheartedly.

Preface

"However late you think you are, however many chances you think you have missed, however many mistakes you feel you have made or talents you think you don't have, or distance from home and family and God you feel you have traveled, I testify that you have not traveled beyond the reach of divine love. It is not possible for you to sink lower than the infinite light of Christ's Atonement shines" (Jeffrey R. Holland, "The Laborers in the Vineyard," *Ensign*, May 2012, 33).

This book came about because of a spiritual impression. I had been praying about pursuing professional opportunities, and the answer I received was, *Write a book*. I was reluctant—authors abound, and publishing offers do not. And what would I write about, anyway? *Write about what you know—infidelity and redemption*. No, there are a zillion of those kinds of books. *Listen to me. Write about it, but from his point of view.*

I was stunned. How could I go through that, remembering what happened, conjuring up where he had been and what he had done? How could I open his wounds again? A complete story would have to include abuse, addiction, infidelity, and betrayal trauma. I wrestled with what that would look like and how to do it delicately. Yikes! So I'd have to fictionalize it, for sure... When I finally had a rough outline in my mind, I told my husband about my impression. And he said, "You should try." So I wrote a few chapters. The tough ones. He read all fifty pages out loud to me. He looked me in the eye and said, "You have to write this."

As we have shared each draft of the manuscript with others, time after time we have heard, "This happened to me too, but I thought I was alone." We are confident that you will identify with many parts of Joseph and Paul's stories. We have also had some emotional reactions to the first section. That section is intended to introduce you to the main characters, and a portion of it is unsettling. Please be aware that it is there, but it is in no way graphic or glorified. Its presence serves a purpose.

Throughout our journey, as reflected in the following story, we were met with love and support from family, friends, and neighbors, which in turn amazed us and reminded us that God is good to all His children. The thought of it takes my breath away! We pray that you find that same caliber of support in your journey.

I welcome you into my family room. Pull up a chair, and let me tell you one such story of God's amazing love.

Part I:
Joseph and Paul

Joseph

November 2009

"Lower, lower. Like the Four Corners area, but don't tickle."

Rachel moved to the lower right of my back and scratched.

"Now go up to Box Elder County. Big circles. Yeah. That's good. Maybe down to Tooele County. Hm. Nope, the Great Salt Lake. Yeah, that's it. The whole lake. Big circles."

As Rachel scratched, she began our nightly debriefing session. "I got a call from Mary today. They're thinking about coming for Memorial Day weekend right after their kids get out of school. I know it's still seven months out, but you know how my sister and I like to plan. If they push a trip later into the summer, it'll be tricky to work around camps and youth conference."

I nodded. "I could get a couple days off. It'll be good to see your sister. Now just rub all across the north. Harder. That's good. Would they stay here, or at your mom and dad's?"

She rubbed. "Don't know. We didn't get that far. How was your day?"

"My day was tough. More stuff piled on my plate. I've got more than I can do. Now rub Brigham City."

Rachel zeroed in on the spot between my shoulder blades and said, "That reminds me—when is camp for the Young Men next year? I heard something about the stake doing it and calling it 'Helaman's Camp.' What do you have to do? Just show up? I haven't seen a date yet, and families need to plan their summers. Are you going to have your secretary send that out? I can help you, if you need it." I didn't answer right away. She sensed her barrage of questions was bordering on overwhelming, so she withdrew my need to answer by saying, "Sorry. I'm just thinking out loud."

Rachel was good at task organization, and I learned early in our marriage that her skill was invaluable. But at the moment, it was all too much to think about, so I simply replied, "I think the stake will announce it at the beginning of the year. Can you rub Wyoming more? And Daggett County. That's tight today."

"Sure." She worked my right shoulder.

I have loved Rachel my whole life. She *is* my life. We met in high school, and she turned into the best friend I always needed. I soon felt the more-than-friends attraction. It was seemingly unexplainable when Rachel began to warm to the idea. She pictured herself with an urbane professor, and I am not that. I am a small-town farm boy. When she met me, I had grease under my fingernails and cowboy boots on. It's a good thing she didn't meet me on a dating website. I can hear her saying, "My turn-ons are trips to the beach and poetry. My turn-offs are rough hands, short hair, and flannel shirts." She never would've chosen me. But it turned out that our differences complemented each other, and we became high-school sweethearts. She made me want to be a better man.

I'm the youngest of twelve in my family. My parents named me after Joseph of Egpyt. There were lots of jokes about my Technicolor dreamcoat and being the spoiled favorite child. I was anything but spoiled. I constantly compared myself to my peers, and it was clear I worked harder than any kid I knew. Being on a farm and doing my part to provide for our big family meant there were endless chores. Life was tough, but I also *learned* more than any kid I knew. I was taught how to pull an engine and pull a calf and everything in between. And I have stories about it all.

Even though I was from a big family, I didn't feel true companionship until Rachel. I became the center of her world, which was just fine with me. Not many teenaged girls would look beyond the things they didn't like, but she saw goodness in me and drew it out. She told me how smart I was. She was incredibly sweet and kind, and her attention made me feel unique. Needed. For our first real date, I asked her to the Harvest Ball. I remember wrapping my arms around her, swaying to the music. Her sweater was soft and fuzzy, her hair smelled like lavender, and I felt like I was falling into heaven with my arms wide open.

Rachel wrote to me all during my mission. When I got home, I felt a strong sense of equal companionship when we were together. We had already been talking about marriage, but this confirmed it for me. She was my best friend, perfect for me in every way, and I needed her with me for the rest of my life. She had always planned on serving a mission, but after five years of dating, we decided life would be much happier married to each other sooner rather than later.

And Rachel has always been good at Utah geography, which my left side now particularly needed. "Scratch Delta. Hinckley. Holden. Fillmore. Delta. Oak City. Delta. Delta. Okay, the whole Sevier Desert. Awesome. Thanks. Ready for bed?"

She yawned. "Yeah. I've gotta go shopping tomorrow. Any special requests?"

I yawned. "Get me some of those ready-made salads. I'd like to eat healthier lunches instead of going out so much, but I also need to eat fast. So those are perfect." We settled into bed, and Rachel scooted her toes over against me to warm up.

I was proud of this bed. I had built it with Josh—my brother from another mother since college. When we ended up fifteen hundred miles away from home working at the same company outside of Chicago, we became *real* family to each other. Our wives became great friends and our kids played together, and having each other helped us not feel so homesick. Once, Josh's wife, Jesse, found a huge deal on fancy new mattresses. So Josh and I spent a couple weekends in his garage, making fresh sawdust, creating bedframes. We started calling it sawdust therapy, and we assured our wives we needed frequent sessions.

I could tell Rachel was almost asleep. I, however, could not sleep so easily. I always had a million thoughts crashing around in my mind, and when the room was dark and quiet, they were a relentless bombardment...

The stake hadn't exactly been clear about what they wanted from the ward Young Men's presidencies for youth conference. What should I plan on? Am I in charge of my ward's food? Activities? Transportation? What should I have my counselors do? Are they even going?

Work. I'm up to my eyeballs at work. I have more than one man can do. I'm not ready for the meeting tomorrow. How do I fill up thirty minutes convincing them to spend ten million bucks to move a production line to a different building? Why can't I just say, "Trust me, it makes sense. Do it"? Only half of the Power-Point slides are ready. I'll have to finish the rest before 9:00 in the morning. No pressure—just the boss's boss's boss will be there, and my recommendation is going to the CEO. I don't even want to think about next week. Why won't the guys at facility management return my calls? I feel like I'm doing this huge project alone.

And the car is leaking oil. It's making a mess on the concrete. I hate that. Aw, dang it—leaks. The tile has got to be replaced in the kids' shower, which means ripping out the whole bathroom. Or does it? Yeah, it does. It should be done before Mary and her family get here for Memorial Day. So do I try to save the baseboard? Or just replace it at the same time?

Relentless. To calm my mind, I concentrated on Rachel holding my arm, which she did every single night, and I listened to her breathe.

Rachel stirred, squeezed my arm, and mumbled in her sleep, "I love you, honey." She loved me even when she was unconscious.

"I love you too," I whispered.

In the morning—I assumed it was morning—my alarm woke me up. Although, could it wake me if I never truly fell asleep? I willed myself out of bed. I have functioned on very little sleep my whole life. My mornings were spent in solitude since Rachel was not a morning person. I would have loved to spend a few minutes with her, but it was not the schedule we were used to. She didn't need to get up with me. There were plenty of other things I loved about her. I grabbed my gym bag and headed out while it was still dark, closing the door softly behind me.

Paul

I get bounced around at work a lot. Today I'm in a cubicle that isn't mine, staring at a guy's pictures of a big fish he caught on some boat and a party where everyone is raising a glass. But the cubicle is empty, and I've got reports to do, so I'm borrowing his desk and his chair. This is the glory of working company-wide, consulting at all the production plants. I know everyone; I know no one. My computer bag is my office, and the phone on my hip is my desk phone.

Today is especially rough. I'm feeling alone, and I'm staring at a big, ugly, dead fish. I feel no motivation to do anything. Nobody in this office knows me. They only call me by name because it is emblazoned on my safety uniform.

I feel like I've spent most of my life alone. I'm not especially loveable. I'm almost forty-eight years old, and as I look back on my life, it's clear that I'm a failure. I lucked out that The Wife is awesome and The Kids are great. Somehow, they think I'm a good guy, and that makes life bearable. But I'm terrified of the day they find out how wrong they are.

Sitting here, staring at that stupid fish picture, seeing this guy with the smile on his face, I wonder, have I ever been that happy? Why can't I be this guy? His life seems pretty easy. Has he ever had anything harder to do than fish and go to parties?

This office smells like a damp basement. I can't breathe.

I go to very dark places in my mind. I can't stop the memories. Lately, it's this one, and it's loud. I was six. The cool kid in the neighborhood was twelve. He had spent a few months hanging out with me—showing me the new stereo in his room, letting me shoot his new BB gun, feeding me candy he had raided from his kitchen cupboard. One day, he showed up in my front yard with a magazine in his hand. He said, "Hey! Meet me downstairs in your room. I found something!" He seemed really excited, so I left my chores and met him in my room.

He opened this magazine. There was a woman on the page,

and she wasn't wearing a shirt. She sat there with a look in her eye I had never seen before. I have sisters and a mom, but I have never seen that look in a woman's eye. It was curious to me. Very curious. She was looking straight at me. Into my eyes. Into my head. I felt like I didn't have a shirt on either.

The cool kid flipped to another page, and there was another woman who wasn't wearing any clothes at all, but she was leaning against a wall, so I couldn't see her front, but I could see the curves of the back part. I had never seen anything so smooth, and that shape was very intriguing to me. And she had that look in her eye too, which went straight into my eyes. Into my head. I felt like I was leaning with her against the wall. My heartbeat had never been so loud in my ears before.

When I saw the cool kid from across the yard a few days later with the magazine in his hand, he motioned to me, and I knew what he meant. We went downstairs to my room and sat on the floor against the wall. He turned right to a page that had a different picture than those I had seen a few days earlier. The lady was pretty and was wearing a lot of makeup, but for the first time I saw her whole front. I asked the cool kid a couple of questions, and he told me some answers. We flipped through more pages, taking our time, looking, saying few words. Each lady looked straight into my head.

Fast forward a few months later, and the cool kid was meeting me regularly in my room. Sometimes he brought a new magazine. Sometimes he didn't bring anything. He would tell me what to do, and how to do it. And a few months after that, he told me other things he wanted me to try, and I did it.

When I was twelve, the cool kid stopped "visiting" me because he got his mission call and left town. We never spoke again.

My childhood was discovering a world full of things I didn't know, and I was schooled. Indoctrinated. I learned that when you're sad, there's one way to feel better, even if it's just a quick dose that doesn't last. I learned that when you're bored, there's something interesting to do. I learned that when you're tired, there's one way to relax. I learned that when no one listens, there's a lady who looks into your head, and she is very interested in everything about you. My thorough education was that there is one medication, and it takes care of whatever it was that brought you there.

But I was just a kid. I couldn't possibly have understood any of the powerful, contradicting emotions. I felt horrid. I felt inquisitive. I felt shame. I felt excitement. I wanted more. I wanted to stop. There were only two things I knew for sure, every day, since the age of six—I knew I could tell no one, and I knew I was broken.

Now I am an adult, and I have finally figured out what happened. My brain created indelible paths of dopamine-laced self-hatred; my body found this behavior as essential as breathing. I found a medication that had become physically necessary to function emotionally.

Why have those things been coming up now? Why can't I push them away? Why can't I just forget about it forever? I've got phone calls to make, reports to draft, and I am sitting here staring at a stranger with a fish and feeling… broken.

I decide to change my surroundings—maybe that will help. I close my laptop and head to the break room. Maybe I'm hungry. I heard a rumor that someone brought a birthday cake to share today, and I'm in desperate need of a Mountain Dew.

I sit down to an obscene amount of cake on my little plate when I notice Joseph. That's the name showing on his work ID badge. He doesn't seem to judge me as he looks at my heaping plate of blue frosting. The picture on his badge shows a smile on his face, and it looks genuine.

I decide to break the silence, and with my fork in midair, I openly confess, "I love it when somebody has a birthday."

He smiles, and we sit there amiably eating cake. He seems like a friendly guy. I had some friends in college. They were good guys. I miss them. The Wife says it's not easy for guys to make friends, and she's right. If you don't drink or watch a lot of sports, there's not much to do together. I spend my evenings with The Wife, helping The Kids with homework, dabbling in my own projects. I spend a bit of time on whatever church assignment I have. Not much time left to hang out with the guys, even if I wanted to.

Between bites, Joseph says, "This is pretty good cake," and then, "What are you working on today?"

He speaks like he knows me. I answer by abbreviating my dismal workday. "They want to move the production line to another building, and I've got to find out if it's feasible to make room for it."

Joseph perks up. "Hey! That's my area! I've got ideas about that. You're the guy I need to talk to!"

I work with Joseph for the rest of the afternoon. And that's how most days go for me. I sit until I can't sit any longer, and then things seem to fall into place to get a few things done. I'm glad to feel busy, and I'm glad to feel needed.

And today, I'm really glad Joseph found me eating cake.

Joseph

Rachel stood at the table and gave directions. "Okay, Hannah, you clear the plates and fill the dishwasher. Sarah, let's play Hi-Hi-Ho."

Sarah walked over to the fridge, opened the door, and assumed the catching position. Rachel picked up the mustard bottle, called, "Hi! Hi! Ho!" and gently threw it to Sarah. Sarah put it in the door of the fridge. Rachel picked up the package of leftover hamburger buns and threw it high. "Hi! Hi! Ho!" Wild, careless throw, but easy catch. I loved watching this. Rachel picked up the plastic mayo bottle—not glass, never glass—and called, "Hi! Hi! Ho!" Sarah caught it and put it away. Everything throwable was thrown and caught. "Sarah, now clear the rest of the table. Thanks, doll-face."

We have never made a big deal out of family home evening. We don't have a chart that rotates prayers, songs, and the lesson. We don't have a snack. We don't make a big to-do. That's just not our style. But every Monday, we talk and laugh after dinner for a while, have scripture time and a prayer, and then go about our evening. It's not much different from our normal evening routine, but we sing a song on Mondays, so it counts. Watching Hi-Hi-Ho gave me an idea for our lesson. I went back and got the glass ketchup bottle out of the fridge. After the food and dishes were cleared, we sat back down at the table and sang a song.

"Look at this ketchup bottle here in the middle of the table," I said as I moved the bottle around like a chess piece. "This is you. You have a lot of choices in your life. You can move forward, backward, or around in circles. You're pretty happy here in the middle of the table. Life is good. Lots of places to go. What if you move closer to the edge?" I made a dramatic move and placed the bottle about a foot from the edge of the table. "How much freedom do you have to move around now?"

"Less." Hannah, our quiet and studious middle child, was a senior in high school. "You can still move backward, but not as far forward.

"Right. I can also move side to side with no problem," I danced the bottle around, "and I can always go back to the middle of the table where I was happy. But I've gotta be careful how far I go…" I zoomed the bottle. "…forward." I perched it right at the edge. "What are my choices now?"

Sarah, fourteen, who had adored me since the day she was born, said, "Well, obviously you can't move forward anymore. Just sideways or backwards."

"True. But notice that I've been on a trajectory, and I seem determined to get to the edge. Now I'm here. What do I do? It's pretty dangerous here on the edge."

"Turn around. Repent." The girls thought they knew where this was going.

I pushed the bottle off the edge.

I couldn't have scripted it better. It hit the tile floor awkwardly, the glass shattered, and a blood-red mess splattered on the floor, on the legs of the chairs, and on the table legs. And dang, some on my pants, and Rachel pointed at stray splatters on the cupboards ten feet away.

"Dad!" Hannah was shocked. "Now we have to clean it up!"

"Wait! Hold on. That's the point I'm trying to make. Sometimes in life, people make choices that make a mess. We are supposed to correct our trajectory before we get there—yes, repent and turn around—but sometimes the edge is too alluring, the pull too strong. I don't think anyone ever means to dive off the edge. But it happens." We stared at the mess. "Do I need help getting cleaned up?"

Sarah got it. I could see it in her eyes. "We need Jesus."

"We do." I made eye contact with both of my daughters. "He will pick us up, fix us, make us clean, fill us, and set us back on the table to try again. He doesn't mind the mess. He loves to help us. Think about it—He literally lives for it. It is His mission and His purpose." But then another thought dawned on me. "Hey. Who else can help us get cleaned up?"

"I guess whoever is willing to get messy," Sarah said.

"Like…"

Sarah wasn't sure what the right answer was. "Our family, I guess?"

I nodded, but I wanted to make her think harder. "But they didn't create this problem. You did. You fell off, or maybe jumped off, the spiritual cliff. Is your family obligated to help clean it up?"

Sarah wanted to give the right answer. "Ummm… yes? Wait… no?"

Hannah gestured to the red-splattered floor. "You'd have to love somebody a lot to want to get mixed up in this mess."

"Exactly. Girls, no matter when, no matter where, no matter how hard…" I paused. "You are not alone. If you find yourself in a place where you've made a giant mistake, God is right there to help you get clean and whole again. And maybe 'obligated' is the wrong word, but isn't that what your family does? If you ever find yourself getting too close to the edge, or falling, never be ashamed to ask each other for help. That's what families do. Plus, Mom and I are pretty smart." I winked at Rachel.

I told them to sit still while I cleaned up as many glass shards as I could, and then I brought them their shoes and some rags. We spent ten minutes chasing down the splatters with rags in hand. It required care. Ketchup doesn't wipe easily because it smears and it's sticky, and I had to keep reminding the girls to be sure to watch for glass. The parable was complete.

After we were satisfied that we had eradicated the kitchen floor of anything sharp or dirty, we read scriptures, had a closing prayer, gave hugs and kisses all around, and scattered to do homework and other important things, like watch TV. While I dozed in front of some PBS nature program, Rachel wrote to Abby, who had just been transferred from Bend, Oregon, to Eugene and needed some motherly advice about her new companion.

I was getting ready to brush my teeth at bedtime when Rachel hugged me from behind. "I keep thinking about your family home evening lesson. You are brilliant! How did you come up with it? I told Abby about it in my email. She could probably use it in a discussion, although it would be best not to actually splatter ketchup at an investigator's house."

I smiled. "It just came to me. I wanted the girls to know that every choice is important. It's important to stay on the table." I replaced the cap on the toothpaste. "The Atonement of Jesus Christ helps them when they fall and make a giant mess, and so do we."

"It was a great visual. Very sensory. And I have an extra ketchup bottle in the pantry, and it's plastic, so we all win."

We prayed and got into bed. I sighed when Rachel took hold of my arm, and I had an overwhelming sense of joy as I thought about our daughters. "Rach, sometimes it's surreal to me. This is what we've worked for all these years. They like us. They believe us."

She stifled a yawn and whispered back, "Sarah hangs on your every word. She likes me just fine, but you are her hero. Hannah tells me everything, but she knows I'm just going to turn around and tell you, and she likes it that way. And have you noticed how Abby's letters have changed over the last year? Our stubborn child is putting into practice all the things we taught her. We're lucky."

"Yeah, but we've worked on it. You've always been about communication. They're teenagers, and they *still* look forward to Rock and Talk with you every night. That was *your* brilliant idea fifteen years ago." I took her hand, placed it on my chest, and covered it with my larger hand. "I'm positive they listen for your footsteps coming down the hall to their bedroom door. I've sneaked a peek while you sit on their bed, rubbing their feet or playing with their hair, asking them questions, or just listening to their day. I love seeing that. They know they are valued and loved. It makes them actually want to tell you things." I leaned over to kiss her. "I think it's important that we've never shielded them from anything. We just talk. We've all learned that from you. I love you, Rach."

She kissed me back. A lot. Peace is made of these moments.

Paul

The light from the window casts shadows above our bed. I watch the distorted black trees sway on our ceiling. The Wife has been asleep for a while.

> Paul: I'm married. I'm just looking for an escape for tonight.
>
> Amy: That's disgusting. Get a life.

From the time I was about twelve, I was assigned to work with my uncle, Sam. Sam was bitter, angry, and demanding. I loathed working with him, but he needed my help on his construction crew, and my mom and dad would send me with him. I learned everything about home construction from Sam, but my biggest education was that I was a failure.

The cool kid in the neighborhood had just left on his mission, so I was already mired in self-hatred and guilt. But then I started working for Sam, and he let me know that I was a poor excuse for a human being. I knew Sam had a huge burden on his shoulders, and I was well aware that he was taking it all out on me.

My first assignment was as the "go-fer" for him and his crew, to maximize their time. I tried to be observant to keep nails and screws stocked, electric hand tools prepped, lumber and supplies hauled to each area, wire and pipe pre-measured for easier installation. I thought that for a twelve-year-old, I was doing pretty well. Sam didn't. It started with muttering to himself, but really toward me, about how worthless I was. And it progressed to calling me names, cursing me out, and threatening me. And then he would backhand me when I was slow with the nails or kick me on my way to grab a board. It was especially bad when it was just him and me. What could I do? He was my uncle. It wasn't like I could hit him back or yell at him.

But more than that, I knew he was telling the truth. I *was* worthless. I was slow, stupid, useless—a waste of good air. I was good for absolutely no one. The cool kid in the neighborhood had taught me that.

Time passed and experience progressed, and I knew as much as anyone on his crew, plus I was faster. I took on huge responsibilities and was indispensable on every job. But he didn't pay me—I was family. The least he could do was thank me, but I didn't get that either.

One day, when I was eighteen or so, he was particularly angry at something and he began to hit me. It dawned on me then that I could've knocked him out cold and walked away. I was now much bigger and stronger than he was, but he was my uncle. I decided that he couldn't beat me forever, so I just waited for it to end. I leaned against the work truck with my arms in front of my face and took it. I think my parents knew what was happening, but we never talked about it. Sam would call for me, they would tell me to go, and I would go.

> Paul: I'm married, but don't let that stop u...
>
> Blair: So wut. im married. Wanna meet?
>
> Paul: No meeting, just chatting.
>
> Blair: Can I get a pic? ;)
>
> Paul: Just sent it. Can I see u?
>
> Blair: Sending.

I was a teenager. The girl across the street was lonely and desperate for love, and I knew exactly how that felt. But I had no interest at all, other than she was available and willing. After a while, my mom figured out something was going on, and she told me to stay away from her. I knew I should, so I started making excuses and didn't go over as often. But the girl thought she was in love, so she started calling and coming to our house. I would step outside the back door so my mom could truthfully say, "I don't think he's here." It took a couple of years for the girl to quit calling. I hated myself for doing that to her.

> Paul: I'm married, but looking for adventure.
>
> Carrie: Im full of adventure
>
> Paul: Tell me more.

There was a corner store in our one-horse town where I grew up. They had a small video section. Beneath the cover of night, I would walk half a mile to the store with a screwdriver in hand. There was a back window that was old and loose, and by removing a few screws, I could let myself into the store. I "borrowed" a few videos once in a while. Not all of their videos were bad, but enough of them were. I would replace the window, walk home, and watch one on our only TV, which was in the front room. It was just a few steps down the hall from my parents' room, so it was brazen on my part, but it was my only choice. I ran the risk.

When the movie was over, I would walk back to the store and replace the video so no one missed it. I constantly worried about what I would say to my mom or dad if they found me gone in the middle of the night—or worse, found me in front of the living room TV watching dirty videos—but they never did. The momentary rush was worth it. No one ever found out. I was good at covering my tracks. More than feeling tired in the morning, I felt bad. No surprise there.

Nighttime is usually when the memories kick in. The sadness is fierce. I know the easiest way to escape. I've been doing it off and on for years, but I started looking at stuff online again almost a year ago. I'd made it ten years "sober" somehow, but I always find myself back here. It's much easier now than breaking into a corner store when I was a kid—it's in my house, anytime I want. Any kind I want. This time, I find myself supplementing my fix with chatting. I have been leaving the bed and going to the den. I close the door and the curtains, and I find the medicine I seek.

> Paul: I'm married, but I'm lonely tonight. U have any ideas?

> Dot: Go to bed, get a life. Single people looking for rela-
> tionships only, LOSER.

I'm a logical guy. I know it doesn't make sense to turn to the very thing that makes me sad, but this is what I do. This is the only way I know how to feel better, even just for a little while. And I would give anything to feel better for a little while. Anything. I'm so deeply sad, so utterly full of hatred for myself, so buried in shame, I just need medicine. This isn't permanent. I'll get what I need, and then I'll stop. I've stopped lots of times.

> Paul: Is anyone out there?
>
> Emilee: What can I do for you?
>
> Paul: I don't even know. Can we talk for a while?
>
> Emilee: Tonight, I'm not here for talk.
>
> Paul: You know what? I'm not either...

I'm also in love with The Wife. So in love. I told her about my childhood pornography problem, and she knows I've slipped a few times. Once, she came home from a weekend at her parents' house, and she put in an old video for The Kids to watch while she unpacked. The video wouldn't track correctly in the machine. She turned to me and said, "You've been watching dirty videos!" She had meant that I had used tapes with unclean surfaces that gummed up the heads in the VCR. But as soon as she said it, there was a big moment of truth, and it got ugly between us for a while. Since then, our agreement has been to be honest about being tempted.

How could I tell her this? I don't think she could take it. I feel like my only choice right now is to protect her from this part of me, and that means hiding my identity from the people I meet. I've been telling subtle versions of the truth—I was abused as a kid, I love The Wife but I'm trying to find myself, I just need an escape.

But lately, I've started to venture out from my own life story. I'm in a pseudoworld where I can be anyone, so I have begun to tell a story about someone I'm not, a fantasy guy I am curious to be. I'm finding it absolutely liberating to be someone else for a while. It truly is the medication I crave. So the new narrative is that I graduated from college as an engineer but became an EMT because I like saving people, I have had a couple affairs, and I am cryptic about experimenting in my encounters. When I enter that world, it is so much better than the life I have been living. It's exciting. It's fascinating. It's dangerous and daring. I meet all kinds, and I decide where it goes. It can go anywhere, innocent or... not.

Paul: I'm married, but I'm looking for friends.

Fiona: Same. Looking for friends, I mean. Recently divorced.

Paul: How was your day?

Fiona: Pretty good. Busy. I run a pediatric dental office. Scared kids come in all the time, so I get to draw cartoons and bring out the puppets.

Paul: That's so nice! Anything interesting happen today at the office?

I have always prided myself on being a good provider. I grew up poor, and I always figured that I could avoid that as an adult because I have a pretty extensive skill set. My last job, though, I found out how much apple-polishing you have to do to climb the corporate ladder. I got so annoyed when people were promoted right past me, and it wasn't because they did a better job than I did—it's because they did what they needed to do to make the boss look good. I wasn't willing to do that. I wanted to be recognized for my hard work, plain and simple. I was no good at the game.

> Paul: I'm married. Gigi... Is that ur real name?
>
> Gigi: u can call me anything u want ;)
>
> Paul: Tell me about ur best night ever, Gigi.

So, I quit my job. I started a company on my own. It scared The Wife because she likes security, but I had to leave corporate America. I got my contractor's license and found a couple of jobs. Things were going fairly well. I feel strongly about precision and perfection, and my clients were pleased. I got referrals and did a few more jobs. I worked on my own, and I enjoyed the solitude. After spending years jumping through the hoops of job performance reviews and stats and reports, I now felt an amazing sense of accomplishment from the sweat on my brow. I liked setting my own hours, and yes, being my own boss. It was liberating, fulfilling, and satisfying.

> Paul: I'm married. I'm also looking for a little something extra on the side, right here, right now.
>
> Holly: Go tell your wife you're a jerk.

But it wasn't paying the bills. All my hard work, all the labor of my own hands wasn't enough to provide for my family. *I could not take care of my own family.* My talents were useless. This was yet another example of how I'm not good enough. I am such a huge disappointment to myself, to everybody. I am a waste of air.

> Paul: I'm married. Tonight I'm lonely and need someone to talk to.
>
> Izzy: What's going on?
>
> Paul: Just lonely. What about w/ u
>
> Izzy: Had a long day so watching movies
>
> Paul: What movie

> Izzy: Ironman robert downey jr is sexy I dig his goatee
>
> Paul: I have a goatee
>
> Izzy: Ur married, ya?
>
> Paul: Y. U?
>
> Izzy: I was ive gave up on guys
>
> Paul: What happened?
>
> Izzy: U rlly want to know
>
> Paul: Y

I had to swallow my pride and go back to corporate America with the job performance reviews and the promotion games and the endless reports, for the health insurance and the 401k and the salary. The Wife was sad for me, but the reality was, we needed the financial security. As I said, I'm a logical guy.

> Paul: I'm married I'm here looking for a good time
>
> Jezebel: I just made a prity hot video w/my ex, id luv to show u
>
> Paul: Wanna send it to me? Or just describe it for me.
>
> Jezebel: I uploaded it go watch n tell me what u think

I love The Wife. She has stood by me through everything, but she's tired, and I don't just mean that she's in our room sleeping. Life has been hard. I feel like the only thing I'm good at lately is disappointing her. That's all on me, though. I feel guilty for what I'm doing. I know I'm lying to her. And I'm also unbearably sad.

> Paul: I'm married. I want to get lost for a while.
>
> Kyra: You're married? I hope you figure out your life. You don't belong here.

Paul: I know I don't. I'm just really going through tough times. I'm here because I need a friend.

Kyra: I'm actually here to find a friend or two. What's going on?

Paul: I feel lonely. Life is hard sometimes.

Kyra: Same. I've got a pretty good life, but sometimes, everything just gets to me and I get sad.

Paul: Me too. That's exactly how I feel.

Kyra: School is rough.

Paul: School? Are you a teacher?

Kyra: Um, no. I'm in college.

Paul: What are you studying?

Kyra: English lit. I like reading.

Paul: I've never enjoyed reading. My dad told me I should read more.

Kyra: My dad too. Are you in college?

Paul: I graduated a long time ago. I studied engineering, but I'm an EMT now.

Kyra: So, you're a smart guy?

Paul: Sometimes, but I do dumb things I know I shouldn't.

Kyra: We all do. Hey, I gotta go. Catch ya later.

Tonight, as I slip out of bed and into the den, I have a purpose. I started chatting with a woman named Lila last night, and I want to revisit the experience.

Paul: Hey, u there?

Lila: Ya what took u so long? I been here 15 min waiting for u i missed u werent sure if u were coming

Paul: I had to wait for The Wife to fall asleep

Lila: I cant believe ur married. If ur so miserable, why don't u leave

Paul: She doesn't make me miserable I do that all on my own

Lila: I wish i could make it bettr

Paul: Me too. Last night helped a lot thx for being there for me

Lila: Anytime. I liked it alot to. My life is prtty terrible n i could rlly use a fiend right now

Lila: *FRIEND Lol!

Paul: haha Whats going on?

Lila: My ex is out of jail n wants to see me

Paul: Do you still have feelings for him

Lila: Hes the father of my kids, thats it

Paul: What does he want

Lila: I think hes lonely. Not much girl action in jail LMAO

Paul: Do you want him back

Lila: Not ever! Hes not like u

Paul: U dont know me that well

Lila: I know that ur a nice guy who just needs a friend

Paul: ...I guess

Lila: U guess??

Paul: I dont feel like a nice guy. Ive got a past

Lila: Dont we all

Paul: Whats ur past

Lila: Well, my ex getting out of jail says alot. I hooked up with some guys I met on here

Paul: Like, hooked up?

Lila: Ya there was a guy in salt lake that I was hoping was serious, but he was just using me :(

Paul: I'm sorry. That must feel horrible

Lila: Y. Im a sngl mom just trying to make a good life for me n my kids. Men r jerks

Paul: Most men are

Lila: R u a jerk? Whats ur past?

Paul: ...

Lila: U there?

Paul: I guess I am a jerk look what we did last night

Lila: We dont know each other. We arent in the same room. Its just... feeling better... together ;)

Paul: Oh crap Wife just noticed im gone.

Lila: Can i txt u? I need ur phone number

Paul: I gotta go... cant txt its a work phone. Just leave me a msg here

Lila: TTYL

I keep thinking about Joe, the birthday cake guy at work. I need a friend. But we have little in common. That picture on his ID badge tells me everything I need to know—he's got that confident smile, that million-dollar twinkle in his eye, that pressed button-down shirt that exudes a life of ease. It's probably for the best. I'm a mess. I'm sure if I were more like Joe, I'd be so much better than I am. But I'm nothing like him.

I'm broken.

Joseph

My cell phone rang in the middle of the night. It was my oldest brother. "Hey, Joe."

I was still trying to wake up and find my voice. "Hi. Is everything okay?"

"Sorry for waking you. I wanted to let you know that our dear mother has gone home."

I gulped hard. The news was unexpected, but not surprising. She hadn't been well. My voice cracked. "When's the funeral? What do you need me to do?"

At the word "funeral," Rachel sat up and reached for me.

He answered, "The funeral will be next weekend. We wanted to give extra time for everybody to come. I'll see you when you can get here. Love you, brother."

I gave my love and thanks in return and told him I would be in touch in the morning.

I didn't have to tell Rachel. She just knew. She turned on the lamp and got the tissue box. We propped ourselves up in bed. Rachel held me, and we wept together. Rachel loved my mother as much as I did. My mom was a strong and gentle force of nature who brought me into this life. She taught me the gospel through her untiring example. I always felt like I held a special place in her heart, but I knew each of my siblings would say the same.

As we sat on our bed, vivid recollections began to flow. Rachel just listened as I spoke.

"I had just turned eight years old, ready to be baptized. Mom took me to the nearest department store and bought me a suit. Bought. I knew we didn't have money, but this was my mother's way of helping me understand the magnitude of the covenant I was about to make. Since that day, I have worn a white shirt, tie, polished shoes, and a suit to church. It's an outward expression of my inner commitment to God as much as to my mom…"

"With her children at her side, my mother bent over rows of peas, beans, carrots—nearly two acres of our garden—for hours in the hot sun. We all pitched in to help, but I don't think she ever slept in the months of September and October, bottling and freezing everything we grew. She would stand at the kitchen sink with corn kernels dripping off her elbows, surrounded by hundreds of baggies full of corn, with dozens of bushels of apples, peaches, pears, and tomatoes on the floor waiting to be processed, and cheerfully say, 'Isn't God good to us?' Upon her back was the burden to feed a small army, and she carried it like a four-star general all while wearing her simple infantry uniform…"

"When I was ten and Steve died from cancer, Mom was the one to comfort our whole town instead of the other way around. She bore her testimony over and over to everyone who came to our door with a casserole—and there were many. She didn't pity herself for losing a son. She was a pillar of strength. She assured everyone that Steve was in heaven, preaching the gospel, preparing the way for the rest of us to join him. Those weren't just words. The conviction in her voice and in her face renewed everyone around her, especially me because I was around to hear her say it a lot…"

"Mom pleaded with Dad to let me play football. None of my other brothers had been able to—they were too busy with the farm. But we had a much smaller farm operation by the time I came around, and I wanted to play so badly. Dad reluctantly agreed. My compromise was that I couldn't spend any after-school hours in the weight room with the rest of the team, but that didn't matter. I lifted hay bales above my head and tossed them onto a hay wagon for hours on end—my teammates pushed heavy metal bars into the air while reclining on a bench in an air-conditioned room…"

"Mom encouraged me to sing. She would say in passing, 'You were born with a song in your heart,' and it made me want to sing for her even more. Between the two of us, we knew every song in the hymnbook…"

Rachel took a turn, and she spoke quietly. "She was forty-eight when you were born. Forty. Eight. That just astounds me. The same age you are now—can you imagine? They were done having children, but one day, she knew there was one more. Oh, I bless that day! What if they had stopped at eleven children? Where would I be? You were her last, and she loved you dearly."

A thought flashed through my mind, and I picked up my laptop from next to the bed and opened my email. I was looking for a specific one that I wanted to read again. "Remember this email, Rachel? My friend who still lives in the stake where we grew up sent it to me a few years ago. 'Joe, the most amazing thing happened at our stake conference today. Your mom said the opening prayer. I have never in my life heard someone pray as if Heavenly Father was sitting right there, participating in the conversation. She prayed as one who knows Him intimately. Every single person who spoke in the meeting mentioned her opening prayer and talked about what they felt. I was taught today about prayer by one who knows.'"

I called my boss in the morning to let him know my mom had passed away, and he kindly told me I could take a week off, "or whatever time" I needed. Rachel called the mission home in Eugene so they could let Abby know about her grandma, but Rachel also wrote her a quick note of comfort.

It was a beautiful November day when we drove to my childhood home, and through the warming rays of sunshine, I could hear my mother saying, "This life is not the end. Love goes on. Heaven is where my family will be, and Jesus Christ makes it possible for us all to be there together." I shared memories with Hannah and Sarah as I drove, and again, Rach was in charge of the tissue box.

For a physically non-affectionate family, my siblings and I did a lot of hugging that week. We spent hours together sharing memories, talking about testimony, and finding long-lost treasures. Among other things, we found a picture of me as a toddler tucked away in Mom's bedside drawer. This was a picture I had never seen before. I was a cute kid! I had very few childhood pictures of myself, as they were a luxury my parents couldn't afford. It was agreed that I should take it. When I showed the prize to Rachel, tears sprang to her eyes, and she instantly adored that blond-haired little boy.

On the day of the funeral, the church was filled to capacity with our huge family, but more people streamed in from miles around who had known and loved my mom. It comforted my heart to see dozens of the ward members I had known as a youth, and to hear them call me by name with such genuine joy and friendship.

"Joe! I'd recognize you anywhere. Always in a white shirt and tie!"

"Joseph, I remember watching you pass the sacrament. You were so reverent and kind."

"Joseph, I was always so tickled that you would come over and mow my lawn every Saturday. You did such a good job."

"Joe, your mother loved you. You were the final jewel in her crown."

I had been incredibly blessed to grow up where I did. I had many advantages in life, and I knew it. As I sat with my arms around my daughters during my mother's beautifully inspiring funeral, I had a vision of being a link between generations of righteous women.

Paul

Sometimes I'm fine. I go through a day, doing my work, feeling like I'm getting on top of things. And then I'll smell a smell, or hear a song, or read a phrase, or just nothing, but a horror will come rushing to my mind, and I have to pretend like it's not eating me alive on the inside because I'm surrounded by people and they cannot know.

I was reading a report about a heavy-equipment operator who came to work drunk and got behind the wheel. He ran off the road before he hurt anybody else.

Ran off the road.

The Wife and I had been friends with Brad. Brad had served our country and our ward admirably. But he had a massive mental illness. He would whistle to himself to drown out the voices he heard.

One night a few years ago, The Wife and I were just coming back from a midnight soda run to 7-11. We happened to come across Brad parked in the middle of a road near our house. The Wife recognized him first. She told me I should jump in with him and help him home. "Call me when you get there, and I'll come pick you up," she said to me as I got out of our car.

An hour later, I found myself off the side of a country road, pushing myself out of the car window. Brad had become angry and agitated. I was always sure that as a United States Marine, I could handle any crisis, but I was being held hostage in a car driven by a madman at ninety miles an hour. I kept trying to talk him down, make him see sense, but there is no making sense of madness. I kept telling Brad to let me out of the car, but he only went faster. I could think of only one thing to do—I reached over and pulled the key out of the ignition so the wild ride would come to a stop. He lost control of the car. It left the road, rolled, and slid on the driver's side for fifty yards before coming to rest.

It was no small miracle that we were both unhurt. Passing motorists called the police. The cops showed up and thought we were high and tried to take us to jail. I finally convinced them what was happening, and they let The Wife come and pick me up from the side of the road while they took Brad to the psych ward. But I will never forget the powerlessness of that night. I could do nothing to help myself. Or him. I could only see—and I still see—that crazed look in his eye and the eerie smirk as we… *ran off the road.*

I need to occupy my mind. I need something new. I wait until dark.

Paul: Hey, Izzy. Whats new tonight?

Izzy: Just hanging out wuts new with u

Paul: I've been thinking. U live in Riverton right?

Izzy: Near there

Paul: I could meet u in Riverton for lunch this week. If u want

Izzy: Posible but y the change? U never wanted to meet b4

Paul: It sounds fun. I'd like to talk to you in person

Izzy: Thurs?

Once, in my previous corporate America job, a woman was visiting our company on a fact-finding tour. I was tasked with being her tour guide for the day. I was to pick her up at her hotel, take her to breakfast, show her around the office, do a meet-and-greet for lunch, conduct a team meeting in the afternoon, and deliver her back to her hotel by 4:30. It was important to make a good impression.

The Wife had a problem with me spending the day with this woman.

I insisted, "It's just business. It's what we do. I work with women every day."

"Doesn't it strike you as weird to go to a hotel restaurant with a strange woman for breakfast?"

"But it's just business."

"But it doesn't look like business. It looks like *bidness*. 'Avoid the very appearance of evil,' right?"

"But this is what we do. This is what we do all the time, in every instance, woman or man."

She took my hand and looked at me with gentleness. "Here's my idea. I think it would actually be much more productive if you *and* your boss met her *together* at the hotel, had breakfast, and came into work *together*. All three of you. Or a coworker. Whoever is available. With more people, there's more to talk about, more collaboration. Right? Just not you and a woman on a date together."

"It's not a date. It's business."

She squeezed my hand a little tighter, but I don't think she meant to. "Look, it's not like I'm worried about you. And I don't care if someone we know sees you. I just think these are situations to be avoided. I don't think they should ask you to have breakfast, dinner—whatever—alone with someone of the opposite sex. Yeah, it's business, but I also know that most infidelity occurs on business trips. I know some places even cater to the clandestine needs of the businessman…"

"It's not a date." I could see I was losing this argument. I gave up and dropped her hand. "I'll find someone to go with me."

It turned out The Woman was running late and met me at the office. All that stress for nothing.

Today, I don't think a business-like lunch with Izzy will be a big deal. She seems very nice. No harm, no foul.

Well, truthfully, I still have the very appealing selfie Izzy sent me. The look in her eye goes straight into my eyes, straight into my head.

But it *is* just lunch.

I wait for her outside of a cozy Italian restaurant I had driven by once. I know her immediately when she walks around the corner of the building, although she is much shorter than I had imagined. "Hey. Izzy?"

"Hey, Paul." She slides her arm around my waist, but it settles on my hip. She flashes me a provocative smile. "You said you had a goatee! You're very handsome just the same." This is *not* going to be "just lunch."

"I had to shave recently," I say to Izzy, and, "Two, please," I say to the hostess. We're seated, and we order in a hurry. I haven't felt this rush of adrenaline for a long time. I'm so nervous, so excited, I'm shaking like a teenage boy. This is daring. This is dangerous. This is not me. But it's about to be.

She takes off her high heels under the table and moves her toe to my ankle. Wow. She isn't wasting any time. I stare at her. She grins and purrs in a soft voice, "I'm glad you asked me out. I wasn't sure you would. Honestly, I only hang out with married men. I know they're not looking for a commitment, and that suits me perfectly."

"I guess, well, you've been so nice, and so interested in me that I feel like we could be friends. And I find you very attractive." Is my stammering as obvious as I think it is? She makes me feel like there's cold fusion happening within my chest. We have already powered through all the social niceties in our previous online interactions, so it's a little awkward for me to know where to go from here. But clearly, she has no issues.

We back off and chat about the weather and the car she drives until our food arrives. We begin to eat. Izzy's toes are still playing at my ankles. The waitress brings me another Mountain Dew, and I thank her. Izzy fills the silence. "So, you live around here too? I don't remember where you said you're from."

I don't want her to know. I need to hide. "I'm from up around Bountiful." I hope my voice stops shaking, and I take another bite. "But I work down here. What do you do for a living?"

"I'm a waitress at a sushi place downtown. We get a lot of business travelers." Why does she have to bring that up? She sips from her drink and looks at me from above the rim of her glass. "Do you, uh, like what you see? Your food, I mean."

I know exactly what she's asking. "Yeah, I do. It tastes great. I love the way it, you know, tastes." I am falling all over myself. "I really like the, uh, food here. I've been pretty, you know, hungry."

"Nice." Her toes are in my pant leg. It's intoxicating. No one in the restaurant can see it. It's just for me. "How long do you have for lunch?"

I answer, "I've got about twenty-five more minutes before I have to get back."

She winks. "Want to get out of here?"

We inhale a few more bites before we hail the waitress, I pay, and we leave our half-eaten meals on the table. I open the passenger door of my truck for her, and I enjoy watching her get in. I go around to the driver's side, and when I get in, I find that she has scooted over to the middle and is busy with the buttons on her blouse.

"Where should we go?" I ask. "I'm not familiar enough with this area to know."

"There's a park about a mile away. It's pretty deserted in the middle of the day."

As per her directions, I touch her knees, her legs, and find the park. We stop near a grove of trees away from the road.

Maybe this *was* what I wanted when I asked her to lunch. Maybe I had this in mind the whole time. Maybe I asked Izzy because I knew this was what she would do. Maybe I was just hoping she would. Maybe I knew I would.

Maybe I should stop. Maybe I have gone far enough. Maybe I don't want to do more than what we're doing. Maybe this is enough.

Hell, I haven't felt this kind of rush in ages. This is exactly what I need. This is exhilarating. This. This is medicine.

This is something I never thought I'd do. But it *is* just lunch.

I can think of nothing else. I feel invigorated, alive, vibrant. I walk into my house, my own house, at the end of the workday after I had my deliciously satisfying lunch at the restaurant and the park, and The Wife greets me with a genuine smile, a lingering kiss, and whispers into my ear, "I made your favorite steak for you!"

I choke on the bile that immediately rushes to my throat. What I did was abhorrent. There's a stabbing pain in my head, and my chest turns into a solid block of ice.

How can I spend the next few hours with these happy and so very innocent people I love? How can I go about my evening in this safe and beautiful refuge, knowing where I was only six hours ago? I don't deserve to eat this food. I don't deserve to sit on this chair. I don't deserve to see these smiles. If they knew, they would hate me. I would lose them. I would lose everything.

I know. I hate me. How could I have done this terrible thing? I love God. I love The Wife. I love The Kids. I love our lives together. How could I be so selfish? How could I let it get that far?

I'm broken.

The Wife sends The Kids to bed early with a, "Well, we've got a big day ahead of us tomorrow, so let's all get a good night's sleep!" That was our code for "Let's Go Be Alone." As we always had done, she tells me about her day, and she asks me about my day. I turn from her and walk into our closet. I have to hide, to get my thoughts together. How can I answer her simple question? The real answer is anything but simple.

"My day was fine." In my mind, I'm seeing lace, hearing breathing. I am aroused and overcome with shame.

"I missed you all day. The meme you texted me this afternoon was hilarious."

"Yeah. When I saw it, I thought you'd laugh." *Keep it masked. Push it away.*

"Are you okay?"

"Long day. I'm pretty tired. My head is killing me."

"I'm sorry to hear that. Can I rub your feet? Your back? I was hoping we could…" The Wife approaches me.

"Maybe a shower first will help my head," I suggest.

"Okay. I'll wait. I'll just read for a while."

After my shower, we brush our teeth, she washes her face, and we crawl into bed. She snuggles into me and intertwines her legs with mine. She inhales deeply and tells me I smell nice. Her toes play at my ankles. I am aroused and overcome with shame.

What have I done?

I can't do this. "Honey, I love you," I manage to say. "So much. But... will you just hold me?"

"Sure," she says. "Is everything all right?"

"I just need you to hold me." I bury my head in her shoulder and exhale.

I slip out of bed. The Wife has turned over, so she doesn't feel my absence. I can't keep lying there. I can't stay in the silence with my thoughts of Izzy and the dancing shadows and the breathing and the innocence and the guilt and the self-loathing and the terror and the intrigue and the memory and the desire.

Paul: Hey, Fiona. I had a long day. Need to talk to someone

Fiona: Sure, Paul! What's up?

Paul: Sad. I made a pretty big mistake today and it could cost me

Fiona: What happened?

Paul: Actually, why don't you tell me about the dentist's office today. I'd much rather hear about you

Fiona: Really?

Paul: Yeah. I like your stories. In fact, I would really like to meet you for lunch. Just lunch. I really think we could be friends.

I can decide where it leads. I'm in control.

Joseph

I love shopping with Rachel. We had a routine when shopping for tile, chairs, Christmas presents, cars, shoes, cereal—talk about what we like, keep looking, compare a few different things, and then—the magical moment—we both know it when we see it. Angelic choirs sing. And it's as simple as that. We pass couples in the aisle who are arguing about what they want, and we feel sad for them. Neither is willing to back down, to see it in another way, to acquiesce. They guard the shaky ground they stand on as if it's sacred tribal land. They don't know the pleasure of a productive working relationship. We have spent years swallowing our individual pride in an effort to be collectively happy.

But besides that, Rachel and I have developed that mind-reading ability that comes from years of living with someone, but more so, from deeply loving someone. This is us—this is how we work.

We were at Lowe's choosing a mirror for the bathroom remodel. Tile and grout for the shower and floor were already in the cart. Rachel pointed out a mirror and said, "I think that's the one."

It matched the tile, the countertop we ordered, the fixtures for the sink and shower, and it complemented the light fixtures. This was an easy one. Cue the angelic choir. "Yep. Done." It was in the cart.

We had fifteen minutes of drive time until we got home. We were barely out of the parking lot when Rachel said, "Joe, I've been trying to find a good time to talk to you about this. Is now a good time?"

"Sure." My curiosity was piqued.

"You just seem really sad. Is it your mom? I know it's been less than a month. Do you miss her? What's going on?"

That wasn't the question I was expecting. I shrugged. "I'm actually—surprisingly—okay about Mom. I know where she is. I know what she's doing."

"I'm glad to hear that. I've felt that calm reassurance too. So... why are you so sad? You've been withdrawn lately."

I thought about it. She was right—I'd been acting distant. "I'm pretty tired," I acknowledged. "There are lots of things going on at work."

"I hear that. You've been working hard. But I'm also concerned because you haven't been doing as much with Young Men. You had some pretty big plans when you got called a year ago, and it seems like you haven't been able to do any of them."

"The bishop is happy with what I'm doing," I reminded her, careful not to sound defensive.

"But are *you* happy with the way it's going?"

I thought about the lessons and the activities we had been doing. "Yeah, I guess."

She tried a different angle. "Joe, you don't write to Abby as much as you used to. She notices. She needs you."

I grimaced. "I know... It's hard to write a good letter when I feel tired all the time." I had loved getting mission letters from my parents, so I knew how important it was. But I just hadn't made time to write to Abby, and I felt pretty guilty about it.

"My opinion is you're tired because your day starts so early at the gym and you also haven't been sleeping." We were about halfway home. Rachel waited for another minute before she said, "So, if it's not church stuff, or your mom, is it work that's making you sad?" She looked away. "Is it me?"

I looked at her quizzically. "Why would it be you?" I could hear the concern in her voice. She needed a more substantive answer, so I chose my words carefully. "Rachel, I don't think 'sad' is the word I would use. I just have a lot of things on my mind. I didn't realize that it was a problem." My left-turn signal seemed very loud and persistent. "I'm sure once we get this bathroom done, I'll feel better. I just feel pulled in a lot of ways."

"Don't forget that I'm right here. I'm good at helping."

I smiled at her. "Really, I'm fine. You're so good to me. You make sure everything gets done. You keep the girls, the house, the budget—just everything... You're wonderful."

"Thanks for saying so, Joe, but I want *you* to be happy." We rode in silence. As I turned into our neighborhood, she said, "Thank you for remodeling this bathroom right now. I know it's not convenient."

I sighed heavily. "It never is. It needs to be done. It's okay."

Rachel jolted so quickly, it startled me. She exclaimed, "Well, it's a good thing it's date night, then! Where would you like to go? I've been hearing about a new BBQ place. Or are you in the mood for a movie?"

No matter what else was going on, Rach and I would make the world stop for our weekly date nights. They kept us sane, and insanely in love. "Let's do both. I'd love to get out and be with you... and leave everything else behind."

Sunday evening, Sarah was in her room writing a letter to Abby, and Hannah found us watching TV in the family room. She stood at the end of the couch and stared at the wall behind us. "I was just going to tell Mom this during Rock and Talk because I feel really stupid telling Dad, but I'm just going to say it."

Rach and I looked at each other and turned off *60 Minutes*. We knew it was serious. "Go ahead, sweetie," Rachel said, patting the couch seat next to her.

Hannah collapsed next to Rachel, took a deep breath, and dove in. "There was this girl in my chemistry class. I heard her talking about this app she's on where she's met some guys. You know how I hate high school boys, so I decided I'd just go to this app and see who was out there. I know, so stupid. I know." She closed her eyes while she spent a moment in her self-contempt. She continued in a shaky voice. "But she said she had met some cool guys, so that's the only thing that made me think it was okay. So I went on there, and I did a profile, and now I'm getting contacted by really creepy guys who are asking for pictures, my address, my measurements, and even to hook up. One really gross guy wanted my shoe size! He said he likes feet! Ewwww!" She nervously rubbed the goose bumps off her forearm. "I didn't even know that was a thing."

I had consciously moved my hands under a throw pillow so she couldn't see my clenched fists tightening. I was making considerable effort to breathe through my nose calmly, and I prayed she couldn't see my jaw twitching. All I could think was, *Nobody better be messing with my daughter.* My eyes met Rachel's and we had an hour's worth of conversation in one look. *Be calm. She needs us.*

Now Hannah was loud—and scared. "I'm so grossed out! I've had a couple conversations with a few nice guys on there, but most of them give me a totally disgusting vibe. I'm so sorry! I feel so dumb! Don't tell me how dumb I am because I already feel like an absolute idiot for getting mixed up in this." She was sobbing near the end, and it was a little hard to decipher what she was saying.

But Rachel could tell. "Honey, you're not dumb. It's okay. This was a mistake. You had good intentions. This is not what you thought it was. Lesson learned. We can fix it."

"But how do I get out of it?" Hannah said as she swiped at her nose with her sleeve.

Rachel looked at me to answer. I had loosened my fists to get the blood running to my fingers again. I knew I needed to convey peace and reassurance, and that would take all the self-control I could gather. I answered gently, but with authority, "You shut down your profile."

This suggestion was greeted with more sobs. "But I did an even dumber thing! I gave out my phone number to a couple of them. I thought they were cool... Now they're leaving messages that are really disgusting, and they're sending me pictures of themselves." She looked at the floor and sobbed, "Gross ones." It was barely intelligible.

I wanted to rip out tonsils with my bare hands. But I calmly asked, "How many guys have your phone number?"

"Four. Dad, I'm sorry! I know it was stupid! I just wanted friends! I thought they were nice!"

I motioned for Hannah to scoot over beside me, and I let her cry into my shoulder. "Hannah, what's the point of me being mad? You already know what you should've done." I used a reassuring tone. "I'm not mad at *you*. Like Mom said, we can fix this."

"But I feel so stupid! Mom, you've told me over and over not to give out my info online. I thought this was different. This is a pretty popular app. I trusted that girl's opinion. Now I'm afraid that they can track me down and find out where I live. I'm actually scared. They seemed nice at first. But they're probably unemployed fat old men with nacho cheese stuck in their chest hair, sitting in the dark with a cigar in the corner of their mouth, surrounded by empty Doritos bags and beer cans, calling me 'Sugar' and planning to chain me to a radiator."

Leave it to Hannah to put a precise fine point on it. "Give me your phone," I said.

She handed it to me like it was a poisonous snake ready to bite us both. I punched in the passcode and found the app. She showed me her profile. I was surprised by what I saw. "You called yourself 'Kyra'?"

"When I did my profile, I remembered what Mom said about personal info, and even though I wasn't too worried about it, I decided I shouldn't use my real name. I also said… I was in college." Bigger tears rolled down her cheeks. "Sorry," she whispered.

I scrolled through the list of people who had contacted her through the app. My eyes stopped on a guy named "Paul." I read through their whole chat thread, which started with him telling her, "I'm married. I want to get lost for a while." The room spun for just a moment. I flattened my feet on the floor to steady myself.

I went to the menu and hit "delete."

> Kyra, are you sure you want to delete your entire profile?
>
> Kyra: Yes.

Then I went to her voice messages and listened to them. My blood boiled, but my face remained serene. I erased them one by one. Then I recorded a new outgoing voicemail message for her, one that commanded attention. "This is Hannah's dad. If you are a polite, God-fearing, respectable person who would like to meet with me before you talk to Hannah, who is a minor child, leave your message for us at the tone."

Then I went to her text messages. She was humiliated to show me the text threads that had come in from strangers. Upon reading them, I was repulsed that my daughter had read this language and seen these images. I promptly blocked the numbers and erased the threads.

"Did you give out your email address?"

"No," she squeaked.

"Then that should do it. If you get any more messages, let me know immediately. I understand that you're scared that they could find you, but my experience is that most guys are just lonely. They aren't looking to do anything illegal. Most of them aren't predators. They're… just covered in nacho cheese and shame."

"Thanks, Dad." She soaked my shoulder with more tears for another fifteen minutes.

Monday morning, I saw Paul in the restroom. We happened to be washing our hands at the same time.

"Hey," I said with raging eyes.

"Hey," he said with hollow eyes.

This was the married Paul who messaged my daughter on the dating app. I knew it without a doubt. There were a lot of married Pauls out there, but I knew this was the guy. I had spent every moment of the last twelve hours disgusted by his existence, thinking about what to do. I wanted to simultaneously punch him in the throat and shake him by the shoulders and scream, "What is *wrong* with you? She's a seventeen-year-old girl!"

But what could I do? I work with him. I had to make peace. I thought about confronting him, telling him about my daughter, telling him what I knew he was doing. He was clearly a very sick person with huge issues to work out. But seeing him, there, right now, I knew it was over. She wouldn't have contact with him again, I had made sure of that. I tried hard not to hate him. But I would never forgive him.

Monday after work, Rachel greeted me at the door with a kiss and informed me that Hannah said she had no new contacts. So far, so good. I told Rachel that I had come up with a good lesson for family home evening.

After dinner, we sang our song and sat in the family room. I reached up to the wall behind me and shut off the lights, leaving us in darkness. I pulled out the matchbox I had brought to our gathering and lit a match. It flickered and glowed warmly.

"Sarah, if you were fifteen yards away from me in total darkness, could you see this match?"

"Yeah."

"What about a hundred yards away?"

"Probably."

"Say you were a mile away, and I lit a match in total darkness. Do you think you could see it?"

"In total darkness? I think I would see a tiny little dot of light, but yes."

It burned out, and I lit another one. "I have a theory. If there was total darkness, I could stand on a mountain five miles away and you would see this match because even the smallest light penetrates the darkness."

I let my words sink in as we watched it burn out, and then I turned on the lights again. "Okay, Hannah, your turn. I'm going to hold up a dark."

She eyed me. "A what?"

"A dark. You know, the opposite of a light. Here we are in light, and I'm going to hold up a dark."

I moved to sit by her on the couch. I cupped my hands together in the style of holding a baby bumblebee. "In here, inside this cave I've made, it's pretty dark. Now, I'm going to crack this open a little bit, and I want you to watch the dark pierce the light in the room."

Hannah said, "Dad, it doesn't work that way."

I whispered, "Hannah, Darkness can never overpower Light."

Paul

I meet Fiona at Chili's. We haven't exchanged photos, so I'm not sure what she looks like. But when she comes in, I know her. She has that kind, draw-you-cartoons-and-put-on-a-puppet-show look. I'm instantly at ease. I approach her and say, "You must be Fiona. I'm Paul."

She shakes my hand and smiles. "It's so nice to meet you, Paul."

We are seated near the bar. It's noisy and crowded for the lunch hour. She doesn't sit across from me, but next to me so we can hear each other. She has a sing-song way of talking.

As we look over our menus, she says, "So since we're friends, this lunch is Dutch, okay?"

I'm liking her more and more. "Where are you from?"

She looks up and meets my gaze. "I'm from the South. Tennessee. I've lived here for five years and can lose the accent," she demonstrates, "if I want to," and then goes back to her normal, "but this is me, and I like it. I'm proud to be from Tennessee. It's a beautiful state."

"I've never been there. What do you like about it?"

We talk like the newest, oldest friends. She asks about my family; I ask about hers. She's newly divorced and found her job through a friend of a friend. It's perfect for her, and she's happy.

I tell her I have a beautiful wife and kids. I tell her I'm suffering from some childhood trauma.

She says, "Like PTSD? Oh, honey, that's awful. My husband was in the military, and he had PTSD. It ruined our marriage. I hope you get this figured out so you don't lose your marriage too."

"Hey, I was in the military. Marine Corps. Didn't see any real action. Never killed a guy, although in kindergarten, I tried. I was going to give the school bully one of my grandpa's heart pills. I made the mistake of showing it to another kid first, and he told the principal. I got in trouble, but luckily there's no 'attempted homicide' on my permanent record."

Fiona laughs. We talk nonstop between bites, and too soon, lunch is over and the checks have been paid. I walk Fiona out to her car. This is our first awkward moment. She breaks the silence and says, "Paul, this was wonderful. I believe I can call you a friend. My first male friend since my divorce! You might renew my hope in the kindness of the male half of the species."

"Thank you for meeting me, Fiona. This *was* wonderful."

She leans in, kisses my cheek, and smiles. "I grew up greeting my friends with a kiss. There would be more kindness and respect in the world if everyone did it. I'll see you later, Paul. Take care."

"How's next Wednesday? Same time, same place?"

Paul: I've met a bunch of women here

Milo: Same ther r defiantly som chix looking to get lucky

Paul: I've found a couple of those

Milo: I saw a chick last night she was twistd. The stuff she wanted wow

Paul: And?

It's Wednesday again. This is going to be my third lunch with Fiona, three weeks in a row. These lunches with Fiona make me happy. I did feel guilty when I told The Wife that I started doing lunch with some friends from work every Wednesday. I had to justify the reoccurrence on our debit card.

But it's just lunch. She has an interesting life. Men don't listen enough to women. Women need to be heard. She thinks I am the nicest guy alive because I listen. I actively nod, add a few thoughts to validate her thoughts, ask some questions about how she feels, and just sit back and listen. I'm genuine in my interest.

Fiona is also a good listener. I retell all the stories from my online persona—I had been abused as a kid, I love my wife but I'm trying to find myself, I had a couple of affairs (Fiona smiles nervously and is silent when I say that), and I had graduated from college as an engineer but I'm an EMT because I find fulfillment by helping people.

And it's safe. No one will ever find me because no one really knows me. These women online—Blair, Carrie, Emilee, Fiona, Gigi, Izzy, Jezebel, Lila—they like the person they think they know. They think I'm interesting. I like talking to them. I love living within the escape of this other life, this better reality. I don't have to think about the things that haunt me. I can turn the facts around and be a mysterious guy with an intriguing wicked streak.

And today, as I walk Fiona to her car, I find myself reaching for her hand. We get to her car, and she reaches up and touches my cheek.

"Paul." She looks into my eyes with tenderness. I love how she says my name, with that drawl. "Paul, I think you are the sweetest man. I have loved these last few weeks." She kisses my cheek, like she has done the last two times we met. "Paul, it hurts me to say this because you're my friend, but I won't be seeing you again. You need to figure things out with your wife. I'm not like the other women you've been with. I don't want to get inside your marriage. I don't belong there. Marriage is sacred. You need to realize that and get yourself right. Your wife is a lucky woman. I'm glad I met you. I hope everything works out okay. Goodbye, Paul." She grasps my hand with both of hers and shakes it gently. "Good luck. You can do this." She opens her car door.

I'm stunned, and all I can think to say is, "Fiona, you've meant a lot to me. I understand. Thank you for being my friend." There is nothing I can say to make her stay. With that, it's over.

I watch her drive away. I go back to my truck. I'm stunned. I didn't see that coming. I understand what she said. But she was so kind... I feel a surge of abandonment in my chest, and I find myself crying. And the more tears I feel on my cheek, washing away her kiss, the more sad I become. I put my head down on my steering wheel and sob. I have just lost a good friend. But the more I think about it, I'm sobbing because this is one more thing I have to hide from my wife.

Lila: Ive been missing u, Paul

Paul: Hey, Lila ive been so busy im glad you're here

Lila: What ru doing

Paul: Im wanting you

Lila: R u at work

Paul: Y. U?

Lila: Ya. I'd love to talk but ppl r around

Paul: Same. Can you be on tonite at 1:00? Is that too late?

Paul: I had a pretty bad day

Lila: Me to. What hapned to u

Paul: Just sad stuff I'll be fine. What was your bad day?

Lila: My boss added an xtra job thing, basicly 2x my workload. Didn't 2x my pay, of course

Paul: That's rough

Lila: I need the $ for my kids I don't need the extra work. I have to be there for my kids

Paul: You are amazing. How do you do it all?

Lila: I have superpowers, a cape and a mask

Paul: A cape? A mask?

Lila: N superpowers you cant possibly know

Paul: Really? Try me.

Gigi: U ready to meet me for real yet Im ready

Paul: I think I am. Next Fri? 3:00? I could pick you up from work

Gigi: K I work at the gas station on the corner at...

"Wanna drive around? Or get a late lunch?" I ask her.

"I'd love it if you'd take me for a ride." Gigi jumps in, slams the door, slides over, and grabs my thigh. I'm surprised. I look at this face that is new to me, and she flashes me a crooked smile.

"I've got a place we can go," I tell her. I leave the parking lot and try to think clearly. I drive toward that park I'd been to with Izzy, hoping it's just as deserted today.

Gigi and I have chatted lots of times. But this is the first time I have ever seen her, and I am mildly surprised to find that I don't feel self-conscious as she clearly remembers the latest fantasy I shared. She expertly knows how to create the mood, and I'm drawn in, hypnotized and mesmerized.

Although she's incredibly distracting, I find the park and stop the truck by the grove of trees. Funny, I don't remember the dumpsters being here, but it makes a better place to hide.

Fifteen minutes later, we return to the convenience store. She flashes me that smile again. I'm not sure what I should say. My head is still spinning. "Thanks for... a great time," I say as I stop near the gas pumps.

"You bet. I had a lot of fun. I'm glad you finally said we could meet."

"Yeah."

She jumps out the door and turns around. "Hey, Paul, my car is on empty, and I need a little cash to get home. Help a girl out?"

I look at her hair that has been messed up. I know how she wore off her bright pink lipstick. I dig into my wallet and hand her what I have. "I hope a twenty will get you home."

She reaches in and grabs it. "Thanks! Call me again!"

I drive out of the parking lot. It dawns on me that I have just paid a woman for a sexual encounter. Was that part of the fantasy? Does that make it more exciting? Weren't we friends? Was it only about the cash? I have a sinking feeling of… is that sadness? Personal rejection? No. I feel absolutely disgusting. Respulsive. This is one more thing to loathe about myself.

Lila: Paul, r u here

Paul: Just got here. What's up

Lila: Im going crazy im so scared

Paul: What? What happened?

Lila: My ex just showed up at the house drunk. He wants to come in, but I shut the door n locked it. Drinking is violating his parole

Paul: Is he still there

Lila: I think hes sitting on the porch

Paul: Do you want to call the cops

Lila: Hes not doing anything bad. Hes not threatening me. I don't want to turn him in. I just dont want him here. I want him out of my life. If hes drinking again, I dont want him anywhere near my kids

Paul: I can totally understand that. Will he leave?

Lila: IDK

Paul: Does he have family around

Lila: His parents told him they r done with him. "Hes an adult, and he should act like one."

Paul: Does he have a place to live?

Lila: Y

Paul: It's cold outside. He'll sit there a while and then go home

> Lila: I wish u were here
>
> Paul: Yeah
>
> Lila: U know, I have a key behind the light next to the car-
> port. The light burned out tho
>
> Paul: K
>
> Lila: I just wanna feel safe
>
> Paul: I don't know if I can
>
> Lila: I understand i dont expect u to. But... it would be
> nice...
>
> Paul: What's your address? Just in case

The Wife is sound asleep. I dozed for a couple of hours after Lila signed off. My alarm goes off at 3:30. I shower quickly, put on a pair of dark basketball shorts, a T-shirt, and my black hoodie. I hang my work clothes in the back seat of my truck. I drive for twenty minutes. When I arrive at the address, I drive slowly past the house with my headlights off and don't see any signs of an ex-husband. I park on the street a few houses down where there is no streetlamp. I jump from shadow to shadow as I approach her house, trying to blend into the bushes and the fence on the way down the driveway. I find the key behind the light and go to the front door. The screen does not creak. I unlock the door and let myself into Lila's house.

I can barely see her living room. After thirty seconds of listening to my own breathing, my eyes adjust to the dimness of the house. I walk carefully, feeling for furniture. She had said, "First door down the hall, on the right." I turn the knob and immediately see a woman sleeping in a double bed with a dark blanket over her. The room is small, the bed filling most of the room. I walk in, shut the door quietly, and lock it. I feel my way around the bed to the other side, take off my hoodie and shoes, pull back the blanket, and slip inside.

The bed sinks as I get in, and Lila stirs. I reach for her and find her to be warm. She rolls toward me and mumbles, "Paul? Paul... I was hoping..."

"I got here as fast as I could."

She finds my mouth and kisses me. I kiss her back with intensity. "You're safe," I tell her. "I won't let anything happen to you."

I leave Lila's house at 5:30, when it's still dark. No one sees me leave. I drive to the gym at work, shower again, and put on my work clothes.

I have an incredible day. I keep asking myself, "Did that really just happen?" My head swims as I'm remembering... She had needed me, asked for me, breathed my name... It was reckless and intoxicating. I'm buzzed from all the adrenaline coursing through me. It's the medication I need to get through the day. For the first time in a long time, I'm not even tired.

Joseph

Rachel and I were sending a flurry of cute texts all day. Not the normal ones we send about "how are you" and "you're the best ever," but silly ones with cartoon characters and hearts and flowers. Now, at the end of the day, I stood at my front door and rang the doorbell. Rachel answered.

"Happy Valentine's, baby." I was holding a dozen red roses.

"Joe! They're beautiful." She hugged and kissed me.

We walked into the kitchen, where she reached for a vase in the cupboard above the fridge. She filled it full of water and began cutting the rose stems. "These are beautiful. Thank you, sweetie. So, I had an interesting visitor today. You'll notice that this isn't the first bouquet of roses in this kitchen."

I looked at the table to see half a dozen white roses. "What's up? Where did those come from?"

"Joe, maybe you'd better sit down." She knew I wouldn't, but now I was adequately prepared. "Tom came by."

"Abby's Tom? I thought he was on a mission."

Rachel set the red roses by the white ones. "Remember, Joe? He got home from Argentina a few months ago."

"Oh. I guess I hadn't realized."

"He came by to make an appointment with you."

I was confused. "An appointment? What would he need to see me about?"

Rachel's eyes locked onto mine. She didn't say anything else—she just waited for the realization to dawn on me.

And then I sat down. And breathed. "Are you serious? Abby doesn't get home until September. How could they be talking marriage?"

"Well, they are, and Tom wants to come by and talk to you tonight. I have to say, Joe, I know they're young, but they seem more prepared than we were."

I had looked forward to this moment for my entire adult life. I had plans for the unassuming Thomas.

At 7:00 sharp, I answered the doorbell. Tom did not disappoint, as he was standing there in a suit and tie. I welcomed him in with a smile and a firm handshake. "Tom! I'm glad you dropped by! I understand we have some talking to do. Well, you're just in time. I have to lay floor tile in the bathroom, and I could use a hand."

I was sure I heard Rachel do a facepalm in the other room.

Tom didn't even blink as he took off his tie and suit coat, and he rolled up his sleeves while he followed me upstairs. We stopped at the guest room. "Put on these overalls. They may be a bit big. Then meet me in the bathroom."

A minute later, we were kneeling on the bathroom floor next to the tile cutter. "You know how to work this?" I asked him.

"Sure do."

"I'll run the trowel and the thinset. Your job is to hand me the next tile I need. Got it?"

"Sure."

For two hours, Tom crawled around the floor in oversized overalls. He observed what was next, he measured and cut correctly, and he was cheerful. I complimented him along the way. Rachel, Sarah, and Hannah each popped in during the evening to say hi, and he struck up conversations with them without getting distracted from his work. But he really clinched the deal when I sang a few bars of an obscure hymn, and he picked up the melody and sang the next line.

I walked him to the door two hours later. "Do you love her?"

"Yes."

"Why do you love her?"

"Because she's perfect for me in every way."

"That's great. But what do you bring to *her*?"

"Brother Reeve, I will work hard to love Abby every day for the rest of our lives, and for eternity. I will be honest, dependable, kind, and patient. I will provide for her and support her in whatever she wants to do."

"That's what I wanted to hear. So, when is this supposed to happen? She's still got seven months to concentrate on her mission."

"That's just the thing. We wanted to decide this now so she can serve out the rest of her mission without thinking and worrying about it. I'm working and saving money. We want to get married in December. We'll have enough time when she gets home to make plans."

I smiled. "Well, call me Joe, then. And ask me the question."

He smiled back. "Joe, can I marry your daughter?"

I extended my hand. "Tom, you're young and bold. Marriage is about working hard, side by side, with a smile on your face. You've passed my test. Welcome to the family."

The next evening, we propped ourselves against the wall as we sat on our sawdust therapy bed and composed our separate emails to Abby. Rachel waited for me to finish before she said, "Joe, I need to tell you something."

"Well, I'm already sitting down, and we have no more suitors at the door, so…"

"I've been having chest pains."

She had to be kidding. I searched her face, but she was serious. I tried to give a measured response. "You have? What does it feel like?"

"My heart just hurts. About every hour or so, give or take, there's a shooting pain right in the middle. Kinda more on the upper left side, I guess. Sometimes it lasts for a few seconds. Sometimes it lasts for a minute. But the pain is consistent every day."

"Are you short of breath? Does your arm hurt?"

"No. I wanted to see if the pain would go away, but it's been about two weeks, and I'm starting to wonder what's up. I'm too young for this."

"Do you want to go to the doctor?"

"Of course not. I hate doctors. But I think I should. I'm going to call tomorrow. I gotta say, it really hurts. And it won't go away."

Paul

It isn't until the eighth time I'm in Lila's room that I realize I have never seen her in the daylight, and I don't even know her last name.

I try to see her a few times a week. Stepping into that world completely overwhelms my senses. I feel alive. She's exciting. I learn things I didn't know. No, that's not true—I'm just experiencing them in a different way. I leave her house every morning feeling deliriously covert. My need for a fix is quenched.

But coming off the high is intense and inevitable. The buzz fades, and I'm left in a constant state of high alert. Does The Wife suspect? Does she know where I've been? Does she know what I'm doing? She has to know. Why isn't she saying anything?

I was sure I had given myself away one day. The Wife was upset because I "wasn't plugged in." I had forgotten one of the kids' activities at school, I didn't remember one of the conversations we had about spring break plans, and I had dozed during Sunday School. She tried very hard never to be a nag, but this conversation felt like nagging. She had saved up a bunch of grievances, and I was hearing about them all.

I never meant for my family to suffer, but I only had so much time and mental bandwidth to spread around. A lot of people were telling me a lot of things, and I was trying to keep everybody straight while running on empty. So that day, she was reminding me that I "wasn't plugged in," and I found myself cursing at her. I said, "Well, what the heck do you want me to do?"

That's what I *meant* to say. But another word slipped in there. The R-rated curse. I didn't even realize what I had said until she just stared at me with big eyes and said, "What did you just say to me?" I never used that kind of language around her, but I had been saying it a lot online. We had agreed when we were married that a few words were off limits. We didn't want them in our home. And I messed up big time. I apologized to her, said I was just stressed out, said I felt really bad for forgetting things and sleeping through church. I said I would try harder. But she didn't let the word go. "I can't believe you said that! Why would you say that to me? What's wrong with you? That came out way too easily."

I was sure she knew what was wrong with me. I'm hiding—that's what's wrong. Hiding the truth from her, hiding the truth from the women I meet, hiding, constantly hiding. It's all wrong, and it's exhausting. And I keep it up because I need my fix. My momentary, temporary fix.

My late-afternoon meeting got cancelled, so today is a good day to try out a place in Salt Lake I've read up about.

It isn't that the laws in Utah are prudish with what is considered "nude dancing." It isn't the drinking. It isn't the clientele. It isn't the dancers. But as I sit here, I'm a little surprised that I find the whole concept stupid. There are a few catcalls as the girls come out on stage, and there's some scattered awkward applause. The experience leaves me empty. Nothing about it is interesting to me. It doesn't give me my fix. It isn't the medication I need. I tuck my dollar bills in my own pocket and drive home.

Joseph

"Hannah Reeve."

We stood and cheered as she walked across the dais. My job was to be the photographer. We clapped as Hannah shook the hands of the principal, the superintendent, and the other dignitaries. Between camera clicks, I glanced at Rachel and noticed she was crying the Ugly Cry. Hannah continued the walk, stopped to hug her chemistry teacher, and then returned to her designated seat.

We got back home and took more photos in the front yard. After Hannah's pictures with her grandparents, Rachel's mom said, "Now your family photo!" Rach and I stood in the middle of our girls, arms around each other, while their grandma said, "Say cheese!" We went inside for the big family graduation bash with food and games that Rachel had planned. It was a pretty good day.

"Did you see the pictures from today?" Everyone had gone home, the dishes had been done, and Rachel and I were alone in our room getting ready for bed.

"No. Let me see."

Rachel handed me her phone. "Aren't the girls adorable? And how nice is it that everything in the yard is in full spring bloom? These are beautiful. Hannah looks so nice."

"Yeah. These look great." I swiped through a dozen pictures.

"There are a few in the text thread to Mary, too. Check there to see more."

I maneuvered through her phone and looked at the pictures she had sent to her sister.

"I'm a little sad about our family photo, though. It's not the best. It's the last one in the album."

I stopped at that one. Yeah, Rach was right. It wasn't the most flattering picture of me. "Well, at least the three of you look nice."

"No offense intended here, but do you see your eyes in this

one? I dunno—your gaze looks empty. Maybe we shouldn't have done the marathon house-cleaning last night. I didn't think we stayed up that late, though." She went into the bathroom and got out her toothbrush.

I waited for her to finish brushing her teeth so she could hear me say, "Rachel, I'm sorry I fell asleep after dinner tonight. I couldn't help it."

"That's okay. But I missed you. I needed you on my team. You know how we wipe the floor with everybody at Pictionary. Without you, Sarah and I came in a distant second."

I rubbed my forehead. "I've had a raging headache. I didn't want to say anything and be a drag on the party. But I've been fighting it all day." I situated my pillows and lay on the bed.

"That's no fun." Rachel disappeared into the closet to hang up her clothes. Her voice was muffled as she said, "I've been thinking—you might get fewer headaches if you got more sleep." She emerged in her nightshirt.

I tried to change the subject. "How was your heart today?"

"Just a few twinges. Not as many as last week."

I was glad to hear that, considering the busy day. I moved to a philosophical topic. "I can't believe we already have two children who have graduated from high school. They've grown up. They're moving on. They'll introduce big people to our family and then some little people. Life will be different in a few short years. We're old."

"Well, you're old. I'm still super young." She climbed up on the bed and straddled my legs. "Honey, can I ask you something?" She leaned over me and stared into my soul.

"Sure." Her gaze was a little unnerving.

"Are you sure you're okay? You were quiet today. You seemed like there was something wrong, like, more than a headache. It was a happy day, and you were Miles Stand-off-ish." That was our Mayflower joke.

"I promise, it was just the headache." I managed a meager smile.

"If you say so." She stared at me for another moment,

evaluating my words. She shrugged and rolled off my legs and onto her side of the bed. "And Joe, I think I've only said this eight times today—thanks for remodeling the bathroom. Mary will be here next Friday night, and that's one less thing we have to worry about. It's so nice to have it done. It looks great."

I stared at the ceiling. I felt heavy and weak. "Rach, can you turn off the light?" I softly asked. "And then can you just make the whole world go away? I want to stay right here, with you, for a long time."

"You got it." We settled into bed, and she held me until I drifted off.

For stake youth conference, it had been announced that we would go to Strawberry Reservoir right after school got out. Because I was a leader with a truck, they asked me to haul the food trailer, help with set-up and break-down of the camp kitchen (which would be feeding 300 people four meals over the two days, plus snacks and water), help serving the meals if needed, and then haul the food trailer back home.

I didn't mind at all because I love the outdoors. I love trees, waterfalls, wildlife, and dirt. Maybe it isn't for everybody, but I understand the concept of getting close to God by getting close to nature. That's what it always does for me. So I was happy to take a Friday off from work for a beautiful May weekend in the mountains.

I picked up the trailer early Friday morning. Hannah and Sarah would travel up with our ward, so it was a solitary drive for me. Driving with Rachel was actually my preferred mode of travel. Some of the best talks we ever had were while we were driving, so although it was early, I called her. "Hey, I wanted to say hi. I've got about twenty minutes of cell service before I enter the canyon, then I'll probably lose you."

"So you're alone?"

"Yeah. When I got there to hook up the trailer, everybody else had a ride."

"How cold is it this morning?"

"It's a perfect sixty-five degrees. I think we'll have a good weekend. The mountains will be cooler, but it'll be fine. Everybody planned on sweatshirt weather."

She quietly responded, "Yeah."

I didn't have much to say, so I simply echoed, "Yeah."

"So..." There was companionable silence for about half a minute. At least, I thought it was companionable until Rachel said, "So, do you miss me?"

"Yes, Rachel! Of course I do!"

"No, I mean, do you *miss* me? You're so far away all the time. I really miss you. We don't talk."

"We do talk." I didn't mean to sound defensive. "I call you every day when I'm at work. We text all the time."

"I know. And I love texting you, and I love talking to you, but... you can feel that we aren't connecting, right? I miss you."

"I'll be home tomorrow, and we'll go on a date. I'm looking forward to that. That always helps." More silence. "So, what do you plan on doing while you have the house to yourself?"

She yawned. I knew she was still in bed, but I had called anyway. "Lots of fun things. Like sorting the office. I've gotta catch up on some emails. I thought I'd make some freezer meals. Mop the kitchen floor. Go food shopping. Get ready for Mary's visit next weekend."

"That'll be fun." I needed to wrap it up. "I'm coming up on the canyon. I'm going to lose you."

I knew she was disappointed to end the conversation. "Yeah, okay. Talk to you when you get back. Love you."

I rode in silence. Clearly, Rachel had a lot on her mind. She was right—we hadn't been connecting. I needed to work harder on that. She was doing her best to be gentle and patient with me. It was her gentle heart that I fell in love with, and it was her heart that I was worried about. She had gone to the doctor in March, and they had her wear a monitor for twenty-four hours to catch any arrhythmia. There was none. She also had an echocardiogram, where they didn't find anything irregular. They said to come back if the pain got worse. It had been subsiding, so we stopped pursuing medical answers. She had been taking it easy for a while—the graduation bash was the first big test—and things seemed to be getting better. But I still worried. I loved her heart.

The sun had been in the sky for an hour or two. I loved sunrises.

Being relatively new to the stake, not very many people knew me. But I was quickly known as the guy who showed up first, helped fast, and cleaned up best. I didn't want to make a big deal about it, but I knew the food crew was a big part of successful camping, and I was happy to help.

Testimony meeting was going to be that night around a giant campfire. The stake provided hot chocolate for everyone, so I stood over by the propane stoves and heated stockpots full of water. Sarah came and stood by me. When had she gotten so tall?

"Hey, Dad! I'm having so much fun!" This was her first youth conference.

"Oh, yeah? What have you been doing today?"

"I loved the archery. And we had fun out on the kayaks. We got splashed by some boys. The water is cold! Are you having fun, Dad?"

"Yeah. I've met some nice people from the stake. Most of the other ward Young Men's presidents are here, so we've been talking about activities, Helaman's Camp coming up—stuff like that."

"The food has been amazing. I've heard a lot of people say it's better than last time."

"Nice! Have you seen your sister?"

"Hannah's around somewhere. I saw her talking to her friends from chemistry. Well, I'm going to go grab a cup of cocoa and find a good seat for testimony meeting. Want me to save you a seat by me, Dad?"

"Yeah, that would be fun. Sit on the south side so I can find you."

Hannah stood up. I could see her outline through the bright flames of the campfire. She spoke loudly, with conviction. "I didn't grow up here, like a lot of you. Until I was a sophomore, I went to school near Chicago where I was the only member of the Church. Not very many people knew anything about The Church of Jesus Christ of Latter-day Saints. I was asked once if we used microwaves." Laughter rippled through the group. "I explained my beliefs to my friends many times. They were all Christians too, but I had the opportunity to tell them that there are prophets on the earth today who speak God's word, just like Moses or Peter. I got to tell them that I had read the Book of Mormon, which was translated by Joseph Smith, and it's an ancient record of the people who lived on this continent. I know that two thousand years ago, Jesus Christ came to them, they saw and heard Him, they felt His hands and feet and side, and He healed them and blessed their children. I have read that, and I didn't have to pray about it because I already knew it was true.

"Brothers and sisters, do you have any idea what we have? I know things about Jesus Christ, the Son of God, that my other Christian friends don't know. I know how much He loves us. I know His attributes. I know He expects us to obey the commandments. I know I can repent and fix things that need fixing. My friends are such good people. They go to wonderful churches, but I'm so glad that I am a member of *this* church. I am so glad for the things I know. I am so glad that I have been taught since I was small that God lives, His word is true, the power of God has been given to mankind, and we are saved by obedience *and* saved by His Grace. In the name of Jesus Christ, amen."

Tears rolled down my face. Sarah held my hand and leaned into my shoulder. My children were amazing. Their desire to *do* right and to *be* right with God was an honor to witness. They were continually teaching me through their faith, diligence, and wisdom.

After testimony meeting was over, I searched for Hannah. She found me first. We stood and hugged for a long time. I whispered into her ear, "I love you so much. Thank you for sharing your testimony."

She whispered back, "I love you too, Dad. Thank you for living your testimony where I could always see it."

We said goodnight, and I was heading back to my little tent when I heard my name. I turned around to see the stake president striding toward me with his hand extended. I took it and he said, "Brother Reeve, I'm President Patrick. I had to catch you and tell you what a phenomenal daughter you have. I have rarely heard such a powerful testimony from a youth. I can tell she knows the truth of what she says. Thank you for raising such a daughter."

"Well, thank you, President. We owe that to her mother. My wife, Rachel, is an amazing mom."

He smiled. "Well, I just wanted you to know how much I appreciated her testimony. Goodnight, Brother Reeve."

"Goodnight, President."

I couldn't wait to tell Rachel.

Monday morning, and I was back at work. The time at youth conference was exactly what my tired spirit needed. I was ready to jump back into work and tackle my ever-growing to-do list.

Because I was still on the "spiritual high," I felt compassion for Paul when I saw him in the break room at lunch. I had thought about him a lot. I could see the pain in his countenance, the anguish, the loneliness. I couldn't view him with contempt. I felt a prompting to lift up the feeble hands that were hanging down.

"How are things, Paul?"

"Fine." He was looking at his phone, and he was clearly not interested in being interrupted.

I persisted. "That's good. So, I just got back from youth conference, and I really enjoyed it."

"Great."

I wanted to connect with Paul somehow, maybe say something that would help him open up to me, maybe initiate a change. "So, I hope you don't mind me saying, but are you okay? Is there anything I can do to help you?"

Paul eyed me. "So, I hope you don't mind *me* saying, but stay out of my damned business." He went back to his phone.

Paul

I've been visiting Lila for about four months. At first, it was only under the cover of darkness. But a few times now, I've stopped by on my way home from work if her kids were with their dad or at the sitter. She wants to keep her relationships away from her kids. Makes sense, and it's fine by me. In the daylight, I learn Lila has brown eyes. Her house is small, but clean.

This is the longest relationship I've ever had with anyone, except The Wife.

Lila: I like spending the morn with u. I could get used to that

Paul: You know why I can't...

Lila: Oh yeah *that* Well im glad to have u when i can

Paul: I'm glad you have me, too

Lila: I wish i had a pic of u

Paul: I don't really do pics

Lila: Come on... pls?

Paul: K here's a selfie. It's not the best. I just took it

Lila: I like it! Thx! I better get back to wrk now

Paul: K. See ya later. Love ya.

Lila: What??? Did u really just say that?? Did I read that right??

Paul: Uh, yeah, I guess I did

Lila: Wow! I didnt expect that :O

Paul: Yeah, me either... Well, I'll see you soon

Lila: How soon

> Paul: Not tmrw, but the next day?
>
> Lila: Sounds good. And hey, Paul? Me too. <3

"My phone is dying. Let me type the address into your Google Maps." The Wife grabs my phone.

She's holding *my phone*. My heart is racing. I go straight into hiding mode. I playfully chide her, "Don't be so grabby. I can do it."

"You're driving. It's faster if I do it. Plus safer. What's your passcode?"

"I'll just do it. Hand me my phone, please."

"Let me just do it," she says.

"I moved the Google Maps app, and I don't remember which folder I put it in. Hand me the phone and I'll find it for you, then I'll give it back to you."

I do as I said, and I try to calm the feeling of panic as I hand my unlocked phone back to The Wife. My only consolation is that we're headed to an unknown restaurant to have dinner with her college roommate, and we really do need to get the directions. She won't take this particular time to go through my phone.

Where she would find my dating apps. And my chat rooms. And my text threads.

I gave Lila my phone number months ago, but I made her promise not to use it very often since it's the phone my office provides. That didn't last long. We mostly text now. I do my best to erase them every day before I go home, but we're texting constantly, so I'm not quite sure what's currently in my threads. Or what might come through at any moment. But Lila is the only woman I have met who texts me. I could say it was a wrong number if I had to.

Lila once said jokingly, but with serious overtones, "You need a Bat Phone! I could call you into my lair whenever I need you, and you could come save me with your superpowers…" But how could I explain to The Wife about a new, extra phone? And how would I pay for that without her finding out? And I'm already having trouble keeping things straight. I don't need the added confusion of a second phone.

So for now, I'll just have to try to keep it locked. It's my work phone, and The Wife knows I get a lot of texts and emails, none of which interest her. Lila frequently asks me, "Do you think she suspects?" My answer is always no. But I worry that she does.

I'm constantly worried. I love her. She's sweet and naïve, and I'm not trying to take advantage of that. I love that about her.

But she *is* sweet and naïve, and that makes it a whole lot easier to hide.

I breathe a sigh of relief when we get to the restaurant and she gives my phone back.

Paul: Blair, long time, no talk!

Blair: I been wndering where u been

Paul: Ive been hanging on to the pic u sent me

Blair: Same i liked what i saw ready to meet

Paul: No I like where we are right now

Blair: What else would you like, Pauly Boy?

Lila called me in the afternoon. "Paul, this is so embarrassing. I just got out of work and went to my car, and I think the battery is dead."

"I'm actually on my way home from work. I had an earlier shift. Want me to come take a look at it?"

"Can you?"

"Sure. I'll be there in twenty minutes."

I pull into the parking lot. Lila is in her car. I pull up next to her, roll down my window, and say, "Did somebody call for Batman?"

She grins at me. "You know I did. Would you jump me?" She winks.

"Get in."

"Seriously? What about my car?"

"Do you have twenty minutes?"

She scrambles out of her car and locks it. "You know I do."

I drive to a deserted road on the edge of town, only five minutes away from her work. I have always been glad that my windows are tinted to keep the sun out of my eyes, but today, we hide behind the darkness at midday.

Thirty minutes later, her car starts and leaves the parking lot.

Forty minutes later, The Wife greets me at my front door with a kiss.

Sixty minutes later, Lila texts me a series of suggestive emojis that make me smirk, and I immediately erase them. Then she sends, *Thanks for the jump. Love you*, which also gets erased.

I'm happy all evening. I feel bold and spontaneous.

Until I find myself in my bedroom with The Wife. She lights the candles and has our favorite music playing. She touches me and kisses me tenderly. I return her affection. But it isn't enough.

Again.

She wipes away tears and sits on the edge of the bed. "Is it me? Are you just not attracted to me? What's happening? I've tried not to make a big deal about this, but I'm starting to take it personally."

"It's not you. I love you deeply. I just can't. I don't know what the problem is." I'm lying. I know what the problem is.

"Should we get your hormones checked? Is there a physical problem? Is your mind wandering? What's the deal?" she asks again. "I need you."

"I know. I'm so sorry." I reach for her. I want to hold her and fix this. I'm determined to show her that she is beautiful, wonderful, and desirable. She lets me kiss her and push her backwards onto the pillows.

She is patient, but nothing has changed. She ends up crying

again, turns on her lamp, blows out the candles, puts on her Mickey Mouse pajamas, grabs her latest book, and says, "This is frustrating down to my core. I'm going to read my book. Goodnight."

I lie down next to her, facing the wall. "I'm sorry," I say. This is torture for us both. "I wish I could fix it." And I drift off to a fitful sleep.

On Saturday morning, the text reads, *Paul, I'm not trying to make this a habit, honest I'm not. But I just got my lawnmower out for the first time this year. If I don't mow my lawn, I think the neighbors are going to vote me off the island. And it won't start. What do I do?*

She needs me. I look at my watch. It's only 10:00. I'm just starting my own yard work, and I have to go out and buy some mulch and a new hose. I return her text. *I can be there in half an hour.*

I call out, "Running some errands! I'll be back in a while," and I shut the door behind me.

I park in her driveway, which is my regular space now. I'm a bit surprised that her kids are home. This is the first time they have seen me. I wonder how she explained who I am. I get out of my truck and walk over to Lila, who's standing by the lawnmower.

"Hey, Paul. Thanks for coming."

"Sure. Let me take a look." I check the gas, the spark, and the air filter. Her three-year-old boy is fascinated by what I'm doing. He studies me intently. The older kids have disappeared inside. Lila stands back and watches the two of us silently interact.

The carburetor is clearly overdue for a tune-up, but that will have to wait for another day. After tinkering with it for half an hour, I get it started. Her little boy stands by me the whole time. I'm impressed by his attention span.

"Wow!" Lila gushes. "Thanks!"

"You're welcome. I guess I'll see you around." I head to my truck.

"Yep." She smiles and winks at me. "See you around, Paul."

A few days later, Lila calls to say she finished work early, her kids are still at the babysitter's, and she wonders if my shift is over. Her tone is mysterious, and I have the feeling she has planned something extraordinary. I leave work early. I take the key from my pocket and enter her front door, my heart pounding.

Lila is standing in the living room wearing something silky. I lock the door behind me and slip out of my shoes. "Well, this is a wonderful surprise," I say.

She walks toward me, pushes me into the door, and leans hard against me. She puts her lips near mine and says, "Hello, Paul," only kissing my mouth when she sputters my name against my lips with emphasis. "I was thinking we could play a game, Paul," she whispers. "How about... I'm a lady in trouble. Do you think you could come help me, Paul?"

"Well, I'll certainly do my best." I flip her around and pin her against the door. I feel her heart beating.

She whispers into my ear, "How about you call me... 'ma'am'?"

I'm eager to play along. "Yes, ma'am. Anything you say, ma'am."

"How about I call you... Joseph."

Joseph

No.

No.

No.

No.

I let go of her and sank into a chair.

No.

No.

No. I can't…

I stared ahead. How did she… But… Paul is here.

No…

She was laughing. "Well, you didn't honestly think I wouldn't find out, did you? I'm pretty smart."

I just looked up at her. At this woman who was half naked, standing in front of me. I couldn't speak.

"Yes, you hid it pretty well. But it was actually the funniest thing. I was on LinkedIn because we had just done a team-building exercise at work, so I was following up on a friend of a friend of a co-worker. And there I was, on his profile, and I found a picture of a guy who looked oddly familiar. But his name was Joseph Reeve, an engineer. So weird… I was pretty sure his name was Paul, and he was an EMT. So I've been looking you up, Joseph. I Googled you. I drove past your house in Provo yesterday."

She was standing above me. The floor would not stop moving beneath me. And I was somewhere—drifting—in the void of space between.

"I understand why you said your name was Paul. But I would think after all this time, after what we mean to each other, you could've told me your real name." She laughed again.

"No." My first attempt at speaking. "No, I couldn't. No, I can't. You don't understand. My family. My wife. I can't."

"So, I saw that you really do have three girls. At least that was the truth."

"Of course that's the truth," I croaked. "I would never lie about my family."

"Yeah, but you never told me their names. I see your wife's name is Rachel." She had no idea... the gravity of what this meant... what this was doing to me...

"Yes. Rachel..." It felt like sacrilege to say her name while I was sitting in this place.

She rolled her eyes. "You love *me*, I know you do. You tell me you do. You clearly have an unhappy marriage—otherwise, why would you keep coming back to me? I do things for you she can't do." She stepped toward me.

I looked past Lila and stared at nothing. "She's not the problem." I shook my head and tried to absorb what was happening. "I'm broken. I hate myself. I'm self-destructing. And I just need an escape from my life for a while. But never from her."

"Well, she obviously has no idea what you need. She sounds clueless. I mean, come on. She doesn't even know what you've been doing all this time... Wait!" Lila reached down and grabbed my shoulder. "Think about this! What if she's not clueless—what if she's actually permissive? What if she knows I'm the only one who can make you happy, so she's, like, giving you permission to be with me?"

"That's absurd," I mumbled. "She doesn't know. I've been good at hiding." *Rachel knows. Deep down, she knows.*

Lila crouched in front of me. "Well, I like you here. I *need* you here. It meant so much when you came and helped me with my car. I watched you with my son when you fixed my lawnmower. It changed things for me. We could be really happy, Paul. Uh, sorry! Habit! We would be so good together, Joseph. Do you go by 'Joe'?" She smiled. "We could be an awesome family."

I met her gaze. "I *have* a family, Lila."

"But I need you here. And I know you like it here..." She gently ran her finger up my leg.

I grabbed her hand. "I can't. This is just... I'm just... I..."

Her face registered the rejection, and her eyes narrowed. "I also found you on Facebook. Your middle daughter just graduated, and she's going to BYU. I saw that you're the Young Men's president in your ward. That took me a second. I didn't expect that one."

The air felt thick. But Paul! Paul. It was working so well. Paul was happy. Paul was doping and getting the fix. But in one word... one word... my name.

Joseph.

"Joseph, wash your hands before you hold the baby. This is your new nephew!"

"Joseph Paul Reeve, having been commissioned of Jesus Christ, I baptize you..."

"Joseph, run down to the storage room and get three bottles of peaches for me."

"Joseph, your mission call came today!"

"Joseph, I love you. You are my life."

"Hey, Joe. Sorry for the late hour. I wanted to let you know that our dear mother has gone home."

"Joe, can I marry your daughter?"

Joseph...

That name, whispered into my ear from the mouth of a woman who wasn't my wife.

Oh, what have I done?

"Lila, I love my wife."

"But you said you loved me."

"I know I did. But it's different."

Lila balled her fist and punched my leg. "Are you serious right now? Really? So if you're Paul, you're into me, but Joseph is a self-righteous Mormon who's too good for me? So it matters what name I call you? You are such a hypocrite." She spat out the word.

"Lila, it's not like that. Listen to me. I'm broken. You know what I've told you about my past. I needed to be someone else for a while. I hate who I am. I hate who I've become. It's not about you. I care for you. You're a talented person, a hard worker, a great mom. I've kept coming here because I care for you. I know we're friends."

"Friends?" she shrieked. She punched my leg again and then retreated to the couch, where she held a pillow to her chest. She looked very small. "Friends? Seriously? I'm sitting here in a negligee I bought for you, and we're *friends*? Why did you say you loved me? Why? You're just like all the other guys who've used me." Mascara had started to run down her face.

I was defensive about that comparison. "I wasn't using you. I'm not using you. You're a great person. I said I love you." I scooted forward in the chair and rested my elbows on my knees. "I never meant for this to happen. Lila, look at me."

Her brown eyes looked up at me from behind her pillow. And I suddenly saw something I had never seen before—I saw into her soul. I saw a lifetime of pain and rejection that made me gasp. To see the depth of her misery was devastating.

"How could you do this to me?" she breathed.

I replied softly, gently, "I wasn't trying to hurt you. I was just hiding. I didn't know it would get this far." But there was no way to justify or explain. My words sounded empty.

She hurled the pillow at me. "I swear, I'll just slit my wrists! I swear. Then I'll be out of your hair and you can go back to The Wife you love so much with your three girls and your perfect life and lie to all your church friends and be a huge hypocrite, and the only person who knows your dirty little secret will be dead!"

"Lila, I don't want that." I got up and sat next to her on the couch. All I could think was that I needed to fix her. "You've made me feel alive these last few months. You've been my escape. You're one of the reasons I could get out of bed. I needed you, and you were there for me. Please, Lila. Listen to me."

She looked at me through her tears and smirked. "Did you know that we have mutual friends? Facebook is a gold mine of information. Mark and Anna are in your ward, right? I went to high school with them. Wouldn't they be interested to know what you really are?"

Mark and Anna? I had to do a mental double-take to make sure I had heard her correctly. Mark was serving in the priests quorum with me, and Rachel had become very good friends with Anna as her visiting teacher. "Lila, you wouldn't do that to me. I know you love me. You wouldn't hurt me like that."

She wiped her face with the back of her hand. "Yeah, well,

I want to. You deserve it, you lying snake. I feel like an idiot. I thought this was exciting. I thought you were different. I thought you were, well, in love with me."

"I do care, Lila. I do love you. I'm sorry I hurt you." I pulled her toward me. "Can I hold you?"

And after she let me hold her, I found myself in her bed.

Me. Joseph.

Part II:
Joseph and Rachel

Rachel

Ten years earlier, I was attending a Relief Society "get to know you" activity. We had a sheet of paper with questions on it, and we had to mingle to ask and record people's answers. A sweet lady approached me and read the question to me. "Rachel, where is your favorite place to be?"

I looked her squarely in the face and quite innocently said, "In my bedroom with my husband."

She giggled, fanned her face with her paper, and said, "Oh, my! Did anyone else just hear that? Oh, my!"

I'm sad for her that isn't her answer too. But how could it be, when she misunderstood?

There is no other feeling in the world that compares to being with Joe in our room. There is truly no other place I would rather be. It's just him and me, alone, and the world disappears. We breathe better, we see better, we think better. We relax into each other, and it's pure bliss. It's where we go to get healed. It's how we communicate. It's when we're in sync. It's the way we listen. It's the way we recharge.

Just us. Alone.

Our favorite place. Our sacred sanctuary.

"The girls haven't seen you all day. They miss you. Could you at least go down the hall and say goodnight to them?" I was in the closet hanging up Joe's shirts. He had just come home from the regular Wednesday night Young Men's activity, but had stayed late to chat with the bishop about Helaman's Camp.

"Yeah, sure."

The moment he walked out of the room, a stunning, crushing, excruciating feeling overcame me. I felt the words in my head before I audibly heard a voice say, *He's gone.*

I fell to the floor. I had never had such an experience. It was completely unexpected, and confusingly real. I stayed in a facedown heap in the closet and rocked back and forth, trying to regain my breath while sobbing into my laundry pile. I knew I had a few minutes to get control of myself before he came back. But all I could do was wonder and cry.

He came back too soon. He walked into the closet and stood near me. "Rach, are you okay? What happened?"

I tried to gain control. I tried to speak clearly through my tightened throat. "Joe... Is it over? Are you gone?"

This was not the response he expected. "What are you talking about?"

"I have no idea! I keep asking you to talk to me, and you say you're tired. I keep asking you to tell me what's wrong, and you say you have a lot on your mind. I know there's something wrong, Joe!" I didn't mean to start screaming. I really didn't. It was just the panic in my soul. "Why won't you tell me? Why won't you let me help you?" I reached out, hugged his knees, and pleaded, "Please, Joe. Tell me. Where are you? Where have you gone? Please."

He squirmed out of my grip. "Rachel, listen to me. I'm just going through a tough time. I'm not going anywhere."

I let out a forlorn howl that I didn't recognize from myself. "Why won't you let me in? This is what we do! I'm your best friend. Why won't you let me help you? Why won't you talk to me?"

"Rachel, there's really nothing to say. I'm just sad."

I threw a shirt against the closet wall and yelled. "You can't even make love to me! It's humiliating. What have I done? What's going on? Why won't you tell me?"

And Joe did something Joe never does. He walked out of the room.

As I sat on the floor in my closet, I knew the feeling I had, the voice I'd heard, was truth.

It was Friday, so it was date night—no matter what. Things had been uncharacteristically chilly between us for a few days. My very good questions had gone unanswered, Joe had weakly apologized for walking out of the closet while I was crying ("I didn't know what to say, and I didn't want to make it worse"), and he kept smiling at me in such a way that was probably supposed to be reassuring—but it wasn't worth much. So I requested ice cream and a drive. I would have his total attention, which was what I liked about our drives. I had been impressed that we needed to be reminded what we meant to each other, so I had been working on an idea.

"Joe, I want to read you something." I turned off the radio.

"Okay." He slurped the bottom of his strawberry shake and returned the empty cup to the center console.

"I wrote this today to share with you. I just... I just want to remind both of us, I guess, what we have together. I want you to hear what I love about you. I'm trying to... I need to... Well, it helps to remember these things, doesn't it?"

"Okay." He seemed cautious, but willing to go with it.

"I want to read it slowly, though. Stop me if you have a comment. Here goes.

> *Joe is the most brilliant man I have ever met. He has great ideas. He is always thinking.*
> *Joe knows everything about the gospel of Jesus Christ. He gives great lessons. He is filled with the Spirit and with insight. He has an amazing—*

"Rachel."

> *—spiritual charisma.*

"Rachel, thank you for this, but this is hard to hear. I don't feel so awesome right now."

"Look, I know we're in a rough patch. There's a point to all this. Just keep listening."

He was obviously reluctant, but he knew I was determined. "Okay," he acquiesced.

> *Joseph is the most sensitive man in the known universe. He cries all the time. He cries with you. He cries for you.*
> *Joe's hands are huge and wonderful. I think of all the things those hands know how to do, and have done, and it boggles the mind. He is a hard worker. His work ethic is astounding.*
> *He observes, then applies. Thus, he knows how to do just about everything in this whole wide world. And do it well.*

"You learned that from your dad, and I have always been amazed by you," I added. "I miss your dad."

"Me too."

> Joe has a booming bass voice, and I love to lie on his chest and listen to him talk. His voice resonates through him.
>
> He will go through the kitchen smelling the herbs and spices, and when he finds the combinations that match what he's looking for, he adds it to the dish. He makes the most amazing food that can never be duplicated. He taught me how to cook steaks.

"I love to cook with you," he volunteered. I could tell he was softening as he listened to my list.

> I love to hear Joe laugh. I get such a kick out of his quick wit.
>
> He's warm all the time. Like, his temperature is warm, which is wonderful for me and my cold toes. But indeed, he is warm and genuine all the time too.
>
> He's not shy to meet and greet strangers. People feel instantly comfortable around him.
>
> Joe is a good driver. He's been doing it since he was four and couldn't see over the dashboard.

"I'm sorry I tell you how to drive," I apologized.

"It's okay."

"By the way, turn left here."

Joe laughed.

> He is brave.
>
> He is an amazing father to three strong daughters. They love and trust his advice, they seek his approval, they think he's hilarious, and they use him as a measuring stick for the boys they consider.
>
> I have only seen him mad, really mad, a handful of times. He is kind.

"I'm sorry you've seen me mad," he apologized.

"If you were never mad, I would wonder if you were human." I continued reading.

> *He helps with all the math and science homework.*
> *He does dishes. He makes beds with perfect hospital corners. He scrubs bathtubs. He does laundry and remembers not to put fabric softener in the whites. There is no job too hot or dirty or stinky or 'below him.'*
> *He trusts and validates me. He speaks to me with respect. He treats me kindly and as an equal.*
> *He has always earned our income, but he never says, 'This is my money.' I usually pay the bills and spend the money, and he has never questioned me or second-guessed me.*
> *He is an incredible, selfless, and generous lover. I am so in love with him, and that makes EVERYTHING SO GOOD.*

"And for that, I thank you yet again," I reiterated.

"Thank *you*. I love being with you."

"Joseph, seriously, about that. People call it chemistry, but I think it's more than that—I love the colors of us. I feel like we're the perfect crayon box, right? Every shade to match our mood. Sure, we ebb and flow like everyone else, but we have figured it out. We always end up reaching for each other. We have great colors together. Our relationship is beautiful whether it's muted or vibrant."

He looked over at me, and by the light of the dashboard, I could see his brimming eyes. "I love being with you, Rachel. I'm sorry it's been frustrating for so long."

"I'll keep going with the list. I'm almost done.

> *He is my best friend. I am his best friend. He tells me everything. I am simply compelled to tell him everything.*
> *I've always thought he was perfect for me in every way.*
> *And terribly flawed.*

He cleared his throat as he checked his blind spot to change lanes. "So, you know about the flaws?"

"Absolutely. I know you, all the good and bad. I love it all. I love you, Joe. I have always loved you. I'm sorry I have been less than perfect."

"You? You're perfect for me!" he shot back.

"Well, yes, I am, but this is the point I'm trying to make. You have had the patience of Job as I struggled with depression. You have been endlessly encouraging as I've tried to figure out how to be a mom. You have always helped me fulfill my big Church callings even when it took time away from us. I know I've not always reacted kindly. I know I've not always been as patient with you. I know I have double standards in our relationship. But you've always loved me. I had a horrible self-esteem for years, and your wisdom helped me figure that out. You've never told me to be skinnier or prettier, or to... whatever. You've never criticized me! Any part of me! You've always told me that I'm enough, and it took me years, but I believe you. Your example has changed the way I love people. I've tried to love you like you love me."

"Wow." He was moved, and his voice cracked. "Rachel, you're amazing. You hold me together. You are what anchors me."

"I needed to hear that." I felt calm there in the dark as he drove. I knew we were both ready for the next part of my plan. "Joseph Paul, we have to figure this out. We have drifted. That's a fact. This has gone on too long. We need a new start. I've been thinking about something for a while—we need to draw a line in the sand and step over. I've been with you for thirty years now, and we've been married for twenty-five. I look at my wedding ring, and I'm wondering if it's time to retire it."

Joe visibly jumped. "Rachel, no!"

I patted his shoulder. "Joe, just listen. Remember when it broke? I took it off to mix meatloaf with my hands, and I set it on the counter. I was just taking the salt from the cupboard, and somehow a can of soup fell out and happened to land right on my ring and broke the band. The band! Frankly, I took that as a bad omen. I'm done having a sparkly diamond and a delicate gold band. This just doesn't represent me anymore. I have never been a sparkly girl, and at this point in our lives, I think we're much stronger than gold that bends and breaks. I want matching bands, simple and strong. Something that represents us. Something that represents a new start."

He was silent for only a moment. "That's actually a very good idea. The thing that comes to mind immediately is titanium. It's strong. It resists corrosion. It's highly useful. It doesn't fatigue easily."

"That sounds perfect. It sounds like us."

He merged onto Highway 6 to head back home. "I'll do some research and see where we can find them."

We rode in silence for a while. I knew he had heard what I said, and I knew we were theoretically on the same page, but there was still something… something that hadn't clicked for me. Historically, when that's been the case for either one of us, we would initiate one more conversation, figure it out, and move on. But that hadn't been the case for months. Somewhere along the line, Joe had shut down. Tonight, though, I sensed there *had been* a little progress, so I decided to feel hopeful anyway.

Joe broke the silence. "Rach, thanks for all the nice things you said about me. I really want to be what you need me to be."

"You are." I reached for him across the divide of the front seat console. "Let's refocus and simplify. Let's draw a line in the sand and step over together."

He breathed deeply like he was going to say something on his mind, but he paused and simply said, "I'm sorry I've been hurting you, Rachel."

I needed him to keep talking. I *knew* there was more to say. But we were done.

The following evening, Sarah was working on a project with a piece of decorative glass. She used too much glue around the edges, but Joe assured her he could salvage it by using a hand tool to shave off the hardened globs of glue. It was supposed to be an easy fix. He was almost done when his hand slipped, the tool clipped the edge of the glass, and a shard flew directly into his left eyeball. I called our eye doctor's messaging service, and they told me the doctor would meet us at the office immediately.

"So… how did the glass go straight through your safety glasses?" was the first thing Dr. Lewis said as he walked into the exam room and greeted us. He smiled at me in the chair in the corner of the room.

"Yeah, I know. It was supposed to be a quick job. I was almost done," was Joe's embarrassed reply.

Dr. Lewis put in an eye drop that deadened Joe's excruciating pain. "Now I'm going to put in a phosphorescent drop that will illuminate the exact location of the shard, which I can see when the lights are turned off." After doing so, he used his penlight to see it. "That's a pretty good-sized piece of glass stuck right in there, but I don't think it's deep enough to have done any permanent damage. Let me remove it first, and then we'll take a closer look at the cornea." He deftly used his tweezers to remove the glass from Joe's eye. He set it on a tray and said, "I'll show that to you in a minute. Let's look in that eye again."

As the doctor was peering into Joe's eye with the slit lamp, tears unexpectedly started streaming down my face as words started forming in my mind like a prayer. *Dr. Lewis, I know the eye is the window to the soul. Can you please tell me what you see in there? Can you please look into his soul with that piercing light and tell me the sorrow he won't share with me? Surely you can see what I can't. I beg you, please, please tell me. I can't see it, but I know it's there. Please, please look hard into all the deep recesses and tell me what it is. Why is he so sad? Why can't he sleep? What is it? It's the not knowing that's killing me. If you'd just find it and tell me, I could deal with it. Please...*

And then the lights went on, and I wiped my cheeks. Opportunity lost.

Joseph

My understanding of what I had been doing was slowly dawning.

I had a very visual image of a wall that I had built between the two parallel men inside my head. It came crashing down when Lila called me by my given name.

Paul had done all those awful things. *Paul* carried the blame. *Paul* was lying to The Wife. *Paul* was hurting himself and everybody around him. *Paul* was on a destructive rampage.

I would never do that.

Joseph had an awesome life. Joseph loved God. Joseph honored his heritage. Rachel was the choice of his heart. For heaven's sake, Rachel had read me that list of all the things she loved about me, and I had to admit that they were all true.

Lila had unwittingly dynamited the wall when she called me "Joseph," and I suddenly had a very stark, unpleasant, and unmistakable view of both sides—disparate actions I had refused to let the other man acknowledge. I could not fathom how I had gotten here. I would never do this. How had I let it get this far? This duality was not in my mental, emotional, or spiritual makeup.

Living two separate realities? *Who does that?* I did, because that was the only way I could function. It was exhausting, but it had been working, right? No. It was time to get honest. My "realities" never had been separate. I was both Paul and Joseph, and I always had been.

I couldn't keep living like this. Pretending. Hiding. It was destroying me. It was destroying everyone I loved.

The question plagued me during all my waking hours—*How am I going to get out of this?* I was an engineer. I solved problems for a living, right? I had to find a way to engineer it to a stop. I had to help Lila move on, and I had to figure out how to keep Rachel.

Now *there* was a reality I was going to have to face. I was going to lose her. I couldn't keep lying. But… there was no way I could tell her the truth. Maybe it was one of those things that I could tell her in five—no, ten years. I could tell her an abbreviated version of how I had messed up, but by then, she would have living, breathing proof that I was a changed man. She wouldn't leave.

Who am I kidding? I would lose everything.

I needed a fix. A fix that fixes nothing.

> Paul: Hey. How have you been?
>
> Carrie: Life is one awesome crap storm after another. You?
>
> Paul: Same. What's happening with you?
>
> Carrie: My sister just found out she has cancer.
>
> Paul: Oh man. That is bad. I had an older brother with cancer.
>
> Carrie: She has little kids. It's hard to look them in the face and say everything is going to be fine.
>
> Paul: I know exactly how you feel.

Why are destructive memories so relentless?

I was fully aware of how awkward I was in school. I was a pretty good student, but I didn't have the suave charisma other guys had. I was that guy the adults always liked, but I had nothing in common with my peers. So when Rachel started looking past that, seeing *me* beyond the awkward, it was a lottery win. I started picking her up for school, and we'd spend our lunch hour together. But, loser that I am, I didn't know how to have a normal dating relationship. I only knew one way to communicate, one way to spend time together, one way to function, one way to relate to a girl.

> Paul: So, are you still chatting with other guys?
>
> Lila: Yeah. Most r total idiots. A few r cool.

> Paul: Have you thought about going out with any of them?
>
> Lila: Yeah. There's one. He wants to meet.
>
> Paul: I think you should.

I was Rachel's first boyfriend. She was a few years younger than I was. Her innocence was refreshing. She was very patient with me, and I subconsciously used that. I didn't mean to take advantage of her nature. That's not who I am. Or is it? Because I *did* take advantage of her. She wasn't like other girls who might've kicked me in the groin, stomped my foot, and cursed me out. She would take my hands and reposition them on her back. She would step away and say, "No. I really don't want to do that." And I tried to honor her kindness. She was different. She would look into my eyes. Into my *soul*.

But I pushed her. And pushed. And bent her will. And wore her down. She often said no. She was too polite to leave. She saw me as a wounded person, and she didn't want to give up on me. She was loyal. She wanted to help me. She was a teenage girl who wanted to fix me.

She didn't know that my problems were way out of her league.

She wouldn't leave me, no matter what I did. When I pushed too far, she would yell at me. And cry. Every time, she would cry. But she never left. She believed I would change.

I loved her for not leaving me.

I hate what I did. Self-loathing is the theme of my life.

> Lila: Joe, he was a total player. He turned on the charm, and I shouldn't have, but we did. And as soon as it was over, he was like, "Hey, I gotta go." Why does this keep happening to me? What is wrong with me?
>
> Paul: Well, what did you like about him?
>
> Lila: He was cool about my kids, like U. He is a family man, like U. He has a good job, like U. He's easy on the eyes, like U.

> Paul: Well, those things are positive. Maybe you just caught him on a bad day. Maybe you should give him another chance.
>
> Lila: Maybe. I can't wait to see U in the AM. Your the only thing good in my life.

> Paul: How are you?
>
> Blair: I've been pretty good lately. My husband wants to get back together.
>
> Paul: So, the separation is over?
>
> Blair: I think so.
>
> Paul: I'm happy to hear that.
>
> Blair: What about you? How's your wife?
>
> Paul: She's still good. And I'm not good enough for her.
>
> Blair: That's rotten. She sounds way too uptight.
>
> Paul: That came out wrong. I'm just saying, she's a good person, and I'm not what she deserves.
>
> Blair: Oh. Well, I hope you figure it out, Paul.

That night, Rachel and I reviewed our day with our heads on our pillows. I spoke toward the ceiling. "Helaman's Camp is next week. Could you get some mosquito repellant when you go shopping? We're about out."

"Sure. Need anything else?"

"Not that I know of."

She pulled her blankets around her neck and said, "I'll get the laundry done by Monday so you can pack. You leave Tuesday? What time?"

"Early. I think 7:00."

"Are you staying at Deer Creek all week?"

"Kind of." I explained, "The stake is sending all the different quorums to different places, but the priests, bishops, and the stake president are staying near Deer Creek for boating. We're coming down to Provo for the ropes course on Thursday. Then the whole stake is meeting back up at Deer Creek for a big, full day together on Friday, then home from there on Saturday morning."

"Sounds like a lot of fun."

"I'm so glad I didn't have to plan this. I guess the stake presidency planned most of this one, too. They made this summer's activities easy on the wards."

She yawned. "Yeah, that's been nice."

I yawned. "Maybe I can stop in to see you for a bit on Thursday when I'm in town, if I get a minute."

"I would like that."

"Goodnight, Rachel."

I was mostly asleep when I realized she wasn't holding my arm, and I couldn't remember the last time she did. A voice popped into my head. *How can we draw a line and step over if I'm holding on to the past?*

I was driving to Lila's in the early morning darkness. I was thinking about Steve.

When Steve died, I wanted to know that everything I was told about life after death was true. I heard my mother's repeated assurances. I heard testimonies borne in sacrament meeting by earnest people. But I wanted to know. I *needed* to know for myself.

Because it was Steve.

I was in my room one day, about a month after he died, and I had a thought to pick up the tape recorder and just talk. I turned it on, and I found myself explaining that Steve had died and that it tore me up inside. He was my favorite, my hero. Although he was ten years older, he was the brother closest to my age. He had been strong and big and tough, and I wanted to be like him. I found myself in prayer, pleading to God and into the tape recorder to know, "Is there a heaven? Will I see him again there?"

A sacred, sure, and overpowering spirit filled the room. My soul heard the calm affirmation of the Holy Spirit. *Mortal death is not the end, but a part of our eternal progression. You will see him again.* And then the Holy Spirit wrote with His finger in the fleshy tables of my heart to answer the yearnings I had not uttered. *Families are created on earth to endure for eternity. The Plan of Happiness is real. Jesus Christ is your Redeemer.*

I have held on to that experience my whole life. That has been my touchstone. I know the Holy Ghost speaks and comforts us, and the gospel of Jesus Christ is true.

I was still thinking about this when I found myself on Lila's doorstep. I pulled the key from my pocket and let myself in. I stepped in and closed the door, and I heard a powerful voice.

What are you doing here? What are YOU... doing... here?

In an instant, my mind and my soul were awakened as if from a deep sleep. I felt an overpowering desire to change, permanently. I suddenly wanted to stand before God, hiding no more, and let Him heal my wounds. I wanted to stand before my precious wife, hiding no more, and let her heal my wounds. I wanted light. I wanted to be found on holy ground. I remembered the love I learned from my mother and the love I saw daily in the eyes of my daughters. I wanted to stop lying and hiding and chasing fantasy and hating myself and medicating with poison.

It couldn't have been any more powerful if, like Alma the Younger, I had seen an angel. This was a direct, undeniable communication from heaven for me. I was being called to change. I grabbed the door handle and turned it.

But I glanced over my shoulder down the hall. I felt responsible for Lila. I had to help her move on. I wasn't sure how to say goodbye, but I couldn't end it like this. I was caught in a riptide. I let go of the door handle and was pulled under by the current.

I drifted into Lila's room and sat on the foot of the bed. "Hey, we need to talk." I tried to figure out where to start. "Helaman's

Camp is next week," I said into the darkness.

Lila spoke from her pillow. "I don't want you to go. I need you to decide, Joe. I need you here with me."

"Lila, I care about you. But I've made my decision. My place is with Rachel."

"So, why are you here?" She sat up and smacked me in the shoulder. "You're saying you love her more than me, even though I'm the one who makes you happy. I'm not the one you're cheating on! I'm not the one you're trying to escape from!"

If I had been in my right mind, I would've known that the implosion of this relationship was inevitable from the beginning. It had only been about me—my pain, my escape. It wasn't supposed to turn into this. I never realized I would cause so much damage to everyone else. Why couldn't it have just stayed "temporary"? How did this relationship become... this? I'd never had to break up with anyone in my life, and I knew I would end up breaking this woman in half. "Lila, I do care about you. You know I love you. But my life is there."

"You've seen my bandages, Joe. You make me do that to myself. You make me bleed. I need you, Joe. You're the best thing in my life right now. You can't leave me."

The wave of guilt crashed over my head, as she intended. But I had to stop letting it have power over me. "What about those other guys you've been with? You can find someone."

"That's just a game. They're not you! I've been searching for someone who can take your place, and there's no one. No one loves me like you do. No one."

I heard the words from the voice again. *What are you doing here?*

I had to find a way for this to end. But I felt helpless. I couldn't watch her heart break. I fell backward onto the bed and began to cry. "Lila, I'm so sorry I've dragged you into my mess." I covered my eyes.

"Joe, it's so simple. Just stay. Stay with me. Rachel will get over it. She knows it's over, right? This is where you belong. You're happy here."

"Lila, I'm not happy anywhere because I'm not happy with *me*. Everywhere I go, since I was a kid…" My tears flowed into my ears. "I'm broken, and I have hurt anyone who has ever touched me. This is so out of control. I've got to stop, Lila." My shoulders began to shake, and I couldn't breathe.

She rested above me on one elbow. "Joe," she said softly. "I'm always here for you. You can cry on me any time you want." She wiped my tears.

It was time to draw my line. I sniffed hard and sat up. "Lila, please listen to what I'm trying to say. Please understand." I stood up and walked to the bedroom door. I turned and spoke with the gentleness I felt. "I… I really need to let you go. It's selfish of me to stay. You need to get on with your life."

Her yelling surprised me. "Then just get the hell out! Go back to your stupid wife and your selfish life!"

I left her house, locking the door behind me. I mindlessly put the key in my pocket and walked away.

Rachel

I waited for Joe.

Even though I was a teenager when I met him, I sensed him. I read the light behind his eyes, and I knew there was gold in there. So I waited. And waited. And waited for that Joe to show up.

I sacrificed too much and too often waiting for him to show up. But I knew he would. If only I could find the right words, be patient enough, be strong enough... Clearly, we were both the victims of youth and inexperience. I had no idea how deep the problem was. He probably didn't either.

I had heard somewhere that it was dumb to date a boy with the intent to change him. But I did that very thing because I felt like I was *supposed* to. I knew his family, I knew his history, and I felt like I knew his heart. I could help him be the man he was meant to be! So I put him first, and I faded into the background. My pain never mattered. I allowed... I allowed my innocence to go up in smoke.

I was a bright girl with intelligence and promise. I loved school, and I wanted to go far. But I fell in love with a guy who simultaneously respected me and abused me, and it only stopped when he went to Marine Corps Boot Camp and then on his mission. I ended up with chronic absences in high school. I couldn't get out of bed to face the day. Teachers loved me and hated me—I was a good student who was capable of doing more, but I could barely function. For years, I had recurring nightmares that I didn't graduate from high school, although in reality I got a scholarship to college because I could play the piano. I went to college and dropped out after a semester.

Depression was a monster; I was sinking fast and gulping water. I had no one to tell. I had to hide to protect... him. At first, I told no one because it would reflect poorly on his wonderful family. Later, I told no one because he might get sent home from his mission. For whatever the reason, I told no one. It was the hardest thing I had ever gone through because I lost myself, and it took years and years to get any of it back. But it changed the trajectory of my life.

But I kept waiting. I worked on forgiving him. And forgiving myself. When he came home from his mission a changed, wonderful man, I knew it was time to marry him. I wasn't caught up in the dress, or the cake, or the decorations, or all the inconsequential whatevers—I was caught up in Joe. I wanted to be with him, in the temple, making this covenant. I wanted our journey to be sanctified by God. I wanted my sacrifice, and his success, to be acknowledged. We had overcome! We had arrived in the right place at the right time!

The temple president, President Kelley, was a family friend, so we asked him to perform the sealing ordinance. He spoke to us briefly in the celestial room before we went to the sealing room. In both places, he said, "Don't let pornography into your marriage." What? Yes, okay, Joe had problems as a youth. It's over! Yay! We are here! Let's celebrate and move on! To my young ears, talking about pornography in the temple sounded crass and ugly. I heard what he said, but I didn't *listen and understand* the voice of prophecy.

So we knelt at the altar, and President Kelley said, "Now, during this ceremony, I want you to look at me so I know you're listening. You've got all eternity to stare at each other and make googly eyes." And so I held Joe's hand and watched President Kelley seal us together with beautiful words. I listened to the marvelous promises. I felt the Holy Spirit of promise. I knew Steve was there for his little brother. I felt Joe's warm assurance. I felt us become bonded—sealed—for this life and forever. I had never been so filled with understanding of God's eternal plans for His children. I felt love. I felt love. I felt love.

It was the happiest day of our lives because it was the very beginning of our eternal lives. We look at those pictures of us skipping about the temple grounds, gazing into each other's eyes, our faces tear-stained, our joy effusive. What happy people.

God gave us the gift of that day to hold on to because it's not easy to watch as prophecy is fulfilled.

Sunday night after our family dinner and games, we found ourselves together in our room, our sacred sanctuary. "Joe, I've been wondering. Do you want me to ask around and find a counselor? For you, for me, for us? Maybe we're at the point where it would help to talk to somebody, more than just talking to each other."

He was sitting in the chair by the window. He looked up from his phone and shook his head. "I don't think so. Rach, I've been thinking a lot lately about our new start, and I'm sure things will settle down after this summer is over. Let's get through Helaman's Camp. I really think it'll be okay. Thanks for giving me time to figure things out."

I sat on the edge of the bed and faced him. "Well, that's the only thing left for me to do—just give it time. I need you to look at me while I say this, Joe." He put his phone down and looked up. "Thank you. Right when I think it might be getting better, you go back to being distant, angry at the world, and disconnected. This has been pretty bad. I don't ever remember you like this. This is not who you are. This isn't who *we* are. We connect, we laugh, we love, we listen, we talk. And we haven't been *us* for a long time. You keep saying you want to fix it, but..."

He knew I was waiting for words of wisdom, an unmistakable sign, or maybe a giant lightning bolt that would suddenly fix this perplexing mess that didn't have a name. But his sad eyes met mine, and he simply said, "I know, Rachel. I feel it too. I miss us. I need us. But I promise it will get better."

So I patiently tried again. "I'm here waiting. I want us, but Joe, it's been hard to keep the faith here. Don't take much longer. I don't know how much more of this we can take. You won't talk to me. You're more distant and abrupt with me than you've ever been. You're making too many withdrawals without enough deposits in our marriage bank account. Something has to change. Instead of making a new start, I feel like we're heading for divorce."

He closed his eyes and winced. Tears fell down his cheeks. He stood and walked to me. "Hold on, Rach. I'll figure this out. Don't let me go."

We held each other silently for a long time.

Go to the temple every week.

I woke from a dead sleep and looked for the shadow of the person who was speaking to me. I saw no one. Joe was asleep next to me. So I asked Heavenly Father in my mind, *You want me to go to the temple every week?*

You will need the strength to save your family.

It didn't frighten me. I thanked Heavenly Father for the direction, and I went back to sleep.

After dinner on Monday, we sat in the living room and sang a song to start family home evening. "Dad has to finish packing for Helaman's Camp so he can leave early in the morning, so we'll be quick. We don't have many more family home evenings before Hannah goes to BYU. You've got your list of what to take to the dorm?" I knew the answer to this—I was saying it as a reminder to Hannah, and also to inform Joe what was going on.

Hannah nodded. "Yeah, I've been sorting through things. I'll be ready."

I began my lesson. "Well, our lesson today is in honor of Hannah's love of chemistry. When I was in sixth grade and we learned about chemical changes, I distinctly remember thinking it was the dumbest concept ever. We had a couple of worksheets where there was, like, a picture of a log burning, and we needed to decide if a chemical change had occurred. Duh, right? I assure you that was my last A in chemistry. But the concept of chemical change has been on my mind lately. You'll remember that many chemical changes are permanent because they irreversibly change the chemical nature of the object. What are some other simple examples of chemical changes?"

This topic was of interest to my family, so the answers came quickly. "Baking cookie dough. Planting a seed. Rotting bananas. Metabolisms. Rust. Hey, Mom, can we bake cookies?"

"Sure. So, are chemical changes bad? I mean, it has taken something and irreversibly changed it."

"Not always bad," Joe said. "It depends on your desired outcome. In simple terms, burning a log is great if you want to roast marshmallows. Burning a log is bad if you're in a dry field."

"Right. So the *best* chemical changes are the ones you cause purposely to change an object's nature and make it permanently something that's more beneficial to you, like baking cookie dough." I smiled at Sarah. "So, let's think about our souls for a minute. God created our souls, which means they're good, right?"

There was consensus on that point.

"Are they ever meant to change?"

"We are always intended to change," Sarah said.

"Yes. Not only is change possible, but it's essential. We are *designed* to change from mortal, flawed, and corruptible beings to immortal, perfected, and incorruptible beings. How do we do this?"

"By baking cookies?" Sarah suggested.

"That may be true. Probably not. Let me rephrase. There is an actual chemical change in our bodies when we die, and again when we're resurrected. But I'm also talking about our souls here on earth. How do we fundamentally, chemically change when we need to?"

Hannah piped up. "Well, you also have to consider the exothermic or endothermic reactions, and if they're ionic or covalent..."

"Whoa there, Nelly. This here is just a simple country analogy. Tie your horses to the hitching post."

Hannah smiled. "Shutting up."

We giggled, but Joe remained quiet. He clearly wanted to say something. The girls looked at me, but I held up my finger and indicated that we needed to wait. He bowed his head, and tears fell through his eyelashes. "There is no way *we* can change. We can try and try, but we are helpless to create that kind of change. The only One who has the power to change the chemical makeup of our souls is Jesus Christ. First, we have to surrender our will to His."

This had obviously been an important moment. I hoped he would share it with me sometime.

Joseph

It was the third day of August, the first day of Helaman's Camp. I felt deep down that this would be a pivotal week. I knew I would get clarity for what my next step should be. I was ready to get my life together, whatever that meant.

President Patrick had prepared a booklet for all the Young Men to work on every morning after breakfast, before the activities of the day. The theme of the week was "Helaman's Army 2010," and every day was a topic from the powerful example of the two thousand and sixty boys who had followed Helaman into battle to save their lives, families, country, and liberty. How had their mothers created such obedient, strong, eager, courageous young men who, fostered by Helaman, had the faith to wage monumental battles and win? How could we follow their examples today? It was a great idea.

Bishop Hanson had asked me to talk to our priests quorum about the first topic in the booklet, repentance. He wanted me to talk specifically about confessing our sins. This topic hit close to home for me, but I wanted to help the boys know how important it was to be honest and forthright about confronting their weaknesses. As I looked into their young faces, I emphasized that it shows strength of character to talk about their impulses, temptations, and sins with their parents, bishop, and God even *before* they have serious issues. I testified that God welcomes us with open arms when we are willing—and ready—to receive help to change. It was the hardest lesson I'd ever had to teach.

Afterward, Bishop Hanson approached me and told me he really liked everything I said. He also said he always liked my Sunday lessons and my comments in ward councils. He looked rather sad, and I chalked it up to feeling tired. I told him how much I appreciated the compliment. We had become pretty good friends in the past year as we had served together.

Wednesday morning, I enjoyed listening to the bishop talk about the next topic in the booklet, obedience. Then we had a full day in the hot August sun playing in the water. I was a little crispy, despite the sunscreen. That evening, I was exhausted and my skin was still hot so I didn't want to spend too much time around the campfire. I was ready for bed.

As I was heading for my tent, I was surprised to feel my phone vibrate with a text message coming through. *I miss you, Joe. I wish you had stayed with me this week.*

Two bars of coverage. That was surprising. I was out of earshot from the group, so I decided to respond by calling her. "What do you want, Lila? Is everything okay?"

"Are you alone? Wanna go to your tent and be alone with me?"

I ignored her proposition. "I'm pretty tired. We've been busy. What do you need?"

"I'm surprised you're even up there."

"I need to be here. This is important."

"No, I mean, I'm surprised your bishop even let you go."

"What?"

"Because I called him last week and told him everything."

My burned skin froze. "No, you didn't."

"Yes, I sure did. He didn't believe me. I talked to him for forty-five minutes. He finally figured out I was telling the truth. There was a lot for me to tell him about the guy who's his Young Men's president."

She wouldn't.

"Joe, are you there?"

I tried to comprehend what she was telling me. "No, you didn't," I said again. My heart began to race. He had asked me to talk about *confessing*... He seemed very sad...

"I asked you not to go, Joe. Remember? I told your bishop that he should think twice about trusting you around the boys. That's why I'm surprised he let you."

I had to hold my head to steady myself. "What?"

"Look, you need to get off the fence. It's her or me. She won't stay around now that your little secret is out. You're free, Joe! You're free to be with me. I'm here, I'm ready, and I'm willing. I want you just the way you are. You in your tent yet?"

"No!" Was she serious? She had just ruined my life.

"Hurry! I'm waiting. I've missed you. I might have already started without you."

Finally, I was able to say the words I had wanted to say for so long. "We are over. Goodbye, Lila." I punched the "end call" button.

And I found myself drowning in horror.

I had just lost everything. Everything.

I began walking up and down hills, stumbling over rocks, seeing only darkness. I had lost my Church membership. My wife. My children. My friends. My life. Maybe my job. Everything.

I felt like I was falling through space. I suddenly remembered the ketchup bottle falling off the kitchen table, and I distinctly connected with the inevitability of a shattering, messy disaster.

I had done this to myself. I had followed my sadness to far-away places. I had spent years in a frantic, futile effort to silence my despair, and I now found myself utterly alone. I began to sob.

I desperately needed my wife, but I couldn't call her. She's my best friend. Nothing is real until we talk about it. My true salve. My Rachel. The only person in the world truly loyal to me—all of me—and I had lost her. How could she forgive this, the grandest of all betrayals? How could anything ever be the same again?

The miserable truth was that her love for me was not as strong as my hate for myself.

I hated being in my own skin. I had been exhaustively living a lie my whole life. I was broken. The only thing that ever made me feel better was fleeting, too fleeting. Like all medications, overuse diminishes potency, and I needed more, more often, higher doses, and experiences that enhanced the effects of the drug.

I had stopped—so many times! In the moments when I wasn't actively medicating, I had been gripping sanity, goodness, and the sheer will to be righteous. I was white-knuckling my way through my life, hoping every day that I wouldn't let go, that it wouldn't all slip through my fingers. I willed myself to believe that I was healed because I wasn't using. So I held on tighter, trying to take care of it myself.

But there was a demon in my soul, and I knew it was there. Slowly, imperceptibly, I had been allowing the demon to devour my light. I had been consumed.

I walked and walked for hours, alternately crying, sobbing, silent. There, in my darkness, a voice said to me, *Pick up your phone and call your brother.* I looked at my phone, and I had battery life left and a signal. On a remote mountainside? Providence. I dialed Aaron. He picked up.

"I'm sorry it's so late…" I breathed in a pained gasp. For five minutes, Aaron listened to my grief-filled sobbing, and twice he said, "I'm here, brother. I'm here." I tried several times to speak, but I could only cry. Finally, I found my voice and said, "Aaron, I've lost everything," and sobbed again at hearing the truth out loud.

My burden was crushing. My defeat had been complete.

I could bear it no more. Standing on a mountaintop, I confessed to Aaron, and God, my soul-suffocating torment. I described the years of agony. The misery… the helplessness… the despair… They gushed out of me like a mighty waterfall. Aaron listened to me and cried with me.

His first words were gently spoken from truth that came from his own experiences. "Joseph, you are a noble son of God."

I didn't expect to hear those words. "How can you say that? I have traveled so far down the path. I'm nowhere near God, and I haven't been for most of my life. I've spent years and years going through the motions, doing all the right things. People looked at me and thought I was some great person because I was talking the talk, but I knew the truth. I'm so far away from God. I'm in hell."

Aaron asked, "Joseph, which way are you facing?"

"What?" I took a moment to orient myself. "I'm facing east."

"No, Joseph. If you're in hell, which way are you facing right now? Are you staring straight in, heading farther down? Or have you turned around to face God?"

"I'm tired of living in hell! I have turned around to face God."

"Then you're closer to God than you have been in a long time because you're finally facing the right way. You're heading toward

Him." He waited a moment before saying it again. "Joseph, you are a noble son of God."

I felt a spark through my grief. And then warmth covered me. The Spirit confirmed those words to my soul. For the first time in my life, I understood that my Father in Heaven loves me—all of me—and I *am* His noble son.

I fell to my knees and wept.

"Joseph, do you understand? You are a noble son of God."

I was awestruck. I finally answered, "All my life I've heard, 'You are a child of God, and He loves you.' Not once, not ever, did I believe that. How could God love me? How could He? But Aaron…" With knees covered in dirt, I bowed my head and spoke quietly. "I am a noble son of God. He loves me." And then I added a thought I had never considered. "He can save *me*."

"Joseph, sometimes only in your extremity can you truly understand that God loved you when you were a young, innocent child, and that He loves you now. The love has always been the same. Unconditional."

And I would know that for the rest of my life, without questioning ever again. It was the tenderest of mercies.

Aaron next asked a gentle question. "Are you ready to talk with your bishop and your stake president? You need their help."

I sat down on the dirt. "I've been ready for months. I've been trying to steer this thing to an end. I'm so tired of living this way."

"Are you really ready? Your soul may be ready for change, but you know as well as I do that changing behavior is the real struggle. You said you've been moving toward making a change, but you've been here before. This time has got to be different."

"After a lifetime of feeling helpless, I'm ready to move forward. All the lying and hiding? It's exhausting. I don't ever want to go back. I've been ready for a while, but I stayed with Lila for so long because I didn't know how to keep her safe and help her move on. I was caught up in how to minimize the hurt I'm causing everybody."

"That was stupid. You should've just said goodbye. Gotten out. Cut your losses. It would've been better for everybody."

"I know… I know." I thought about that pained look in Lila's eyes, and how I thought I could help her make it go away. I realized that only God could heal that—I may have added to it, but I didn't put it there, and I was not capable of fixing it.

"So, how is this time going to be different?" Aaron asked.

I thought about it for a moment. "Rachel gave a profound family home evening lesson the other night about chemical change. She had no idea what it meant for me to hear it. It hit me hard that I, of my own power, can never affect the kind of change necessary to fix myself." I pulled a stick off a nearby bush and began tracing in the dirt. "I'd always thought I had to change my behavior *first*, and *then* go to my Savior for His forgiveness. I've tried my whole life to fix myself, to make myself right, to get rid of this burden, and I can't do it. I need to *come to Jesus first*, with all my horrible, ugly, embarrassing failings, and only then am I humble and pliable enough for *Him* to change me. Only the power of Jesus Christ can make a chemical, *molecular* change to my soul."

"You're right. And now it's time to tell your bishop that exact thing. It shouldn't matter that she called him first. You were going to do it soon anyway, right?"

"Yes. I'm a little mad about that because I wanted to be in control of the way this all happened. I wanted to do this on my own terms. Not like this." I tossed my stick. "I was ready, but… I wanted to be in control."

"Well, regardless of how it happened, your bishop knows now. When are you going to talk to him?"

"In the morning. Definitely. She opened the door to ending this nightmare, and I'm going to take full advantage and walk through. I guess that means…" I took the phone away from my ear and looked at the time. "I'll have to wait four hours. I shouldn't wake up my bishop for this."

"Right. Probably not a good idea."

"I think I've done enough to him this week."

"Yeah."

I was quiet. "I'm going to be excommunicated."

Aaron was tender, but he knew the inevitability. "Yeah."

This was a tough subject for Aaron. We had talked about it a lot when he had been excommunicated a dozen years earlier. Excommunication is not about punishment—it's a gift of time during which all membership obligations are removed to concentrate solely on starting over. At least, that's what it *should* have been, but Aaron's experience had left him bitter for a few years. He had done a lot of spiritual heavy lifting to work through the resentment and anger to reach peace, humility, and rebaptism.

"Joe, the thing I wished I had realized earlier when I was going through my experience is that forgiveness from God is independent of membership in the Church. Neither the Church nor God is rejecting you—far from it. You will be enrolled in a personal, accelerated learning course where you are the only student and Jesus is the Master Teacher. The class goes for as long as you need for your personal, divine tutelage of repentance and forgiveness, and your graduation is ultimate change. The Church has guidelines for timeframes, but your personal journey is up to you. Some of my most powerful experiences with the Spirit happened while I was excommunicated. It's difficult, but don't be afraid."

Aaron was being encouraging, but the thought of it was sobering. I stood up, dusted off my pants, and started walking again. "I know it needs to happen. I'm sad about it, but I've been preparing myself. I made covenants, and I broke them. I know the Church has a right to tell me I can't be a member anymore until I show I'm willing and able to represent the institution honorably."

"I'm glad you brought up covenants. That was going to be my next question—what do you think about your temple covenants?"

I gestured to no one. "That's the thing that has torn me up the most. For years, that was the cause of the guilt. That was the shame. I was such a horrible person *because* I had covenanted to be good. Lila has never been to the temple, and when she found out that I was an active member of the Church, it really shook her. She was beyond disappointed, and it solidified her opinion that the Church is full of hypocrites. I worry that I've hurt a lot of people. I worry that I'm going to damage some souls and testimonies. I feel horrible about that." I kicked at a rock.

"I hear what you're saying. I've definitely been there. But tell me more about how you feel about *your* covenants."

"Ah, man…" I put my forehead in my hand. "*I knew them*! I broke them. It was easier for me to be Paul because he didn't care about them. When I had to face what *I* had done, *me*, it was devastating. Because *I knew* what I was doing. Mom and Dad taught us! I always took my covenants incredibly seriously from the time I was a kid. Not the least of which, I knelt…" A sob escaped my throat. "I knelt and covenanted with God to love Rachel. To honor her. God made promises to me, amazing promises that I can't even comprehend. And I blew right through them. I was selfish. I've felt so much shame because of where I've been and what I've done. Viewing myself with intense loathing is all I know."

Aaron caught me. "What did you say?" He wouldn't let me spiritually regress.

I stopped short. "You're right. No, actually, that's what I *used to know*. I'm a noble son of God." It was surreal to say those words out loud, and to mean them.

"Joe, you know the power of the priesthood covenants you have made. So, remember them and recommit to them. It's never too late. Listen to the Holy Ghost to understand how much God loves you. Listen to what He's telling you. Open your heart and your mind to all the help and gifts He wants to pour out on you. You *are* a noble son. *Noble.* Shame will eat you alive. Get rid of it! Shame is Satan's tool. Nobility is the power and grace of God."

I was silent as this counsel rested on me. Aaron could tell that I was a sponge soaking up all the goodness he could possibly share, so he went into detail about scriptures that had given him great peace—Nephi's lament, Alma the Younger, the prodigal son, Paul's thorn in the flesh, and the woman in Luke 7 who bathed the Savior's feet in tears. These stories came alive for me, and I felt great comfort.

He ended with talking about the Lord's explanation in Ether 12 of why He gives men weaknesses. "Joseph, I strongly believe that *we are given those very weaknesses to drive us to our knees, to submit to the necessary healing only He can provide. Only then* are we humble enough to truly access the redeeming power of Jesus Christ. Only in view of your weakness, Joe, can you truly understand His infinite power and Atonement."

Again, the Spirit wrote those words in my heart. I would hold on to that forever. "Wow, Aaron... I went on a mission, I've been in bishoprics and on the high council, I've taught Gospel Doctrine—I mean, I have a testimony! And for the first time in my life, I realize that this *applies to me*. Jesus will save *me* because He loves *me*."

Jesus also loved me because he told me to call my brother, the only man on the planet who could've helped me in this very moment. But it was 4:00 in the morning, and I needed to let him go back to sleep. "Aaron, thank you so much for picking up the phone. You've... you've saved my life."

"Joe, I want you to do one thing as soon as you can. When I was struggling so mightily, I was given a CD called 'The Lamb of God.' Look it up under the composer, Rob Gardner. Find it. Listen to it every day. It will continue to bring you peace and lead you closer to your Savior. It will replace pain with joy."

"I will. Hey, one more thing, Aaron." I looked up at the stars, and more tears began to fall. "How do I tell Rachel?"

"You just do. Another thing I've learned on my journey is that it takes time to metabolize truth. Say you're eating a protein bar. It takes a while for your body to process that for your good. It's not instantaneous. Between ingestion and metabolization, it just takes time to process it. Be patient with her. This will be a bitter thing to internalize. Give her time."

"I'm going to lose her. I'm going to lose my family."

"Rely wholly on the merits of Christ to save."

I still had a couple of hours before sunrise. There was no way I could sleep. I kept walking and thinking about all the things Aaron and I talked about. I had told him about the worst thing I had ever done in my life, but he just listened and loved me, and he pointed me toward God. But Rachel... the girls... my membership in the

Church… I had found myself, but it was too late. I was going to lose everything else. I needed to come to terms with that.

Aaron and I had talked about King Lamoni's fervent prayer, "I will give away all my sins to know thee." The thought of this was powerful, and it gave me an idea. Walking around, I had been avoiding the outlines of rocks to keep from stumbling, but I began to gather the largest rocks and stack them. I worked at it for about an hour in the early morning darkness, and my pile began to take the shape of an altar.

My mother knew her Father in Heaven because she prayed. When was the last time I had prayed, really prayed? I knelt at the altar. I reached my hands to the sky, wanting to bring heaven toward me, and I began to offer my whole soul to my Heavenly Father. As I communed with Him, the feeling swept over me that my stumbling blocks had *become* my altar.

"Bishop Hanson, can I see you over here for a second?"

He set down the pancake mix. "Sure. What's up?"

"I understand that we need to talk."

He cut me off abruptly and spoke quietly, with intensity. "Not here, not now. We're going to have a good camp experience. We're going to get through this week."

"I just want you to know that I want to get this taken care of as soon as possible." I blinked back tears. "But I have to talk to Rachel first. Give me Saturday to tell her. Then I'll come in on Sunday morning. I don't want to put this off."

Rachel

"Well, hi! It's great to see you! Wait, are you okay?"

Joe came in the front door at 11:30 on Thursday morning, and the moment he stepped in, he was near tears. "We just finished up at the ropes course. We're headed back up to Deer Creek, but I have a minute to drop in and say hi while they're eating lunch. I just… I just had to see you."

"What's *up*? Are you all right? Are you having a terrible time?" I hugged him. He curled around me.

"No. I've just missed you. I needed to see you."

I pulled away to look at him. He did look fine. In fact, truth be known, he looked better than he had for months. His eyes were tender again. The softness had returned to his face. He was crying but seemed no worse for wear other than a toasty sunburn. "Well, it's good to see you. Are you missing lunch? Can I get you something to eat?"

"No. I really just have time to stop in." He reached for me again and nestled his face in my neck. "I love you, Rachel. I love you."

"I love you too, Joseph." He held me as if I were fragile. "Well, I guess I'll see you on Saturday," I said into his ear. "What time will you be home?"

"Noon." He pulled away slowly.

"Hey, our Friday night date can be Saturday afternoon instead! Let's go to lunch, and I can hear all about your week."

"That sounds wonderful." He kissed me wistfully. "There's so much to tell you. See you in two days."

"Rach, it's really good to be home," Joe said as he dropped his camping gear in a heap in the garage. We walked into the kitchen together, and I surveyed him. There was still that palpable difference that I had seen on Thursday. He was uncharacteristically reserved. He was obviously tired. But he looked… delicate. "I'm hungry, but I need a shower before we go to lunch. Give me half an hour?"

"No way. I've missed you too much. I'm coming with." The words came out of my mouth, but my heart immediately second-guessed the offer. I watched Joe walk up the stairs, and I called out after him, "Actually, Joe, I'll just wait for you."

"Okay!"

I waited to hear the water running before I entered our room. I stood in the doorway of our bathroom and spoke toward the shower curtain. "It must feel good to finally get clean."

Joe was slow to answer, but then he said, "You have no idea."

I put his dirty clothes in the hamper, and then I went back to the bathroom doorway. "Tell me about it. Did you have fun? When I saw you on Thursday, your neck and arms were sure red. Do they hurt?"

"No. Kinda. They're okay. It was good. We had a good time. This cool water is helping."

"Well, you're going to love the place I found for lunch. I've never been there before, but I heard someone mention it this week, and I'm excited to try it."

"That sounds really great. Hey, so... I have to talk to you about something."

"I'm listening."

"No, like, later."

"Okay. Whatever you say. Get dressed, and I'll meet you downstairs."

The restaurant wasn't very busy on a Saturday afternoon, and the food was as good as promised. Joe was still subdued. I tried to understand the look in his eye. Calm? Scared? Lost? As we sat at the table in the near-empty restaurant, I took Joe's hand. "So, why were you crying on Thursday?"

"It was a very emotional day."

"What happened?"

"We worked through a booklet for the week, with a different topic each day about how to be spiritually stronger. It just made me think about a lot of difficult things in my life."

I was hopeful. "Like..."

"Like how I need to be a better husband and father. Like how I haven't been everything I need to be." Tears started to fall again.

"I can support that. But seriously, Joe, are you okay?"

"I'm just... I'm just enjoying being here with you, right now." He squeezed my hand.

"So, is this what you had to talk to me about?"

"No. I'll tell you later," he said, very gingerly.

"Okay, but you're scaring me. I know something's up."

"Don't be scared. It's okay."

Joseph & Rachel

This is the last day I will ever spend with my Rachel. Repentance cannot soften the blow of the consequences of sin.

We pass the day getting chores ticked off our lists. Joe is somber all day, but he smiles at me through his tears. "It's okay," he keeps saying. Our last chore of the day is to run to the store, which we do at 9:30, to pick up a few things for Sunday dinner at our house with the extended family. I'm driving, Joe's in the passenger seat, and as I turn a corner about a mile from home, Joe says, "I'm ready to tell you something."

The Spirit speaks clearly to me. *Pull over. Right. Now.*

"Okay, just a sec," I say to Joe. I turn right almost immediately, into the parking lot of a school, where I park under a streetlamp, face him, smile, and say, "Go ahead."

The light divides his face diagonally, half pale blue, half pale yellow. His mouth moves, and his eyes look panicked. Joe is never scared of anything, and he looks terrified. I just watch his mouth move, these foreign words coming out of it, these silly, silly things that could never. The words come forth and fall to the floor and just lay there. I stare down at the words incredulously. Those words could not possibly. Certainly did not. They punched holes in my reality, and disbelief oozed out.

Just say it. Just say it all. Be honest. This is going to kill her. This is going to destroy her heart. Oh, her heart… I hate these words. I hate them. But they are truth, and the truth will set us free.

Surrender to the power of the Atonement of Jesus Christ. Rely wholly on the merits of Christ to save.

"No, you didn't."

"I did, Rachel. I'm sorry."

"No, you didn't. You would never do that to me."

"I will do anything you want me to do to fix this."

"But you didn't. You would just never do that. You wouldn't. You didn't."

I have no idea what to say. All I know is that it's not true. It's not congruent with anything I know to be true about him. Why is he saying this to me? Is he just trying to see what I would say if this had really happened? If I could just think. I'm trying to think. This is a joke, right? Right? But his face... his hands. He's scared to death. This *isn't* a joke? But it's not true. It can't be... but... *what if this is true*? Oh, no... It's *t...r...u...e...* No... I don't want this to be true...

"Oh, Rachel. I'm so sorry. I don't want to lose you. I will wait patiently. I will answer anything you ask me."

"I need a minute to think. You know that split second when you find out your whole life has changed? I just need a minute."
I'm in shock. I feel like I'm at a loud rock concert, and I can't even hear myself scream.

Stay with me, Rachel. I'm trying to breathe. In, out, in. I can't breathe. I'm watching everything I love slip through my fingers.

"I thought you loved me."
"I do, Rachel, I do."
"Don't even say that to me. If you loved me, you wouldn't have done this. What about everything we have together? What about all that? You wouldn't dishonor everything we've been through. You would never do that."
"I do love us together. I'm sorry, Rachel. I wasn't thinking."

That was a stupid thing to say.

That sounded stupid. But it was the truth.

"That's your answer?! You weren't thinking?! I think about you every minute of every day. I have loved you with every ounce of my energy for thirty years. I have done everything I could possibly think of to make you happy. I've been patient and long-suffering. And you *weren't thinking*?"
"I'm just telling you the truth."
"How long?"
"I'm not sure. Probably six months."

"Who is she?"

"Someone I met online."

"What's her name?"

"I don't want to tell you. I don't want you to hear the name and associate this with that name forever. You don't know her. You'll never meet her. I made sure to keep it separate."

"But you won't tell me her name? I thought you wanted to tell me the whole truth."

"I'm trying to protect you."

"It sounds like you're protecting her."

"Rachel, I'm protecting you."

"Do you love her?"

"No. I accidentally told her I did, but I don't. I love you."

"Do you want to stay with me?"

"I love you, Rachel. I love you forever."

Let those words hang in the air. Listen to those words, Rachel. I'm telling you the truth. I'm not hiding anymore.

"I'm guessing you met her somewhere? When did you possibly find the time for her?"

"We met online. I saw her… early mornings, usually. We were at her house."

"You mean, when you were 'going to the gym'?"

"Yes."

"Seriously? No wonder you stopped losing weight. Is it over?"

"Yes. I've been trying to end it for months."

"Is she the only woman you met online?"

"No."

This is not where I want this to go. I'll answer, Rachel, but don't…

"How many women?"

"I don't know. Ten, maybe twelve."

"Did you meet up with any of them?"

"A few. At restaurants for lunch."

There can't be more. There can't be more. *Who is this man?*

"Did you sleep with any of them?"
"No. But I kissed a few."
"Kissed?"
"Well, more than that."
"When?"
"After lunch."

This is agonizing. Rachel, you don't want to know this. You don't want to know. You should stop asking. Don't make me say it. Please...

"What does that mean—more than kissed?"
"Two... were... I took each of them for a drive in my truck... and... I let them..."

This is not happening to me. This happens to other people.

"Two, huh? I see. Do I know any of them?"
"No. I made sure you didn't."
"Did any of them know you were married?"
"They all knew. I told everyone up front. I never lied about having a wife and a family. I lied about my name and other details, but not that."
"But you told them you were separated? Leaving? Didn't love me? What?"
"I told them the truth—I love you, and I'm broken."

Wait, he said he was married? So he *was* thinking of me? Part of him did remember?

So the worst of it is out. Now she knows. I can't feel my arms.
"And they still did this with you, even though you said you were married and having a tough time?"

"Yes."

"Wow, they sound awesome. When did all this start?"

"With her, about six months ago. With being online, probably two years ago."

"Is that where you would go at night? To the den to have cyber affairs? Is that why you're so tired all the time?"

"Yes."

How do I wrap my mind around this? Joe has been sleeping with a woman, engaging in illicit relations with strangers on his lunch hour, meeting yet more women at restaurants, having affairs online in the middle of the night in my house, all while telling people he's a married man. I feel myself slipping back into shock. This just can't be true. This is not Joseph.

"Why did you say you were married?"

"Because I am. Because I have a family. Because that's… that's who I am. But I told them my name was… Paul."

I knew this would hurt. Terribly.

"*Paul*? How could you? How could you do that?"

All I can see is red. We were going to name our first son Paul. Paul was the name of Joe's great-grandfather. We loved the name and all it stood for. Why are tears just now springing to my eyes?

"Rachel, I couldn't be Joseph and do all this stuff. I couldn't. I had to be someone else… It was the first name that popped into my mind. I know. It was asinine."

"So, you, masquerading as some guy named Paul, took your precious time and energy away from me, your wife, your family, your job, your calling, and decided to spend it with her, with them?"

"Yes."

"Are you kidding me right now? This whole time, I'd ask you why you were acting so different, and you lied to my face and kept telling me you were just tired and had a lot on your mind."

126

"It wasn't a lie. I tried very hard not to lie to you."

Justification sounds so ridiculous when exposed to oxygen. We both heard it.

This... I'm trying to remain in control, but this... This is where I can hear his voice as he lied to me over and over and over. How many times had I asked him what was wrong? He knew *exactly* what was wrong all along. He wouldn't tell me. I find myself screaming.

"But all this—this is the real reason we've been miserable when we try to be intimate. You've been with someone else."

"Yes. I felt horrible and guilty, and it was gut-wrenching to make love to you."

"And you made me think the problem was me!"

"I told you it was me."

Actually, *this* was the worst of it. Wait—who am I kidding? It's *all* bad. I see it in her eyes. She's trying to drink from a fire hydrant. She's staring straight ahead, trying to gain control. No more questions yet. She's wiping her face on her sleeve. Rachel, I'm so sorry. I am so sorry. I never meant to hurt you. I don't dare reach for her.

"Did you wear a condom?"

"No. Latex made her uncomfortable."

"And how can you be sure she didn't give you anything?"

"I have no symptoms."

This was shaky logic. I know how disease gets carried—I've seen the filthy, snot-infested carts at Walmart.

"So, Joseph Paul, why are you telling me now?"

And my best friend, someone I haven't seen in a long time, begins to tell me about his life. It pours out and doesn't stop. He has missed me, I can tell. He has so many things he needs to say, so many things he needs me to hear. I watch his diagonal face, and the light from the streetlamp playing in the trees, and the lights on the buildings, and the lines painted in the parking lot, and the contours of the grass. And I listen. I watch the lines on his face deepen, his eyes recalling what he has seen, his mouth recalling what he has done, his palms holding his knees. I listen to the nightmare he has been living, alone, not being able to tell his truth. Until now.

And then my best friend tells me about his Worst Week in History, and about how The Woman called Bishop Hanson and told him everything she thought was true, even though some of it was not. And how he had to give a lesson on confessing. And how he called Aaron because he couldn't call me, and how he finally understood that he was a noble son of God. And how, in the last seventy-two hours, he has died a thousand deaths trying to figure out how to tell me. I know my poor best friend is buried, over his head, in guilt.

And then the little boy from the picture is in my car—the little boy from the picture in his mom's bedside table. That cherubic, tender little boy with blond hair and innocence. That little boy who was his mother's last crown jewel. He's so small that he can't see over the dashboard. And he looks up at me with frightened eyes as he speaks his truth. He's scared and alone. No one is protecting him. He doesn't feel safe. No one is the guardian at the door to chase away the demons he has let in. He's trying to be brave, but he is hopelessly lost. He has no idea where to go.

And then Paul is in the car, and I understand that I have been living with Paul. I don't like Paul at all. Things are starting to make sense.

And then my husband returns. My Joseph. My terribly flawed hero. There is suddenly no question that I will honor his soul. I decide to believe—in him and in Jesus's infinite Atonement.

So I drive home, and he puts away the groceries while I stumble blindly up the stairs.

She's in shock. That was the hardest thing I've ever had to say. I will do anything she asks. I will show her how much I want to fix this. I spent so long thinking she would never be able to forgive me, but she listened. Please, God. Help her. Save us. I don't want to go. I want to stay here. With my Rachel. With our children.

This is strange. Just when I could lose everything, why do I finally feel... safe?

Time moves very slowly.

I sit in the chair in our room, and I stare straight ahead. He sits on the bed in case I have something to ask him. I don't. I have asked enough. I'm absolutely numb. How many hours have passed? Somewhere around half past forever, I consciously examine my soul and decide I do, after all, feel two things—defeated and exhausted.

I silently go and get our good camping mattress from the garage. I put it on the floor next to my side of the bed with blankets and my pillow. "I can't sleep on the bed with you. You're welcome to sleep on our bed."

"No, please. Please, I can't let you sleep on the floor. Please. Take the bed."

"There's no way I'm sleeping on our bed. I just can't." I turn off the lights, collapse on the mattress, and stare into the darkness. I don't want to close my eyes. I feel like my eyes have been closed for years. I pray. I listen. I pray. I listen. I try to accept that this is happening to me.

I feel like a heel being on the bed. I cheated, and she's the one sleeping on the floor? But she feels like I violated our bed. I didn't ever. I wouldn't. But... I did.

The anguish and remorse are smothering.

Somewhere in the fog, I recall that God had told me I needed to attend the temple because I would need the strength to save my family. That made a lot of sense now. I would go as soon as I could. *Strength.* I don't feel strong. I feel a healthy dose of disbelief.

I have never felt so personally feeble and helpless in my whole life. I can only surrender to the power of Jesus Christ. Trust God. Trust. Please, God, hold Rachel. I can't.

Two of my wonderful girls are sleeping down the hall. And one is blissfully sleeping in Eugene, Oregon. They didn't ask for this. *Strength.*

How do I show my daughters strength? I have choices to make. My first choice of strength is to show them how I turn to the Lord in my time of need. He has power to carry me. Only He is mighty enough to save and tender enough to relieve my sorrows.

My next choice in exercising strength is more complicated. I can show strength and send Joseph away, which I have every right to do. I had friends who needed to end their marriage, and it was tough, and it was the right thing to do. I'm trying to hear the Spirit tell me what to do.

I'm struck that if I terminate our relationship at this moment, it will undermine our girls' definition of love for the rest of their lives. They idolize our relationship, as well they should. We are good together. We *were* good together... If I told them it was all a lie, they would never be the same.

None of this will work if Joe still has one foot in Sodom. I pray to know. Is Joe ready to step up and fix this giant mess he created? He seems to be. I sense a distinct change in him, different from the last—wow—how long has it been? He said it was two years. Is that what he said? Could I trust? *Should* I trust? There it is again, the impression that I had in the car—I will honor his soul. I will believe, in him and in Jesus's infinite Atonement. I have to try.

I'm replaying our conversation in the car. I broke the gentle heart of my best friend, the only person who has loved every part of me. Aaron said she would need to metabolize. I will wait for you, Rachel, like you've waited for me. Be strong, Rachel. Draw on your deep reserves. Lean on the Lord.

It's strange to be in our room together, both knowing the other is awake, not saying anything.

"Joe?"

"Yes?"

"Do you think I still love you? Because I thought I knew what that meant, but maybe I have no idea what love is anymore."

"I don't know, Rachel. I hope so."

"Well, to answer the other question that I know you want to ask—I think I'm not leaving. But I have to figure out how to stay."

"Okay. I'll do anything you want."
"Oh, I know. And you will."

Not leaving me? I have an endless supply of tears. How could this be? Thank you, God. Thank you, Rachel. I know I don't deserve this.

"Joe?"
"Yes?"
"How many people did she sleep with while she was sleeping with you?"
"Three other guys, I think."
"You have to go tomorrow and get tested for STDs."
"I'm sure they're closed on Sunday. I'll go first thing on Monday."

"Joe?"
"Yes?"
"I don't think I'm up to family dinner tomorrow. Cancel it."
"Okay."

Sunday morning dawns through our windows, and the initial shock is wearing off. We're going to church together. But he has to meet with the bishop first.

Joseph

"We'll make the formal announcement in sacrament meeting next Sunday. We have to rearrange the presidency, and we need a week to make all the changes. But effectively, as of this moment, I extend you a release from the calling of Young Men's president." The bishop had every right to be angry with me, to be disappointed, to express betrayal. I had lied to him, too. But I only sensed love.

"I expected that. It makes me sad that I can't serve anymore. I loved this calling."

"I'm glad my son has been in the priests quorum with you. We would talk about your lessons at the Sunday dinner table. You know, when I was the Young Men's president, the bishop at the time said to me, 'They always look to see who has been over the Young Men when they're looking for the next bishop.' I've thought about that often as I have worked with you."

"Yeah, I know." I smiled weakly.

There was an awkward moment as he then said, "I also need your temple recommend."

I removed it from my wallet, wriggled it out of its protective case, and slid the paper across the desk. I knew I was far from worthy, but it was hard to give it away. It was a necessary step.

"You know, Joe, I didn't believe her. It took me half an hour to realize it wasn't someone playing a joke on me. I called President Patrick and asked him what we should do about Helaman's Camp. We both prayed about it, and we decided that you should still go. This breaks my heart. This just isn't you."

"No. It's not like me at all." I had an impulse to look at the floor in shame, but I heard Aaron telling me that I was a noble son of God, and I was able to meet my bishop's gaze.

And now, in his office, where we had sat together in council meetings and quorum lessons, I was able to speak my truth to my friend, my bishop. I was grateful for the gift of confession. We both cried a lot. I filled in a few blanks for him, corrected information Lila had misreported, and corrected information that I had lied to her about. He didn't ask me many questions. He ended our talk with, "Is there anything else I should know?" What else was there? I had committed adultery.

As I got up to leave the office, he hugged me for a long time. When he let me go, I again looked him in the eye and said, "I will do everything I can. I promise you. I want you to be the one to give me my recommend back."

I went home, said hello to Sarah on the stairs, and closed the door to our room after I went in. I reported on the meeting to Rachel while she was putting on her makeup. She was somber, but she seemed genuinely glad to hear it had gone well. "What's next?"

"I talk to President Patrick tonight. They'll probably convene a disciplinary council in the next week. I told Bishop that I don't want to wait. I want to move forward quickly."

She put her makeup bag away and found her shoes in the closet. I stood near our bedroom door waiting for her, and she stepped close to me. I could smell lavender. Her beautiful face was full of sorrow as she said, "I'm fairly certain you're going to be excommunicated." We knew the gravity of what this meant for us. As an unintended consequence, my actions were going to punish her.

"Yeah," I said.

She looked up to the ceiling to blink back tears. "Let's be brave. Ready for church?"

I have always loved singing hymns, thanks to my mother. As I sat in sacrament meeting with my family, I realized that singing would more than likely be the only way I could participate in Church services for at least a year. Rachel and I tried to begin the sacrament hymn, "I Stand All Amazed," but we fought back tears as the congregation sang, "I stand all amazed at the love Jesus offers me, confused at the grace that so fully he proffers me." We cried as we listened to all three verses.

While the sacrament was being passed, I read more sacrament hymns and was filled with gratitude for Jesus's grace and mercy for me. Rachel was reading along over my shoulder. I pointed to many phrases, and Rachel nodded in agreement. "For us on Calvary's cross he bled, And thus dispelled the awful gloom That else were this creation's doom…" "And gave himself a ransom To win our souls with love…" "How great, how glorious, how complete, Redemption's grand design, Where justice, love, and mercy meet In harmony divine!" The Spirit assured me of God's love for me, that I was not lost.

It had been a long day already, and I was emotionally spent. But in our priests quorum meeting, Bishop Hanson graciously let me teach the lesson I had prepared. He sat through the lesson looking like he had lost his best friend. We both knew it would be a long time before I would give another lesson, say a prayer in church, or even be able to make a comment. As I looked at this group of boys, I felt a great regret that could have been avoided. They didn't know it yet, but I could not attend another priests quorum meeting to say goodbye—to tell them how proud I was of them, how much I loved them, and that God would be their companion throughout their lives if they would let Him. These boys were more collateral damage in the wake of my self-destruction.

That evening, I sat in President Patrick's office. "Brother Reeve, I have to say, I've been in ward or stake leadership for most of my adult life. I have seen and heard hard things. I go to great lengths not to take my burdens home with me or they would consume me. But when I heard about you, Brother Reeve, I have to tell you, I took it home. My wife was worried about me, and I couldn't tell her. I'm in shock. I love your family. This makes me sad."

I felt he cared about me. I heard the love in his voice, which surprised me a little because I had thought he barely knew me.

"President, I'll do anything you ask me to do."

"I think we'll convene a council on Thursday. Are you available?"

"Yes. Definitely. I want to work with the Savior to heal what was broken. I'm sorry for the hurt I have caused."

"Me too."

While walking home from the stake president's office, I realized I had one last thing to do. This would be the last time I would post anything. I was relieved that it would be over.

> Paul: Hey, just so you know, it's time to say goodbye. I'm fixing my life and fixing my relationship with my wife. I hope you find peace in your life. My best to you and your future.

> Blair: I hope ur reconciling works btter then mine did. I left him last week. I hate men, cept u ;)

> Carrie: Thx for the memories, cowboy good luck

> Emilee: Yeah, whatever. It won't last.

> Fiona: Nice to see this, Paul. It made my day. I'm happy for your future.

> Gigi: aww... my loss call me if u ever change ur mind

> Izzy: See ya i wish u the best

Jezebel: I just broke up with my boyfriend! To bad ur not available

Lila: Just so you all know, "Paul" is actually Joseph Reeve of Provo, Utah. He is married, and he is a huge liar! Beware! He is an active member of the Mormon Church and has a temple recommend. He is a hypocrite and a predator. He will lie to you and break your heart. Beware. Share this picture and information with everyone you know so that Joseph Reeve AKA "Paul" doesn't do to another woman what he did to me. If you have experience with "Paul," PM me and we will talk. I'm compiling all the info I can.

Rachel

Was it really still Sunday? It had been a long day. All my strength, and then some, had been spent going to church. While Joe was talking to the stake president that evening, I sat in my closet on the floor behind my shirts. I just wanted to block the world out for a bit. I needed a quiet place. I needed to call my sister.

"Mary, do you have some time?" She could tell this was big. I rarely used both syllables in her name.

"Yeah. Let me go into my room and shut the door. Just a minute. Hey, guys, count me out on this hand. Just keep playing. They're playing cards," she explained to me as she walked. "Going up the stairs, going, and I'm at my room. Closing the door. Okay. It's quiet. What's going on?"

"Mare." I breathed deeply. "I have something to tell you. I just need you to listen." There are life-changing phone calls you don't want to make, like telling a loved one about a car accident or cancer. Because she's my best friend, I knew that my pain would be her pain, and I was genuinely sorry about that. But I needed her. She listened and listened, and she blew her nose a few times, and I finished with, "And now I've decided that I need to pray to know *how* to stay."

"Wow. Rachel, let me first say, I love you." Her voice quavered. We sat in silence and loved each other from four hundred miles away. "Next, and you know this, the Lord loves you." She let out a long breath. "Wow... What can I do?"

"It'll all just happen. There's not much we *can* do. We're kinda power-less at this point. He'll be excommunicated, and life will go on. I love him, Mare. I can already see the light in his eyes returning after all this time. Dang, everything just makes so much sense now. Just... everything. This is why he's been so distant. This is why he's been so sad. But he really has a desire to fix his life. I see it. I hear it. I know it."

"I'm so.... *sorry*... this happened to you." She was crying again.

I was too. I was also reflective. "I'm sorry it's happened to *him*. I'm sorry he let it get this far."

"Joe?" In the stillness of my second sleepless night, my mind was again trying to fit pieces together. I realized the puzzle was vastly incomplete. From my safe space of the camping mattress on the floor, I asked into the darkness, "Why did you tell her that you loved her?"

He clearly wasn't asleep either. "It just slipped out one day. It was kind of a natural thing because I say it to you all the time. I guess, well, I was with her, and I cared about her. But when I said it, I didn't know how to take it back."

"So, *do* you love her?"

"Rachel, I really don't. If there was ever a part of me that tried to, she has shown me exactly who she is by the way she has treated me this last month. She doesn't care about me. She lied to the bishop about me. Earlier tonight, when I said goodbye to everyone else, most of them were gracious. She was vicious. Let me show you her reply on the app." He grabbed his phone, crawled across the bed, and leaned over the side to show me his screen. "She's mean and vindictive. I know I hurt her, but she didn't have to put my name and picture out there. She... she knows Mark and Anna. She threatened more than once to tell them. She threatened to tell our whole ward."

I was surprised at how heavily The Woman's threat settled on *me*. I couldn't let that happen. Joe's screen light timed out, and we were back in the dark. I asked, "Then why did you like her?"

"Paul liked her. She's nothing like you. You're kind, understanding, intelligent, eager to listen, eager to help. I mean, she's smart, a good mom, a hard worker. But she has a quick temper. She has lived a hard life, and it shows."

"Well, I haven't always been a bowl of cherries to live with."

"It's not even close to the same thing. Our relationship has a maturity that she has never experienced. She doesn't understand why I won't leave you."

"And I can't understand why you kinda did." I thought those words echoed unnecessarily off the ceiling.

Joe breathed out slowly. "You're everything to me, Rachel. All I can say is that I woke up. I don't want to lose you. My biggest fear is that we might lose what we have together because I did this."

I had a sudden conviction, and I sat straight up. I spoke loudly and clearly toward him. "You know what, Joe? I don't want to be anything like her. I want your choice between us to be incredibly stark."

Joe scooted back to turn on his lamp so we could see each other over the edge of the bed. "My choice? What are you talking about? You're the one with a choice here. My choice was made long ago. I choose you."

"Okay, but I want any doubt removed. I want to be absolutely without question the opposite of her. I refuse to be a bitter, angry person. I refuse. I will not let this take away my kindness."

"See? That's exactly why I love you."

"Joe, I'm serious. I refuse to be bitter and angry. I will not give in to that. I will be strong. I will not be like her."

"I know you're serious. And I am too."

Just as quickly as my resolve appeared, a disturbing thought popped into my mind and I couldn't look at him, especially in the light. But I had to ask. "When did it start? Actually sleeping with her, I mean."

He fell back on his pillow. "I'm not really sure. I've tried to figure it out. She says it's been about six months. I think it was February."

"Like, around Valentine's Day? When Tom came over and you made him lay the bathroom tile?"

"Wow," he said. "What timing. I made Tom prove himself when I was privately being a colossal hypocrite. Yeah, I guess it was about then. I do remember that she wanted me to spend the night with her that weekend. She wanted me to tell you I had to work all night. I said I absolutely would not. I never spent a whole night at her house."

"So, all this started around the time that I started having heart pain?"

"Yeah."

Ah. Another puzzle piece fit. "I think my heart knew, and it was trying to tell my brain, but my brain wouldn't hear it."

"That's what I thought at the time. I'm sorry, Rachel. I'm sorry I hurt you."

Tears stung my eyes and I lay back down to hug the pillow. "You broke my heart, Joe. Broke it. I have always loved you. It's always been you."

He peeked over the side of the bed and waited to reply until I glanced up at him. "I know. And it kills me that it's always been me who has hurt you."

"Yeah. That's true too. That's why I need you to be worth it. Be worth it, Joe."

"Can I show you something?" He turned his phone on again and tapped a few things before showing me the screen.

> Paul, are you sure you want to delete your entire profile?
>
> Paul: Yes.

"I wanted you to be with me when I did that. The app is now gone. No more chatting." He breathed out a sigh of relief.

"Why did you wait until now?" I asked.

"I thought I'd wait and see what else she was saying about me. But I've decided I don't care. She can plaster my face on the side of a bus, take out a full-page ad, call me whatever she wants—I don't care. You know the truth, and that's all that matters. I'm not hiding anymore."

I think it was Monday morning. I wasn't hungry. I didn't eat. I drank some water. I think I did. What compelled me to presume that I could have strength and resolve?

Joe had gone to work. He would stop by the county health department as well. I sat in the chair in our room. That's all I felt like doing. I looked at the closet door and I remembered… months ago… hanging his shirts, falling down, hearing the voice, thinking that he was gone, not being able to breathe. I remembered what that felt like, and I began to be crushed again by that thought. *Was he really gone? Was I fooling myself?*

As I stared toward the closet, the light in the room changed. An undeniable feeling of comfort swept over me. My soul flickered to life, and I was enveloped with warmth down to my toes. I was aware that a being I could not see came into my room and rested beside me. I couldn't be sure who it was, but there was peace as they sat with me. My spirit was soothed. I was lifted. I was loved. And they stayed a while until I felt strong enough to get out of the chair.

I looked at my phone before I answered. It was Joe. "I'm just leaving the health department." He sounded flustered.

"Are you okay? It's like a blood test or something?"

"Yes. I felt so stupid. First, I went to the wrong desk. I said to the receptionist, 'I'm here for a test.' She said, 'What test?' I had to talk loudly because the waiting room was full of noisy kids, and I said, 'For STDs.' She said, 'This is the pediatric vaccination desk. Go to the room down the hall.' Great, so I announced *that* to the whole room. So I went down the hall and signed in. The receptionist looked me up and down with disgust when I checked the 'STD' box on the form. It's her job, right? This is what she does every day, right? They finally called me back, and the nurse was a sweet old lady. I felt like my grandmother was giving me an STD test. She was drawing blood and she said, 'Can I ask you a question?' I said, 'Yes.' She said, 'I see your wedding ring. You're married?' I was so embarrassed. I said, 'Yes.' She said, 'Does your wife know you're here?' I said, 'Yes.' She said, 'I see this kind of thing far too often in here. I hope you get your life straight. You don't belong here.' I didn't know what to say. She was just expressing concern about me. She was nice. But I felt so stupid. I wanted to say, 'Yes, I screwed up. I've hurt a thousand people. I'm trying to do what's right.'"

I had a choice here. I could be snotty and say, "Serves you right," or I could assume the position of his best friend. If I wanted him to continue being honest with me, I would have to consciously choose to be a safe place where he could share his story. *Choose strength.* "I'm sorry you were embarrassed. How long until we know the results?"

"I don't know. They call in a week or something. I feel so stupid."

Was this really my life, talking about getting an STD test at the county health department? It was all I could do not to give a parting shot like, "Natural consequences are tough, aren't they?" But that wouldn't help. It would only hurt. Instead, I settled for, "Thanks for going to get tested. I'll see you soon."

"Hey, one more thing. Rachel, I heard from The Woman today. She texted me, and she wants her house key back."

"You had a key?" This I didn't know.

"Yes."

"Well, I'm pretty sure you aren't going over there to deliver it. What's her address?"

"She's afraid of you. She's afraid of you coming over. She thinks you... well, I don't know. Well, that you're mad and you'll take it out on her."

141

"Hmm. I'm finding it hard to care what she's worried about. She doesn't know me at all. How about you drive me over there, and I will hand her the key."

"I think she wants it back tonight. But after her kids are asleep."

I'd held in my sarcasm long enough. "Oh, by all means, let's make sure it's convenient for her." Then I sighed, knowing I had to put on my big girl pants and do something difficult. "After we have family home evening, we'll head over there."

"Rachel?" He was timid. "Do you mind taking the lead with the lesson tonight? We need to prepare the girls for what's going on this week, but I'm just not sure how to say it."

I heard the fear in his voice. I saw the little boy who needed someone to protect him. Our children were no different. I would protect them as well, with information and honesty. *Don't let this take away your kindness. Strength.*

"Yeah, I can do that. I've been thinking about it nonstop. We definitely can't tell them the truth about everything right now. We're not ready for that, and I don't think they are, either. But I have an idea of how to explain about your disciplinary council. Joe, have you thought about Abby?"

"Only a million times. Rachel, it won't do her any good to worry about what's going on here. She'll feel helpless. It will be overwhelmingly distracting. She's already making a conscious effort not to think about wedding plans. I don't want to add this to her load."

"That's exactly what I was thinking. Well, then it's decided. See you when you get home."

Joseph

We gathered in the living room for family home evening. Rachel and I sat next to each other on the couch. Sarah was ready to start with a song, but Rachel said, "If it's okay, tonight this is more of a family council. I want to go straight to a story. Girls, I want to tell you about something Uncle Sam did once. Don't share it—just learn from it, okay?"

They nodded. I wasn't sure where she was going with this, but I trusted her.

"Aunt Tabitha was going into town one day for grocery shopping. They had old cars that ran on old tires. They hardly had enough money for gas. She was almost to town when a tire blew. She pulled over immediately and went to fix it, but the jack wasn't in the car. Uncle Sam happened to be following on the same road in his work truck about twenty minutes later. He saw her and pulled over. What do you think happened?"

Hannah said, "He used the jack from his work truck to change the tire?"

Rachel replied, "Good guess. That's what your dad would've done. Uncle Sam did eventually, but not yet. He stood by the side of the road and yelled at Aunt Tabitha until she was bawling. Why didn't she check the tires before she left home? Why didn't she know where the jack was? Why didn't she wait and go into town with him? A cop even drove by and asked if everything was all right. Tell me, Hannah, why did Sam yell at her?"

"He was frustrated? He was worried about money?"

"Yes, but here's what I want you to learn—*so was she. She* was also frustrated, *she* was also worried about money, *she* had all the same questions he had. So why did he need to yell at her?"

Hannah nodded. "That's true... Good point."

"Sarah, what good did it do to yell at her?"

"It just made her feel bad."

"Yep. And it might've made her wonder if he really loved her. This is one of the things Dad learned from Uncle Sam—and this is what I've learned from Dad—Dad doesn't yell at you if you already feel stupid about making a mistake. There's no point. You'll notice we've tried very hard to do this with you, right? Otherwise, you would be afraid to make mistakes in front of us."

Hannah said, "You've never explained it like that. You don't yell at me, even when I do... really stupid things I wish I hadn't." She rubbed her arm unconsciously.

I decided I could field this one. Easily. Except for the tears. "I want to help you. I love you, Hannah."

Rachel continued. "So, with that story as a preface..." She reached for my hand. "Girls, you can tell something has been going on. Things are a little different. We've been in our room talking a lot." They acknowledged it but didn't seem worried. She went on. "When Dad was a little boy, lots of things made him really sad. We've talked to you about quite a few of them, right?"

They nodded.

"Some things we haven't told you. Those things really had an impact on him. You know how we always want you to talk to us so we can process things together? Dad didn't have anyone to talk to, so he made some bad decisions along the way. When he got older, he felt like he had figured things out. That worked for a long time, but a few years ago, he went back to old habits and made some more bad decisions. But now he's ready to get things fixed once and for all." Rachel paused and asked, "Do you have any questions so far?"

"No," Sarah said. Hannah's eyebrows furrowed and she shot a sideways glance at me, and I involuntarily looked at my shoe.

Rachel was showing the resolve and strength they needed to see, and she was doing a beautiful job explaining things. I knew I also had to find my voice and speak with surety, which was difficult through my tears. But Rachel had set it up beautifully, and I knew it was my turn to say the rest. I raised my chin. "Girls..." It was more of a croak, so I cleared my throat. "I have talked to the bishop and the stake president. To get this fixed properly, I'm having a disciplinary council with the high council on Thursday. I might be excommunicated." I swallowed hard and looked at my children. They were motionless. Stunned. Two more hearts break-ing. "Hannah, Sarah, my testimony is strong. As strong as ever. I know Jesus Christ loves us. I know... I *know* I am a noble son of God."

Rachel could also see the shock on their faces. She dropped my hand and reached for Sarah, who was sitting next to her. "Dad will be going to church with us every Sunday. We will still laugh, pray, have family home evening, Rock and Talk, everything. But he won't be the Young Men's president anymore, he won't be allowed to participate in church meetings, and he can't give you blessings for a while. And he... he probably won't be able to attend the temple for Abby's wedding in December. Remem-ber the story about Uncle Sam? Dad already knows where he went wrong, and he's trying to fix it. We're going to support him instead of yelling at him. I'm hurt, and we're sad, and it's okay to feel that way. Do you understand what I'm saying?"

They both searched my face before they answered, and I did my best to look confident. "Yeah," Sarah said.

"I guess," Hannah said.

Rachel tried to sound upbeat. "I want you to know something that I've learned in the last twenty-four hours. We're a stinking awesome family, right? We love each other, and we're very active in the Church. Who hates that?"

Sarah didn't have to think about it. "Satan."

"He really does. Strong families have a target on their door. They're not immune to his fiery darts. Just because you go to church and pay your tithing doesn't mean Satan has given up on you. In fact, it makes him want to try harder. The stronger you are, if he can get you to fall, he's pretty sure you're his. But we're stronger than Satan. Dad is doing brave things to fix what he did. And we stand together. Remember the ketchup bottle? Remember how your family can help you clean up the mess? Asking for help is not embarrassing or shameful. Dad has finally asked for help, and the saving power of Jesus Christ will work a mighty miracle for him. He knows that, and I know that. Understanding this can make us all stronger." She paused. "Does anyone have anything to add to the council? What are you thinking?"

I knew Rachel directed the question to the girls, but I was thinking what a humbling moment this was, to come before my tender children and inform them that my sins were serious. I tried to remove my shame, but it was a boulder that would not be budged.

Sarah spoke first. "I love you, Dad. I feel like... it will be okay."

I managed a smile when all I wanted to do was sob at the love and hope she offered me. "I couldn't have said it better myself, Sarah. Thank you. I love you too."

Hannah knew it was her turn to say something, but she didn't. Rachel didn't want to leave her out, so she coaxed, "Hannah? Do you have anything you want to say?"

"Yeah. Fine. Are we done here?" She got up and went to her room without waiting for an answer.

Rachel and I looked at each other. She was older than Sarah, and with that maturity, she understood that the details were ugly. We would give her time.

Rachel

We had a few minutes before we needed to leave for The Woman's house to return the key. "Sarah, this needs to be a quick Rock and Talk, okay?" I sat on her bed. "Dad and I have an errand to run."

"Can I go?"

"Thanks for offering, but no. How was your day?" I began to rub her feet through the covers.

"Good. I got my room cleaned, and I'm almost done with *To Kill a Mockingbird*. I'm glad they gave us a reading list for over the summer. I always take longer to read books than everybody else."

"You're just reading more closely. So, are you okay with what we talked about tonight?"

"It's fine. It's all been said."

"Really?"

"Really."

"You know where to go if you have a question?"

"Yes."

I leaned up to kiss her cheek. "Love you. Tomorrow, I'll take more time for Rock and Talk. Thanks for being you. Goodnight, Sarah. Want me to leave your lamp on?"

"Yeah, I'll keep reading. 'Night, Mom."

I stepped to Hannah's room. I knocked twice, softly. "Hannah?"

Instead of calling to me to come in, she opened the door about eight inches and kept a firm hold on the doorknob. She had been crying. "Mom, I'm not in the mood for Rock and Talk tonight. I'd like to be left alone for a while."

I spoke quietly. "I just wanted to make sure you're okay. It was kind of a bombshell announcement tonight."

"Yeah, and I need some time. I get that you want to talk more about it, but I just can't right now."

"Honey, that's fine. How about I come in and rub your shoulders for sixty seconds? Or your feet? No words, I promise."

"Mom, I want to be alone."

"Tomorrow, then?"

"Maybe. I don't know."

"I love you, Hannah. I'm still the same. We can still talk about everything. That hasn't changed."

The look she gave me screamed, *Mom, everything has changed.* But she said simply, "Goodnight, Mom. Enjoy your errands," and she closed the door.

There are surreal moments in life when you find yourself doing things you never pictured. Not just like feeding seals in the Antarctic or basking in a Tuscan sunrise. I mean, you find yourself going to deliver a house key to The Woman who had been sleeping with your husband, after you just told your children to expect excommunication, after he was chided by the health department nurse during his STD test. Surreal on so many levels. Not what I pictured I'd be doing a week ago. Couldn't I pick the Tuscan sunrise instead?

Joe turned each corner like he had been there before. Like he could do it in his sleep. And then we found ourselves in a dark driveway, with the form of a woman waiting on the porch.

"Joe, turn off your interior lights. I don't want her to see you when I open the door."

He idled the truck, and I got out. I shut the door and walked three steps to her. She held out her hand, I placed the key in it, I said, "Thank you," and I got back in the truck.

As we pulled away from her house, I started laughing uproariously. "Joe! I handed her the key, and then I said, get this—I said, 'Thank you'!"

"You did?" I think he was grateful that I was laughing. "What did she say?"

I kept laughing. "Nothing! No other words—just mine, hanging out there. Just, 'Thank you.' I guess I didn't think about what I should say, and it popped out of my mouth. Please answer me this—what was I thanking her for?" I wiped my eyes.

When I got home, I slid a note under Hannah's door:

Roses are red.
Moms are smart.
I can help fix
What's wrong with your heart.

Sunrises will come after
Sadness that's blue.
You always feel better
When we talk it through.

It was Tuesday. I had neglected my house for a few days. It would help me bring order to my reeling reality if I brought order to my surroundings. I started a load of laundry, I sorted mail, I moved stuff the girls had dropped on the kitchen table, and as I was starting to dust the bookshelf, I pictured Joe in her bed.

I fell to my knees and said the only words I could think. "Help me, Jesus! Help me! Stay near me, Jesus. Help me not be consumed by sadness. Help me work it through, but then let it be gone. Help me, Jesus. Give me strength."

I knelt there as huge tears dropped on the carpet. And from somewhere, arms surrounded me and gave me strength.

And then I dusted the bookshelf.

An express mail package arrived at our doorstep, addressed to Joseph and Rachel Reeve, from my sister, Mary. In it was a sweet, amazing card. How do you write a card to your brother-in-law who just cheated on your sister? If you're Mary, you do it because you know Rachel loves him, and he's your family. The card said, *You guys can do this. I love you both. We are praying for you constantly.* And there was a box of tissues, a book about forgiving yourself, a bag of chocolate Hugs, and a Tim Hawkins comedy DVD (a YouTube favorite of ours). Joe and I cried, blessed by the magnitude of kindness and love extended to both of us from our sister.

I began every night by trying to sleep, but thoughts would barge in and take over. "Joe?" I asked from my camping mattress.

"Yes?"

"I know this sounds stupid, but I'm a little scared of you. You did something so totally out of character, something I didn't believe you were capable of. I wonder if I even know you. I wonder if you could choke me, or stab me, or kill…"

"Rachel, stop. No! You know me." He rolled off the bed, dropped to the floor, and knelt beside me. He touched me with the warm hands that I have loved for the majority of my life. "I don't ever want to hurt you. I love you more than anything."

"I know. It was just… How could you do that to me?"

"Rachel, I'm sorry to say, I wasn't thinking about you. I *couldn't* think about you."

"I know, Joe. That was the problem."

"Yes, but also the problem was that I hated me. I would never hurt you."

"But you did."

"When you were with her, did you… do The Thing?"

Silence, then, "Yes."

"Oh, Joe… That was ours. That was ours…"

"I know. I'm sorry, Rachel."

I was filled with sadness. "We figured The Thing out together. That was ours."

"I know. I'm sorry."

"Why did you do that?"

"Honestly, I didn't think about it. It was just habit. Every couple has their Thing, and I've never been with anyone else, so it's just, you know, what I know."

I hated that answer, but I knew it was true. "Why did you pick her?"

"She was there."

I was confused. "That's all? There wasn't an emotional connection?"

"Well, she listened to me. And she needed me. And she seemed attracted to me."

"But why her, Joe? She seems, well, troubled. You didn't help her. In fact, I think you messed her up."

"She was already messed up."

"What do you mean?"

"She's had a hard life. A lot of men see women as objects, a means to an end, right? Men do selfish things. She's been hurt many times. I was just one on a long list. But you have to understand that she—well, it goes both ways. There are a lot of sad souls out there selling themselves for pottage, seeking medication, trying to dull the pain of life."

"That is very sad..." But the irony wasn't lost on me. "Not to be rude, but didn't you just objectify the women you met? I mean, it was all about you and your sadness, and you didn't think about who you were hurting."

"At first, I didn't see it as hurting anyone. I was actually listening. I was their friend."

"But by being there with them, in that place, you were disrespecting them. That's what I don't get. You've never been like that. You don't do that. Our whole married life, you've always been so incredibly kind to me. You honor womanhood."

"I know. I was lost."

"That's an understatement." I was quiet. "Joe, that makes me mad. The Thing was ours."

"I know. I'm sorry. I was a fool."

"Joe?"

"Yes?"

"I can't listen to the radio anymore. All the songs are sad. They're too real. There was one I heard yesterday about... about... sneaking away together so their spouses wouldn't find out. I used to like that song. It's catchy. I hate it. I want to smash that song, Joe."

"I know. I'm sorry."

"I hate listening to the radio."

"I'm sorry."

"Joe? Does she smoke and drink?"

"Sometimes. Not around her kids."

In my mind, I heard a chorus of my childhood bishops saying that immorality was almost always accompanied by breaking the Word of Wisdom. So I felt certain of the answer to my next question, but I wanted to hear him admit it. "Joe, did you drink with her?"

His answer surprised me, and it was immediate and emphatic. "I would *never* do that."

And for the second time in a week, I exploded into uproarious laughter until tears ran down my cheeks. "If you're ever again presented with the choice, could you just pick up a damn beer?"

I hadn't spoken to Bishop Hanson directly, and I wanted him to know my side of things. I wasn't sure if it was appropriate, but I wanted to be heard:

> *Dear Bishop Hanson,*
>
> *I'm writing to you to try to give some further information about my dear husband before the disciplinary council.*
>
> *In no way do I excuse his incredibly stupid behavior. He acted carelessly and endangered himself, his membership, his reputation, his marriage, our health, his children, his extended family, and the lives of those he interacted with.*
>
> *That being said, I want to clarify his history. I think he covered a lot of this with you, but I want to add a few things from my very valuable point of view.*
>
> *He was sexually molested by a neighborhood boy from the time he was six until the age of twelve. It stopped only when this person went on a mission. Soon after, Joe went to work with his uncle in his construction business. He was told that he was worthless, an embarrassment, useless, a good-for-nothing waste of air. Anyone who knows Joe knows that he is a brilliant, thinking man who can work anyone into*

the ground. This verbal and emotional abuse continued, escalating into physical abuse. These two events character- ized his childhood and formed a very negative foundation for his self-esteem. It breaks my heart that no one protected this little boy.

He had a pretty significant addiction to pornography through his teens and twenties, but he broke the habit before Sarah was born.

We moved to Illinois to pursue employment. A year before we decided to move back to Utah, Joe was taken hostage in a vehicle by a friend who suffers from paranoid schizo- phrenia, and my big, strong, former-Marine husband found that the only way he could save himself was to cause a car crash. He miraculously walked away, but this triggered a very painful series of events, as that family was very dear to us.

It was following this event that Joe began to shut himself away from God and me. He was still going through the motions of going to church and presiding in our home, but he felt tired, empty, broken, and helpless. Like the situation with his uncle, he felt like no matter how hard he tried, he was a failure in every way. Nothing I said or did could convince him otherwise.

We moved to Utah to save our family. He began a home construction business when we first got here, thinking that the business would be a successful way to provide for us. When it was clear that it wouldn't be enough, he found a great job in Salt Lake. I didn't realize how much the business failure affected him either.

We had many discussions about, "Should we go for counseling? Do you need medication? What can you do to find joy in your life?" And he would cry and say, "I don't know." Unbeknownst to me, this is when he began viewing pornography again and chatting with people online. He had a loving, caring, understanding wife willing and ready to do anything to help him, and he knew it, but he was not emo- tionally or spiritually able to help himself. He was profoundly sad, and profoundly lost. He has been trying to medicate to feel something, anything.

I know that what he did wasn't to hurt me or his family; he did it to hurt himself. He would never commit suicide, but I think this was the closest he could come to self-destruction. This was a tremendous wail for help, and I'm very glad that he will now be getting the help he needs. We have found a fantastic counselor, and his first appointment is next Tuesday.

You know Joe. You know he is a spiritual giant. That is the man I married. These actions are not him. This isn't in his nature. But he says he has been white-knuckling his way through life because he didn't know what else to do. It's an irony that for all his intelligence, he didn't know what to do to save himself.

I'm grateful that you were so loving when he spoke to you. That was very helpful. However, we know this is a long process. We're not naïve. This is going to be rough. He has a determination to save his family. He is willing to submit to whatever he has to do to make this right.

I'm his best friend, and I separate the sin from the sinner. But boy, that was dumb.

Thanks,
Rachel

I had spent time during my sleepless hours thinking about my covenants. I had kept my covenants; not one was broken. I was going to continue in my faithfulness to the covenants I had made with the Lord. I was also going to continue in faithfulness to the covenants I had made with Joe. We had created something incredible. Our family wasn't broken. Our relationship had been consecrated by God, not just on the day we were married, but many times through the years by all the trials and experiences that had tested us. I believed in what we were doing. I believed in where we were going together.

I knew that I had to wait for Joe one more time.

Go to the temple every week. You will need the strength to save your family. The next day was the disciplinary council, so I knew where I needed to be the night before. I walked into the temple and felt an immediate sense of love. I didn't attend the temple alone very often. But since his mom's funeral, Joe had been making excuses. Ah, that puzzle piece fit now. And I'd be going by myself for a while.

I got into my white dress, and suddenly I knew who was standing there with me. Joe's mom came to thank me for loving her son. I quietly acknowledged her with a smile through my tears. She came to be with me so I wasn't alone.

All through the session, I felt pure joy. For the first time in a week, there was no sadness, no guilt, no pain. Ideas and impressions flooded my spirit. *Be patient. Be kind. Learn of Me. Pray. Listen. I will lead you. Have faith. I will not leave you alone.* But curiously, not a single impression was about Joe, like, *Try this, tell him this, make sure he does this.* I had the distinct feeling that Joe was in God's hands, and truly, that was the best place for him. God would help him better than I ever could. My inspiration was about God's love for *me*, and His care for *me*. I did not expect that. I was overwhelmed with gratitude and comfort.

I sat in the celestial room and thanked Heavenly Father for all the love and ideas I had received. I would write them all down and remember them. But I wanted the big questions answered, so I asked the first one just to confirm. *Do I stay with him?* The answer made me laugh because it was the same answer I received when I had asked twenty-five years ago if I should marry Joe. The answer was clear. *Well, duh!* So I thanked Heavenly Father for the humor, and I acknowledged the answer. And then I asked the follow-up question. *How do I stay?* Clear as day, I heard, *I trust you.*

I left the temple knowing *how* to stay. *Knock, and it shall be opened unto you.*

Joseph

We met Bishop Hanson at the stake center on Thursday, August 12th, at 6:25 PM. The three of us waited in the foyer together until President Patrick brought us into his office. "Thank you for coming tonight. I want you to know we have been fasting and praying in preparation for this evening."

"Thank you, President," I said as we sat down and Rachel grabbed my hand. "We have too."

"Thank you for that. The high council is ready for us to come in. We have already discussed the situation, according to what Brother Reeve talked to Bishop Hanson about and what he said to me. Sister Reeve, I've read the letter to them that you gave Bishop Hanson." I glanced at Rachel, and she raised her eyebrows—she was surprised that the bishop had shared it with him. "I'll take you into the high council room, and Brother Reeve, they'll ask you some questions. You'll have a chance to say everything you would like to, and then you'll come back to this office with Bishop Hanson while we deliberate as a council. Then the stake presidency will go to another room and pray until we receive an answer about your membership. Do you have any questions?"

"Actually, I have one," Rachel said. "I don't work outside the home. Joe's income is *our* income. Can I still pay tithing on his income if he's excommunicated?"

"Yes, I think you can," President Patrick said.

"Okay. I wondered how that worked."

"If there's nothing else, are you ready to go in?"

"We're ready," I replied. Rachel squeezed my hand, and it was clear she wasn't going to let go. I needed to hold on to her as much as she needed to hold on to me.

We followed Bishop Hanson into the high council room. All twelve of them were present—three of whom were in our ward, one of those being our loving home teacher, Brother Richards. I made eye contact with him, and we sat down in the three chairs placed for us at the side of the room. Brother Richards looked very somber. I was sorry for the shock this had to be for him. The stake presidency sat at their places at the head of the table. Rachel wasn't letting go of me.

I surrendered. I wanted to keep my faith and my family. But more than anything, I wanted to keep this peace that I had found within myself.

You are a noble son of God.

"Brother Reeve, our decision is unanimous. You will be disfellowshipped for the space of at least one year."

Rachel began to tremble and cry. She was clearly shocked. So was I. I squeezed her hand and murmured, "Rach, it's okay." She stopped shaking, but the tears kept flowing.

It was clear that President Patrick was shocked as well. "We were not expecting this outcome, but this is what the Lord has directed us to do. Honestly, I was prepared to have it go the other way, but we are all in agreement. Understand, Brother Reeve, this is a time of repentance. If there is just one reoccurrence, the Lord will not be lenient. Do you understand?" He looked me in the eye to make sure I heard him. "We will be sending you a letter this week detailing our decision and what progress we expect to see from you during the year. Do either of you have any questions?"

"No," I said. "I'm humbled."

Rachel shook her head.

President Patrick said, "We have felt your spirit and your conviction to repent. We're grateful you're here. We commend you for wanting to return to living in accordance with the commandments. Sister Reeve, thank you for supporting him. We don't see that very often. I hope you realize how lucky you are," he said to me. "Brother Reeve, we want to see you return to this room in a year. We love you. We will close with a word of prayer, then please come to the front of the room so we can each greet you as we leave the room."

Every member of the high council and stake presidency looked me in the eye as they greeted me on their way out. Some spoke words of support, some hugged me, but all of them loved me and were tremendously kind.

Rachel and I went to the foyer, and we couldn't contain it anymore. We stood there holding each other, crying. After a few minutes, we went outside and began to walk the few blocks home. Rachel said, through her tears, "I can't believe it. I can't believe it! Disfellowshipped! Joe, that just doesn't happen!"

"I know. I was totally expecting to be excommunicated. I've actually been excited to get rebaptized. But this…"

"I needed this, Joe, and God knew it. This was a tender mercy for *me*. Remember the day we got married? We were so happy. It was the best day of our lives. We held on to that day during those first few years of marriage that were so rough. This whole week, I've been feeling like the covenants we made *that day* would be diminished if you were excommunicated. I needed to know they were still there, still real, *that my sacrifices mattered*, then and now."

I hadn't thought about it that way. "I do have to say, I wanted to start over. But as you were speaking, I realize that because I understand the Atonement of Jesus Christ, I don't need to be rebaptized to be clean. Repentance does the same thing. And, Rachel, I can see how you needed this."

"I really did. God knew I did."

We walked hand in hand, and I felt like this was a good time to tell her. "Hey Rach, I ordered new wedding rings last week. Titanium. They should be here in six to eight weeks."

She stopped in the middle of the road and hugged me. "Good timing, Joe! It's a new start."

We walked through our front door a few minutes later, and we were almost knocked over by Sarah, and I was surprised to see Hannah close behind. Sarah said, "We've been praying for you. We just saw you hug in the road, so we think it went okay. What happened?"

I smiled, reached my arms around them, and pulled them in. "Girls, it was a marvelous experience. I'm on the journey to forgiveness."

Sarah insisted on more information. "But what happened, Dad?"

I kissed them each on the head. "I've been disfellowshipped, and I love you, and we are going to get through this." I didn't want to let them go.

Part III:
The Journey

Rachel

It had been exactly one week since he had been disfellowshipped. Joe sat in the chair in our room, and his phone pinged with an incoming text. "Let me see it." That was our deal. He would hand his phone over immediately if I asked for it. Or he would tell me if there had been any contact during the day or night, and he would show it to me as soon as he could. No erasing. No lying. No hiding. All apps were gone. And I had password and lock screen privileges forever.

> 801-555-5555: Just come over one more time. I miss you, Joe. It doesn't have to be the end.
>
> This is Joe's wife. He will not be contacting you again.
>
> 801-555-5555: This is none of your business. This doesn't concern you. I'm talking to Joe.
>
> It is all of my business. I am his wife. He's done talking to you.
>
> 801-555-5555: Don't think so. He's been talking to me all week.
>
> Yeah, I doubt that.
>
> 801-555-5555: Go ahead. Ask him.

Surely that wasn't true. I turned to Joe. "So, what's this about you've been talking to her all week?"

He turned white. "She called me twice. She said she was suicidal. She said she still needed a friend. I kept telling her to talk to her family. It wasn't anything else. I swear."

I could not believe these words were coming out of his mouth. I glared a hole into his forehead, and my voice was low and menacing. "Joseph Paul, I will not be made a fool. I am your wife. If you've made your choice, you pull yourself together immediately or so help me, I'm out the door. Do you understand me?"

"Yes." His eyes were big.

I searched his phone. I erased her messages and searched for anything else I should be aware of. I found nothing. My voice was even and solemn as I handed his phone back. He knew it was the first and last warning. "Stand on holy ground. Remember what President Patrick said last week? Not one more thing."

"But it wasn't like that. She just needed a friend."

"Joseph, you hid it from me. To whom did you make covenants? Where is your heart? Where are your feet? Which way are you facing? You have got to take control and get yourself together. God is changing your heart, but you have to step up and act like it. I am your wife. This other stuff? All of it? It's not who you are. Let her go." I stopped and took a deep breath so I could speak more calmly. "Remember who you are, Joe. *Remember*. Be my husband. Be my friend. Be *mine*."

Joseph

Be mine. Those words echoed through my head for a week. I was all in, and I needed to take every opportunity to build trust again. I had faith that every small effort I made would, over time, add up to help repair the damage I had done.

I remembered that Rachel said that too many songs were making her sad, and I didn't want my mistakes to be the reason she cut music out of her life. So I listened more closely to the radio, searching for songs to download to her iPod. I also went back and read a bunch of letters we wrote when we were dating because she had a habit of mentioning what she was listening to. Plus I bought the CD of "The Lamb of God" that Aaron told me about. She would have plenty of good songs to listen to.

And I had another idea as well. After I helped her bring in the weekly groceries, we stood in the kitchen and I showed her. "Rachel, I found an app for you to add to your phone. You can look me up any time on this app and see my location. I promise that I'll always be where I say I will be."

I expected her to say, "That's cool!" But Rachel hugged me with tears in her eyes and whispered, "Thank you." I knew this one would be important, but I hadn't realized how much.

I came in from mowing the lawn and saw I had a text.

I went and found Rachel in the den. "The Woman just texted me," and I showed her.

> 801-555-5555: How could you just leave me?

She said, "Can I respond?"

"Why? It won't do any good. I just wanted to tell you."

"Joe, I don't want her in my life either, trust me! But listen, I feel incredibly threatened by her! Her threats about self-harm freak me out. And remember what she said on the app, that she was compiling information about you? And she wants to tell our ward? I have no idea what she might be up to."

The tables had turned, and it was beyond weird. "Rachel, I don't care what she does. I want her out of my life. We need to block her number."

"But this is my family that she's threatening. I'm sure that I can say something that will help her see that she needs to move on. This is how I can defend my family right now."

Rachel's heart was too big sometimes. I could tell that she had her mind made up, so all I could do was let the record show my objection. "I don't think it's a good idea. I'm telling you, it's not going to help."

So she texted back:

This is Rachel. He won't be texting you.

801-555-5555: Why did he choose me? He knew I was going through a hard time when he met me, and he chose me to use me.

It wasn't like that. You were two massive orbs of sadness who collided with each other. He's married and moving on. You need to let go so you can be happy.

801-555-5555: He targeted me.

Uh, no.

801-555-5555: He lied to me.

Yes, he did. He's sorry. He has moved on. You need to move on.

801-555-5555: He told me he loves me. Did you know that?

Yes, I know he did. But he's staying with his family.

801-555-5555: I held him when he cried. I wiped away his tears. I love him.

Rachel let it drop. She had given the essential information she wanted The Woman to know, and she hoped that would be enough to help her walk away in peace.

A few nights later, another text came through.

> 801-555-5555: I think I'm ready to forgive and let go.

Rachel took my phone and responded:

> That's wonderful. Thank you for saying so.
>
> 801-555-5555: I've been working with my therapist, and I think I can move on.
>
> Thank you. You will find peace like he has in the repentance process. In my own process of forgiveness, the restitution I need from you is for you to stop texting him. I need you to stop loving my husband, and to let us live our lives, beyond this experience.
>
> 801-555-5555: That's what we all need. Goodbye.

The next night as we were getting ready for bed, we were surprised when The Woman texted back:

> 801-555-5555: Joe, my therapist (who is LDS, by the way) says I owe your wife no restitution. She's unreasonable to ask me to stop loving you. That is none of her business. I will always love you. We have something special that she will never understand.

Rachel wanted to respond to that. I begged her to leave it alone. Rachel likes to solve things. This would never get solved.

But the next night, The Woman texted:

> 801-555-5555: Rachel, I can't understand why you're staying with him. You don't even know him. He's been lying to you. I'm the only one who really knows him.

That hit a nerve for Rachel and she gave into it:

> I have thirty years on you. You knew him three times a week for half an hour on a mattress.
>
> 801-555-5555: Once a cheater, always a cheater. He'll do this again and again. He's been doing it for years. You don't even know all the people he's been with. You're so blind.
>
> I know him. I love him. I believe him. You need to let this go. This isn't your problem anymore.
>
> 801-555-5555: You're just staying with him because you're weak.

Rachel turned to me and exploded, "What about this looks *weak* to you?"

"Rachel, she's baiting you. She doesn't know what she's talking about. She's just mad that it didn't end like she wanted it to."

But Rachel wasn't done, and I wasn't about to stop her. She threw the phone on the bed and yelled toward it. "Fighting for a marriage isn't weak! Standing up for your best friend isn't weak! Keeping your covenants with God and your family isn't weak! I'm fighting the good fight! I'm invincible! Is this the best you have, whining that your married boyfriend stayed with his wife and you have to go back to sleeping with random men you meet on the internet? Oh, poor you! I feel so bad for you! Get some self-respect, woman! Figure out your life! If you want something better for your life and kids, stop digging through the garbage heap of humanity hoping for a prince! But how about this—stay out of my marriage! You don't belong here! This is mine! This is sacred! You have no idea what it means to have what I have. You have no idea the price I have paid to get this. Back the hell up and stay out!"

And we did, in fact, block her number.

I got the call from the county health department. All results were negative. We were lucky.

Rachel

It had been a crazy week, and in the effort not to be a walking zombie and miss the important things, my constant prayer was for peace in my heart. Going to the temple that particular week helped more than I thought it could.

Hannah had spent the week alone in her room packing. She had relented and allowed Rock and Talk, but attempts to talk about anything other than school were quickly shut down. This was hard for me because this was not normal for our relationship. Saturday morning, the 28th, Joe carried all her things to the car. She actually smiled, hugged him, and joked with him about chemistry, and we saw this as a glimmer of hope. We drove her to her dorm at BYU where she met her roommate, and it was clear that they would have a good year together. Hannah let us pray with her, and then we left. She didn't see me cry as we walked to the car.

As Joe and I drove home, I was consoled that she was just a few miles away. Oh, how I loved my Hannah. She was the second great experiment of my personal journey to motherhood. She was my daughter and my friend. I wasn't used to being shut out from her life, but I had faith our relationship would rebound. She was patient, loving, honest, and good. I was thrilled for her to march toward Life. I hoped Life would be kind in return.

At least, not brutal all at once.

Since our evening walk home from the disciplinary council, Joe and I developed a taste for walking together. It gave us time to talk in the fresh evening air, away from distractions. It was much more productive than the nightly informational debriefing sessions we were used to. The miles of discussion were healing, full of sharing and explaining to each other what we had missed out on for almost two years. I was so grateful that he would answer everything. So each night, we would have an early Rock and Talk, which was faster because we were down to just Sarah, and by 9:00 we were out the door.

This particular walk's discussion had turned into a disagreement. Joe was sure that I meant something else, but I never said that—I said this, etc. This is the typical disagreement of married couples in the world. And so, as we walked, I made an exasperated verbal commitment. "Joseph, I promise you that for the rest of our lives, I will say what I mean, and mean what I say. You won't have to read between the lines. You won't have to wonder if I really meant something else. I will mean precisely what I say, and I will say it deliberately. Your responsibility is to believe me and act according to the information given."

I was genuinely surprised by his response of relief. "Really? Oh, Rachel! That takes a huge load off me. I spend a lot of time trying to interpret how you feel, and I'm so afraid to get it wrong."

"What? I genuinely thought I had communicated clearly for most of our married years."

Joe was honest in return. "It hasn't always been clear. And that's why I've said and done things that ended up being wrong. I misread the situation and the conversation."

"Why didn't you tell me this before? I could've fixed it."

"I didn't want to hurt you."

I smiled at the irony. "Then we absolutely need a promise number two. And we're both agreeing to these, right? Here it is. Joseph, we are very good at being polite to each other and choosing the right time to have serious conversations, but if you're holding back information, we're not truly communicating. We need to be able to talk about it, even if it's painful. Especially if it's painful."

"That's tough. I don't want to keep being the person who hurts you."

"Thank you, but that has led us to where we are now. We should've had some painful conversations a long time ago."

"I didn't want to lose you." His voice was sad.

"Am I going anywhere?" I prodded.

"No."

"Are you going anywhere?"

"Only if you're with me."

"Okay, then. I'm looking forward to future painful conversations."

"Joe?" I said into the darkness of our room from my queendom on the floor. "Hey, honey?"

He stirred. "Yeah?"

"Do you remember me crying so hard at Hannah's graduation?"

"Yeah."

"It wasn't because she was graduating and it was the end of an era and I was proud, blah blah blah. It was because I felt like I was standing there as a single parent. I was sure that we were done. Absolutely sure of it. It filled me with utter grief. And remember your eyes in that family picture we took that day? You looked so hollow. There was no Spirit in your countenance. And now I know why."

"Yeah." His voice was laden with regrets.

"It was a hard day."

"Yeah."

I breathed deeply, trying to be sure this next part was the right thing to say. "Joe? I've been thinking about something else. I'm done being single. I know you're super tired, but… I think I'm ready. But you have to take it slow, and you have to look at me the whole time. And I reserve the right to change my mind, okay?"

"Like, right now?" He was wide awake. "Are you sure?"

"I miss you so much, it hurts. We need to be us."

It was achingly bittersweet. It was my Joseph, my everything, my best friend, my love. He loved me with his entire soul. The next morning, I put away the camping mattress.

Joseph

I rushed home from my third appointment with my counselor. It was a beautiful evening for a walk, and I wanted to tell Rachel all the things I had talked to him about. For a few blocks, I explained the mindfulness techniques he had explained to me and my commitment to practice them all week, and Rachel was happy to hear about that. Our conversation morphed into our excitement—and nervousness—to see Abby at the airport in three weeks. Before she and Tom got too involved in preparing for a wedding, I wanted to sit her down and tell her I had been disfellowshipped. Plus, we didn't want Hannah and Sarah to feel like they had to continue to keep a secret from her.

After agreeing about Abby, Rachel subconsciously sped up the pace of our walk, so I knew she had something big on her mind. "This is probably going to be a painful conversation. Are you ready?"

I braced myself. "Yep."

"Why did you take the porn to the next level and start chatting?"

I had to recall what was going through my head at the time. "I told myself that I was lonely, and I wanted friends. I was also getting interactions that would heighten my fix."

"You mean, you had online sex with all of them?"

I hoped our voices weren't echoing down the street. I answered quietly, "Not all of them. It wasn't always about sex. We would just talk about life. Many of them were my friends."

"Those don't sound like friends. Friends don't help you down your path of self-destruction."

That characterization made me defensive. "It wasn't like that. They listened to me. They cared about me."

"But how could they? They didn't really know who you were. You were lying to them."

"They cared about me," I insisted.

Rachel abruptly stopped walking. I could see in her face that she was trying to be patient with my answers. She looked into the

172

darkness of the unlit park across the street and spoke toward it. "How much did they care if they were helping you destroy yourself? Friends care about your spirit. Friends want you to succeed. Friends are invested in your happiness. Friends don't help you cheat on your wife."

She had a point, but she hadn't been where I'd been. "I did a lot of listening to them. They didn't have anyone else they could talk to. They were all going through tough times just like I was."

"And how can you be sure they were telling the truth?" She turned to look at me. "You sure weren't."

That hurt to hear. Rachel didn't understand. "But it *was* real. They are my friends. I miss them. I had to tell them goodbye. I told them I was moving on and fixing things with my wife, and they were happy for me."

"Wait. You miss them? You miss your online affairs with them?" She looked at me with disbelief.

I was quiet. "That's not what I mean. I miss talking to them. They were a big part of my life for two years."

Rachel threw her hands up in exasperation. "Joe! Do you even hear yourself? You don't know them! They are *not* your friends!" She started walking fast again, and I fell into step beside her. She finally said, "I *so* don't get that. I kept asking you to talk to me. I know all about your past, and I've loved you through it all. I'm your best, most loyal friend." She was walking so fast that her breaths were short and it was hard for her to keep talking. "You didn't need to create a fictional existence and fill it with strangers who were probably lying just as much as you were. I can't understand why you went there when you had me."

I breathlessly replied, "It wasn't about you, Rachel. You didn't make me unhappy. A lifetime of sadness drove me to doing what I did... For some people, it's meth. For me, it was always pornography. That was the thing, early on in my life, that I learned to turn to when I was sad. That's where I got my dopamine rush, where the endorphins went crazy and made me feel better."

She stopped again and gestured wildly. "But I'm your wife! I love being with you! That's what I'm saying—why couldn't you just turn to me?"

I didn't raise my voice, but I matched her intensity. "Because addiction doesn't work that way. It wasn't about the sex. It was about the high. You make me happy, Rachel, but there was that broken part of me that I couldn't escape and I needed a drug to silence the self-loathing."

Tears brimmed in her eyes and glistened in the streetlight. "But *you left me!*"

My breathing had slowed again, and I spoke gently. "Right when the business started to go under, we had a big talk, and you were crying pretty hard. You told me that you couldn't take one more bad thing. I had just started watching stuff again, trying to get a fix, because I was such a failure. I kept thinking that I couldn't be the one to tell you this 'one more bad thing.' I avoided having a very painful conversation, which just led to, well, this."

"So you turned to these women online instead of turning to me?" She wiped her cheeks.

"Rachel, I have always been able to talk to you. But when it got so… complicated… I couldn't tell you what I was doing. They were the only people in my life who understood me. I know I'm not doing a good job of explaining it, but I need you to understand that they were my friends."

She was emphatic. "And I'm trying to get you to understand that you were deluding yourself. Josh is your friend. Bishop Hanson is your friend. Even our home teachers are your friends. You have a lot of good friends. As defined by their actions, these women did not care about you. True friends don't do that." And with that, she stopped, reached for my hand, and put it on her heart. "This is real."

And it finally dawned on me how wrong I had been. Rachel was first, now, and always, my safe place. My best friend.

It was time to text a friend.

Hey, Josh. Long time, no talk.

It took a few minutes for his reply to come through.

> Josh: Hey, Joe! How are things in your part of the country?
>
> Abby gets home in a couple weeks. Pretty exciting. How are you?
>
> Josh: That's awesome. Kids are back in school. Jesse and I are working on a new lighting feature over the dining room table. She found an antique wagon wheel at a pawn shop and she's got a vision.
>
> To turn the wagon wheel into a light fixture?
>
> Josh: Yeah!

And so it went. He couldn't see me crying. Josh just spoke my language.

On September 22nd, we stood at the Salt Lake airport with our "Welcome Home, Sister Reeve" sign. It was Hannah who saw Abby first, and I got a lump in my throat to see them running through the crowd to get to each other. Sarah wasn't far behind. Rachel and I had waited eighteen months for our hug, and we could wait a bit more. The girls clung to each other until finally, Sarah and Hannah escorted Abby toward us for our turn. For all she knew, we were crying because it was nice to see her again. We were crying because it was nice to have her home—and her life was not done changing. We let go and allowed Tom to have his "my-girlfriend-is-a-missionary-at-the-airport" handshake.

We had asked Hannah and Sarah to let us tell Abby about being disfellowshipped. We were praying for the right time, but we knew we had to do it soon. Her first Sunday home was the day she spoke in sacrament meeting, and then she had friends and old companions over for the evening, so we decided we should wait until Monday. Rachel had arranged for Sarah to go hang out at

Hannah's dorm for the evening and have their own "sisters home evening" together so we could talk to Abby alone.

But at 6:30, Tom showed up. I ushered Rachel into the kitchen and whispered, "Did you know he was coming? We shouldn't do this tonight. It doesn't feel right talking to Tom right now."

Rachel whispered back, "No, I didn't know he was coming, but she's going to tell him as soon as we tell her anyway. And honestly, they'll be married in three and a half months, and they'll need to learn how to go through things together. Why not start with this?"

I wasn't as confident, but she was probably right. We pasted on smiles, walked into the living room, and sat down. Abby held Tom's hand and they sat closely on the couch. Rachel and I occupied the two chairs.

Rachel started. "So, Abby, how are you transitioning to non-missionary life?"

"It's going pretty well. I have to register for school next semester, I need to find a job, we have a wedding to plan, and we have to find a place to live. I'll be keeping busy with all of that, so I think I'll be fine."

"That's great. I'm glad you're planning ahead." Rachel looked at me and silently said, *Ready?* I nodded. She clasped her hands and smiled. "So... Dad and I... we wanted to talk to you about something."

"Yeah, I figured you did. I told Tom to come over because you would be full of marriage advice. I mean, you guys are the most syrupy-sweet couple he's ever met." She leaned into him.

Tom laughed. "I didn't exactly say it like that!"

Abby defended her words. "Uh, yeah, you did. You said they were..."

Rachel cut her off. "It's not marriage advice. Well, not really. It's something that happened while you were gone, and we want to explain it to you. Just know that everything is going to be fine."

Abby kept smiling, but she said a cautious, "Okaaayyyy..."

It was my turn now. I inhaled deeply. *I am a noble son of God.* "When I was a kid, some traumatic things happened to me. You remember we talked about some of those? I never fully processed the way they affected me. I pushed through the issues for years with various degrees of success. Things kind of blew up about six months ago, and Abby..." I paused and prayed that God would bless my oldest child in this very moment. "I made some poor choices that affected my membership. Four weeks ago, I was disfellowshipped."

Neither Abby nor Tom was smiling. Abby looked at Rachel for confirmation, and all she could do was nod.

"Why would you joke about this?" Abby asked searchingly.

"That was exactly my reaction, honey, but we're not joking," was Rachel's quiet reply.

"Dad, what did you do?"

My jaw fell open. I tried to form an acceptable answer as my mind began racing as fast as my heart.

Rachel saw me flounder and jumped in to give me time to recover. "Abby, it's a fair question. We've always been honest with you about everything—we talk about the tough stuff. But Dad and I have decided to explain it to all three of you together someday, and we don't think Sarah and Hannah are ready to absorb the rest of the information yet. If the three of you can get used to this part first... you know? Gain strength by seeing that nothing has changed, right? He's still Dad. You know and love Dad."

I had regained my composure. I had decided to answer her question by avoiding it. "Abby, you've seen Mom and me. We're still in love, we're still a family, we're still us. I have a testimony, and in fact, it's stronger than ever. We're working through this, and we'll allow the Atonement of Jesus Christ to strengthen us all and make us whole."

Tom raised his eyebrows and gestured to Abby. "Actually, Joe, if you're telling us you've been disfellowshipped, Abby deserves to know why. She's your daughter. She needs to know if she can trust you."

I tried to remember that I admired how bold Tom was. I responded evenly, "I'm not hiding anything. I'm done hiding.

I've spent my life pretending that I was doing fine when I was actually broken. I've finally turned my life and my sins over to Jesus Christ. I've experienced a change of heart. My soul is being renewed. Where once I was dead, I am now made alive in Christ."

It was as if Tom didn't hear me. "But what did you do?"

I met his gaze. "Tom, I have three children whom I love very much. Rachel and I have made the judgment call that it would be best to tell them when *all three* are ready to…"

Tom was unpleasantly persistent. "Abby needs to know if…"

It was Abby's turn to interrupt. "No, Tom. No." She stared at the coffee table in front of her and formed her answer. "I know my dad. I know him. He carried me on his shoulders all over Yellowstone when I was six. He taught me how to ride a bike. He baptized me. He was in the bishopric when I was in Young Women, and he taught a few of our lessons, and I remember every single one because he spoke with love and with the Spirit. My dad has tucked me in at night so no monsters would get me. He makes me laugh. He helped me pass every math class since algebra. Whatever my dad did, it doesn't matter. I didn't mean to ask."

Rachel and I simultaneously wiped our cheeks with our fingers.

But Tom was unmoved, and he turned to Abby to respond. "You need to think about this, Ab. I've met a lot of people who have done some pretty awful things. On my mission, there were wife beaters, rapists, embezzlers, and child molesters. I saw the damage they did to their families. With all due respect, we will be having children and bringing them here. We deserve to know what he did."

Rachel and I were silent. We knew what Abby would say.

"You know, Tom, I just got home from teaching people about repentance and forgiveness. The scripture says, 'He who has repented of his sins, the same is forgiven, and I, the Lord, remember them no more.' The Lord remembers a lot of things. He remembers the name, the history, and the feelings of every single person who has ever lived on this earth. He remembers how to create big worlds and tiny sparrows. But when someone repents, He doesn't remember those sins anymore. If the Lord can forgive and literally forget, why shouldn't I?"

Rachel and I remained silent. Abby was doing fine on her own.

She looked at me and continued, "I either believe in the Atonement, or I don't. I either believe that the power of God can save souls, or I don't. I either believe that God has the power to save my own dad from sin and sorrow, or I don't. Tom, I choose to believe Jesus. And I choose to believe my dad."

That's exactly what we thought she would say. I had no idea what Tom would say.

Tom held on to her hand but looked past her. "Abby, I didn't want to tell you this. This is part of my family that I'm not proud of." He took a deep breath. "My dad cheated on my mom, and he lied about it for fourteen years. The man you met isn't my dad. He's my stepdad, but as far as I'm concerned, he's my real dad. I don't ever want to see my biological father again. He caused us so much pain and heartache from all his lies and emotional manipulation." Tears welled up in his eyes. "I will never introduce my children to my own father because I don't trust him. A man who can do that to his family isn't a man. He's a coward and a hypocrite. I'm doing everything I can not to be anything like my dad. I want to marry you because you come from a strong family that I can be proud of. That's what I want for my children."

Abby looked from Rachel to me, and back again. She replied, "I want a strong family too, Tom. And I've got one. I look at my dad and my mom and I see only strength. I believe in the power of forgiveness. I believe Jesus when He said He would wipe away the tears from off all faces. Jesus can make it right, whatever it was. Dad, I don't need to know. You're being honest with God and with Mom, and that's all I need to know. That's what you taught me, and I know it's true from teaching it to people on my mission."

I was speechless. All I could say was, "Thank you, Abby. You're your mother's daughter."

Rachel took her cue. "If you have no more questions for us, it sounds like you guys have some stuff to talk about. We'll head upstairs and leave you to it."

When we got to our room and closed our door, I collapsed into Rachel's arms and cried.

The entire month of September had been perfect walking weather. Even on the one night it rained, we tromped through puddles and raced leaves down the gutters. On the last day of September, the sun was just about below the western horizon, the world was beautiful, and it matched our mood of gratitude. "The image that keeps coming to my mind," Rachel was explaining, "is Peter, sinking in the water. He thought he could do it on his own; he was caught up in the moment of actually walking on water. But when his gaze left the Savior and focused on the rough sea, he sank. I had always pictured that he sank slowly, like sinking in quicksand, but gravity probably meant he dropped hard and fast."

"I've been thinking about that too. The poignant thing for me is that the Savior doesn't say, 'You stupid kid. You disappoint me.' He also doesn't hold Peter's head under the water and yell, 'Have you learned your lesson yet?' Instead, Peter calls out, 'Lord, save me,' and the Lord grabs him immediately. Peter cried out, and Jesus was right there with His hand outstretched."

Rachel agreed. "Afterward, He does tell Peter that he needed more faith and not to doubt. But I think that was said in complete love, not anger or by way of reprimand. Kind of like, 'Next time, and there will be a next time, remember your faith in the God of miracles, who is also your best friend. I will always save you.'"

"I feel like Peter." I began to cry, which we both did a lot on our walks. "I cried out, and Jesus saved me from drowning."

Rachel looked toward the night sky and asked, "Joseph, why do you suppose we've been talking about scripture stories so much lately?"

I furrowed my brow. "It's not out of the ordinary for us."

"It seems like a lot more than it normally is."

I had to think about that for a minute. "Aaron calls me just about every day, and he points out something new for me to think about. We talk a lot about forgiveness, redemption, and the power of vulnerability and humility. I can see myself in the scriptures he reminds me about. I have a deeper understanding of the things I've always known. So when you and I talk, it just feels natural to bring those up."

"For me too. I've never found such comfort from the scriptures before. Conference talks too. Love is everywhere."

I had to agree. "I've never seen it like I do now."

Rachel

I texted Joe:

> Tonight, I need you to take me for a drink instead of a walk.
>
> Sweetums: Sure. Is everything all right? Did Abby break it off with Tom?
>
> No. It's me.
>
> Sweetums: What happened?
>
> It hit me today. Hard.
>
> Sweetums: Was it what Tom said? Do you need me to try to come home now?
>
> Not Tom. He's young and incorrigibly idealistic. Yes, come home. I need to talk to you face-to-face. Painful conversation.
>
> Sweetums: You could call Mary until I get home. I'm worried about you.
>
> Good idea.

Mary listened and helped me reorganize my jumbled, raw emotions into succinct thoughts. I was ready when Joe got home. I didn't wait for him to come inside—I met him in the driveway. He looked at me with concern as I opened the door of the truck. "Are you okay? I hurried as fast as I could."

I climbed in. "Just drive."

One of our favorite places to go was to the small mining town of Eureka because the round trip was long enough to have a good talk. After the first twenty minutes of freeway driving, the traffic and roads weren't distracting. So that's where he headed. We sat in silence for about ten minutes before I was ready to talk.

I began with a cleansing breath. "My mantra is that I will not be bitter and angry, right? I don't want to be that person. I want to be the epitome of strength. But today, it finally hit me. After a month of walking in a fog and blindly feeling my way, the light clicked on. Do you understand that I'm trying incredibly hard not to yell at you right now? I'm trying to be super-human, and be reserved, and choose my words wisely. Just because you hurt me doesn't mean I should hurt you. Just because you disrespected me doesn't mean I should disrespect you. Just because you gave into weakness doesn't mean I need to. In fact, because you did, I can't." I set my jaw and shot him a look.

"I'm supposed to hold us all together," I continued. "I'm supposed to be the pillar of strength that keeps this house of cards from tumbling. I don't want to be like this crazy woman you found on some stupid app. I want to be an example of kindness and levelheaded goodness. But all I want to do is yell at you for your stupid decisions and smash stuff."

I could see Joe brace himself. He knew what was coming. Bless him.

"You jackass! How dare you! How could you? How could you do this to us? How could you come home every day after you'd been with her, or any of those other—and I use this term loosely—women and look me in the eye? You lied to my face again and again! You took my kindness and trust, and you flat-out used them against me. Not for one minute did you think about the future! Not for one minute did you see beyond your crappy decisions. For someone mired in self-hatred," I pointed a forceful finger at him, "you were sure great at caring only about yourself. Why didn't you think about Abigail and Hannah and Sarah? Why didn't you think about what this could do to them? Why didn't you think about what this would do to me?"

I knew my words were powerful punches, and I couldn't keep from throwing them. "If you told everyone you were married, why didn't you act married? You've shown an overwhelming disregard for our life together. We made covenants. We made children, made decisions, made a home—together. We have jokes that only we get! We have places only we've been! We have stories only we understand! And you... you welcomed some stranger into my place, my life, my marriage. How could you?"

I knew Joe could drive through tears, his and mine.

"Why did you choose this... this thing to do? When it's alcohol, you have to physically go buy a bottle, physically put it to your lips, physically swallow. You get the high, but then it's out of your system. Alcohol doesn't have to be a part of your life. You have to make a conscious choice to introduce it into your day. But sex... that's part of us. That's part of who we are. What you've seen, what you've said, what you've done—you can't undo what you did. You can't unsee that. You've warped our relationship! You took what was good and pure and mocked it. How can it ever be right again?"

He didn't duck and dance around my feelings. He listened without his gloves on.

"How could you use the name of Paul? How could you desecrate it like that? You know the agony I went through when we were talking about having another baby. I wanted to have a Paul so much. I always thought I would. When we finally made the decision that our family was complete, it wasn't without tremendous sadness, even mourning. And that? That was the name you chose to use? Were you trying to hurt me?"

My words punched faster. And harder. Tears dripped from my eyes like sweat. The verbal blows I landed made him visibly wince with pain.

"You have never lied to me. You know how much I value truth in friendships. The one time, the one time"—I inadvertently spat saying the T—"that I had to end a friendship was over her inability to tell the truth. So somehow you thought it was a good idea to lie to me? Did you just take it for granted that good ol' Rachel would forgive you for lying over and over and over? You saw what it was doing to me. How could you be so heartless?"

I entered the Ugly Cry and slammed down the armrest. "You saw that I was absolutely ripped up over how we were dissolving. I begged you on my knees to tell me, and you walked away. You have never shown this much callousness to anyone. It's not in your realm of being, but yet you did. To me. To your wife. Your best friend. The person who has sacrificed everything from the beginning to be with you. You are the only one who has ever had the power to hurt me like this because I love you so much. And what did you do with that power, that gift I have willingly given you? For the second time in my life, mind you, you reached inside my rib cage and pulled out my beating heart."

Joe was wiping his face, and I was not done pummeling.

"You shared intimacies with other women. When you were undoing your belt, you didn't think, 'Wow. I'm going too far. This is a great time to stop.' You didn't look into their faces and think, 'They have souls. I'm violating their souls. It doesn't matter that they're consenting. It doesn't matter that maybe they're initiating. I'm taking something precious from them.' You didn't look into my face and think, 'My covenants mean more than my selfishness.' You didn't look at your daughters and think, 'I will never take away from you the security of a father who honors their mother.' Joseph would! How convenient of you to hide behind this horrible man you named Paul!"

I stopped to breathe. I grabbed a wad of napkins from his glove box and used them all to clean myself up. I began to breathe deeper breaths. Joe wasn't saying anything because he knew there was nothing to say. We left the interstate and began to drive west through Santaquin. He suddenly pulled into the gas station on our right. He said, "Stay here," and he disappeared inside. Four minutes later, he emerged with two heavy sacks, which he set in the back seat.

"What are you doing?" I was incredulous that he'd left in the middle of the discussion. To go shopping?

"Sorry. I wanted to get something for you." He turned back onto the main street and continued heading west toward Eureka. "I didn't mean to interrupt you. You're right, I was hiding behind Paul."

I had regained my composure, and I was trying to remember where I had left off. "Today it all hit me. It's like it finally dawned on me what you did. I feel a rage I'm not familiar with, and I couldn't hold it in anymore. I just... You just... Pff. I lost my momentum. What was so dang important that you had to stop for groceries while I was talking?"

His voice caught, full of emotion. "Rachel, you're right. I was a jackass. I can't express the respect I feel for you—for the strength you've given to all of us, for the desire you've had to control the situation." He looked at me with compassion. "But you have every right to be furious. You can simultaneously be an example of strength and be mad once in a while."

"No, I can't! I have to be peaceful and stoic, the ever-wise captain of this ship at sea that's being attacked by sharks on fire. I can't be bitter and angry, remember? I'm just trying to get through every day the best I can. Today was a rotten failure."

"Was it? Is anger bad? Why are you putting a preset value or limit on how you're supposed to react? You once told me that if you never saw me angry, you'd wonder if I was human."

That statement made me pause. It validated me. "Thank you. You're right. Thank you! Mary thought that too." I watched the trees and fields out my window. "But my problem is, I know me. If I give in to anger, it will swallow me whole, and I really don't want to be like The Woman. I want to make conscious choices, have positive reactions." We were a few miles outside of Santaquin, and Joe slowed down to turn onto a dirt road. "Where are you going?"

"You'll see." He drove past the few houses on the road, then a mile more, and stopped as the road curved around a foothill. "Jump out."

By the time I was out, he had retrieved a crowbar from the toolbox in the bed of the truck. "What are you doing?" I asked. He didn't answer. In the back seat of the cab, he emptied the plastic milk crate that held his work shoes, coat, and safety glasses. He carried the milk crate, safety glasses, crowbar, and the two heavy grocery bags to a flat space about thirty feet from the truck. He turned the crate upside down, and from inside one of the bags, he pulled out a bottle of beer. He set it on its side on the milk crate.

I was mystified. "You've lost your mind. A beer bottle? What on earth are you doing?"

He held the safety glasses and crowbar out to me. "Come smash it."

"I don't want to smash it."

"I'm listening to you, Rachel. You said you wanted to smash things. You texted me earlier to take you for a drink, and I recall that instead of being with her, I should've just picked up a damn beer." He smirked. "Here's the damn beer. Come smash it. This will be incredibly satisfying."

"We'll make a mess."

"I'll clean up the glass. Come smash it."

I walked forward and took the safety glasses. I looked at him sideways as I put them on. I took the crowbar. I circled the crate. "I don't want it to get all over my pants when it breaks."

"Who cares? I'll do the laundry. Come on—smash it."

He was right. This would be satisfying. I raised the crowbar over my head. I pictured it coming down hard and landing squarely on the bottle.

I could hear the satisfying crack, glass shattering everywhere, foam oozing out.

And that's exactly what happened. Six more times.

And then, as I suppose he was looking for variety, the eighth through fourteenth glass bottles he placed for me were alternately salsa, queso dip, iced tea, and apple juice. We were laughing hysterically. The front of my pants from the thighs down were soaked with liquid and artfully decorated with various streaks of food. There was a large pile of glass, and Joe was hoarse from matching my screams. He produced the last bottle, a bottle of beer, and placed it for me. I handed him the crowbar. "Would you like to do the last one?"

He shook his head. "But I just want you to feel you're doing well." That was his favorite line from Fezzik in *The Princess Bride*, and his imitation was impeccable.

I laughed. "But what fun is it if we get pulled over on the way home and only one of us is soaked in beer? Come on. You know you want to."

He took the crowbar and playfully missed the bottle a few times before he swung so hard that he not only broke the bottle, but lodged the crowbar in the crate. His entire body had been generously sprayed. We doubled over in laughter.

Together we picked up the pieces of glass and put them in the bags. "Kind of reminds me of the ketchup bottle," I commented.

"I was just going to say that. However, this is one activity we probably won't be having for family home evening," he replied.

After we were sure we'd gotten all the glass, we walked back to his truck, where he set the crate and the glass-filled bags in the bed near the toolbox. He found a roll of paper towels, and we wiped off the best we could.

We headed toward home instead of going to Eureka, being sure to drive the speed limit and use the blinkers when changing lanes. On the drive, Joe was the first one to speak. "You know, we've been dealing with two things here—pornography and infidelity. You're right, Rach—what you said about why porn is so horrible. It damages relationships. You can't unsee those things. It can skew what should be sacred. It breeds disrespect and mistrust. I'm sorry that was my drug."

"It grosses me out to think you're thinking about those things when you're with me."

"You'll find this hard to believe, but I don't. I was introduced to it so young that I actually separate it from you and our married relationship entirely. I see it as different."

"What? But it's the same act."

"But it's not. I don't see you like that. A few months ago, you said something that resonated with me. You said you like the colors of us together; that we were a great box of crayons, with all our moods. Something like that. And that's how I see us. I really like all our different colors when we're together, our sacred art, not somebody's imposter version of neon strobe lights. It feels different."

"That's an interesting way to put it." We drove in silence. The beer and salsa smell was overpowering. I felt like a sports bar in Chicago on a Sunday afternoon. "So, if you love what we've developed together, and it's so unique and sacred and special, why did you do the Thing with her?"

"Habit." He hated saying that. "I'm sorry."

"I'm still mad about that. That turned one of our nice colors into insulting graffiti."

"Do you want me to go buy more beer?"

"Maybe. I'm just that mad."

"I do remember the things I saw, the things I did," he explained. "They don't go away. Many of the memories dim, but you're right—they don't totally go away. But I have a choice how I react to them. This is what I've been working on with my counselor. I can choose to exercise my power to control where my mind goes. I don't want porn in my life anymore. The desire to participate in that is gone. Now, will I still have temptations? Probably."

"That's total crap. Desires and temptations are the same thing."

"No, listen. I've been thinking a lot about this. Remember the people of Ammon? They had done terrible things and never wanted to do them again. They never even wanted to look at a sword again, so they buried them all. Their desire to take up arms and kill people was gone."

"But Joe, you can't bury it. It's there in your mind."

"True, but here's my point. Their desire to commit their sin was gone. Now, when the Lamanites came to wage war against them, they were tempted to take up arms again to defend themselves, but they refused to do it because they knew where it would lead. They would rather die than give in to the temptation."

"Okay. I'm following you."

Joe spoke with emphasis. "The point is that I'm more mindful of what I'm doing. The desire to do that is gone. I'm sure that there will be moments where something sneaks into my mind and tries to tempt me, but I'm telling you, I've been down that road, and I want nothing to do with that pain. I'm done with the drug. I'm done. Nothing about it is alluring. When tempting thoughts come, I will mindfully, consciously remove them. I know where they lead, and I don't want to go anywhere near there. I do not want to dig it up. The desire really is gone."

I was starting to understand.

We were five minutes from home when I said, "This day didn't go like I planned. I had a lot of things that I needed to get out. I didn't know how you would react, but you… you listened and reacted like my best friend. Thank you for letting me tell you about my husband who was a total jerk for a long time. Thanks for letting me be angry. Thank you for not being defensive. Thank you for just listening."

"You can be angry any time. I want to listen."

"I know. But Joe? Please help me take the high road. It would be so easy to get mean and nasty to you, to The Woman, to everybody who will judge you… and judge me."

"Yeah, so we'd better not let it fester then. You'd better talk about it. Painful conversations, remember?"

When we got home, I walked past Abby's room on my way to the shower. She called after me, "Uh, Mom, I lived next to an apartment in Corvallis that smells like you do right now. Is there something we need to talk about?" I just laughed. I'd tell her after my shower.

Joe threw away the glass and did the laundry while I got cleaned up. I found I had nacho cheese in my hair.

It was mid-October, and our anniversary was fast approaching. It was one of my favorite days of the year because it was the anniversary of the happiest day of our lives. Trying to decide where to go and what to do was going to be the topic of this walk. Joe was finishing up the dishes before we left, so I had a minute to text Jesse.

> Hey, Jesse! I don't have time to chat much now, but I
> wanted to tell you I've been thinking about you.

She replied immediately:

> Jesse: Josh and I were just talking about you guys! How
> are things? How is it having Abby home?
>
> I'll call you next week and tell you all about it. We sure
> love you guys.

Joe dried his hands and called that he was ready, so I put my phone down and we headed out. The moment we stepped on the sidewalk, Joe suggested an idea for our anniversary. "Why don't we ask Aaron if we can borrow his cabin for the weekend? He says he's got a new four-wheeler up there."

"Hey... I like the way you think!" The cabin was an ideal destination because there was no cell service whatsoever, and no electricity unless we turned on the generator. It meant playing games, walking, hiking, four-wheeling, talking, or a lot of "not talking." That was very nice too, especially if we were going alone. "So we'll leave after work on Friday?"

Joe nodded. "Yeah. Should we go to church up there and come back Sunday evening? Make it a long weekend? Let the girls fend for themselves?"

"Yeah, baby." I squeezed his hand and bumped him with my hip. He took an exaggerated step off the sidewalk, but he didn't let go of my hand.

Joseph

Early the next morning, two questions pressed heavily on my mind. Why are you fighting for your membership in the Church? Why don't you just give up?

I called Aaron. "Do you have a minute to listen to me? I have to tell Satan to get out of my head, and I figured you could listen in."

Aaron said, "By all means. I'm driving to work."

"Me too. It starts like this. I go to church every Sunday. I sit right next to Rachel, and we hold hands during prayers as we have done for twenty-five years because our first stake president in our first ward counseled us to do that. The reason I go to church isn't because I was told it's a condition of having my full membership restored—I go because I believe Jesus Christ is my Savior, Joseph Smith restored Jesus's Church to the earth, the Book of Mormon is a true record, and I know the authority and keys of God's kingdom are found in The Church of Jesus Christ of Latter-day Saints.

"Our regular spot in sacrament meeting is at the end of a pew near the front of the chapel, right? The first Sunday after my disciplinary council, a deacon came to our row where I was sitting on the end—me, his newly released Young Men's president—and he held out the sacrament tray for me. I took the tray and passed it on to Rachel. The boy looked confused. The next few weeks, the same deacon held on tight to the tray as if to say, 'No, really, I'll hold it for you while you take the bread,' but I just smiled and passed it on. Last week, the same deacon came to our row, and there was an understanding. He knew I wouldn't partake. He smiled at me, and I felt his compassion. I spent all meeting being grateful for the maturity of twelve-year-old boys who represent the Savior's mercy.

"Aaron, I'm where I'm supposed to be, doing what I believe. And this brings me more happiness than I can express. I'm finally free of my burden, and I won't let pride turn me away from God or His Church."

Aaron didn't pull the phone away from his mouth when he yelled, "Waaaahooooo!" It was loud, and I knew legions of angels were in that cheer as well.

"Hey, while I've got you on the phone, can we borrow your cabin in a few weeks?"

"You bet! The key is under the rock, and the new four-wheeler is in the garage. But before you hang up, Joe, you've reminded me of something else I want to tell you. Think for a minute about what we mean when we say the Atonement is infinite. Our human minds can't even process the amount of infinite. I'm sure you remember having Sunday School lessons like I did where we were told there's forgiveness for everything except the big sins—God wouldn't cover you for those. Seriously? So, are we saying the Atonement of Jesus Christ has a limit after all? Absolutely not! The infinite Atonement enables all the penitent to be reconciled to Him."

I nodded. "I like that."

"And after you repent, you don't have a little asterisk by your name. 'Clean, except for, well, you know what you did.' No. You're forgiven. It's over. You're clean. It's infinite."

I loved talking to Aaron.

Rachel

It was the Wednesday before we were leaving for our anniversary rendezvous at Aaron's cabin. I went to the temple in the morning. I was beginning to draw great strength from Mother Eve as an example of how to find God and peace in this lone and dreary world. But that afternoon, I felt compelled to set everything aside and do something difficult. I called Joe to let him know, and he was reluctant, but I felt strongly that I needed to do this. I needed to forgive.

I called Sam, Joe's uncle. "Hey, Sam. It's Rachel. Can I come visit you tonight? Are you busy?"

"Uh, sure, you can come over. To what do I owe the pleasure of a visit?"

"I just really need to talk to you. I'll be there at about 6:00. Does that interfere with dinner?"

"No, 6:00 will be fine."

It took an hour and a half to drive to Sam's house from Utah Valley. I prayed the whole way. I had made notes and rehearsed in my mind a few things, but mostly, I just wanted to go by the spirit of the moment.

Sam welcomed me into his home, and we sat down on the sofa together. I got to the point quickly. "Sam, I want you to know that I love and honor you. But there are things I need to tell you regarding Joe, things that maybe you aren't aware of."

He looked worried. "Okay."

"I also want you to know that I'm aware these things happened thirty-plus years ago. If someone were to talk to me about things I did in my youth, I would be horrified. We all learn and grow through the years, and as family, we need to extend mercy and move on. But these things were significant, and they changed the trajectory of his life, and I... well, I just need you to know."

He still looked worried. "Okay." To his great credit, he didn't shove me out the door.

"Also, Joe knows I'm here, but he didn't ask me to come. I just needed to come for me." Deep breath. "Sam, Joe learned a lot from you. It was a great thing for him to be basically an apprentice for his teenaged years.

193

He learned skills that he wouldn't have had any other way. I want you to know that I recognize that. It was a good opportunity."

"He was a good part of my team."

"Yes, he was. Now, I recognize that I wasn't there—this was before I came into Joe's life—but things happened on the job that were very negative for Joe. I know you were under a lot of pressure. The bank was hounding you all the time, you were trying to run a business, you had a young family, and there were many other pressures that were pushing down on you."

I paused and reminded myself that this was why I came. I forged on. "Sam, my issue is that you were abusive to Joe. You called him names, and he believed you. You said he was worthless, an embarrassment to the family, stupid, a waste of air, and a son of a bitch. These things went into his young mind and stayed there. They've caused him issues for a lot of years. Things recently came to a head, and he's had to face the past. He's been working through his issues, but he's finding that these things rattled around in his head for a long time."

Sam blew out a long breath. "I really was under a lot of pressure. I was asked to do impossible things to help the family. It was all on me to help a lot of people be successful. I know I yelled at him."

"Yes, all that is true. I'm sorry you had that kind of responsibility placed at your feet. That must've been hard."

"It was. I needed all the help I could get. But every day, there was a new set of problems, and it was crushing me."

"I'm really sorry that happened to you. I'm glad Joe could help you out. But you hit him. You slapped and kicked him. You called him names. To his recollection, you never said a kind word of encouragement, or even thank you. Can you understand how that made him feel?"

Sam frowned. "Yeah, and I knew he was just a kid. But we all struggled growing up. We all had stuff we had to do, and there wasn't time for appreciation or nice words. It was just what we had to do."

"I know. Life isn't fair, and I'm not asking it to be. I know that you had it rough too, and I'm not making you responsible for Joe's issues. I guess I just want you to acknowledge that it happened and that you're sorry. I think that's all Joe has needed to get over it. And I needed to talk to you about it to forgive you."

Sam thought a moment and chose his words. "If he was hurt, I regret that it happened. I feel bad that I took it out on him, if that's how he saw it. I probably did. I'd do a lot of things differently if I could do it over again."

"Oh, me too. We all would. Joe isn't angry with you. I just want to move forward with a clean slate, with all this aired out. That's all. I've said what I came to say. Is there anything else you would like to say before we move past it?"

Sam was immediate with his answer. "I've watched Joe through the years, and he's done well for himself. He's a smart guy, and he knows how to work. I would go back and change what I did if I could."

"Sam, thank you for saying that. I appreciate that you've let me come here and you've heard me. Thank you." I got up to leave, and he walked me to the door. I didn't know what to say, so I turned to small-talk niceties as I stepped out on the porch. "It's good to see you, Sam. You're looking good. It was a nice night for a drive. I'll see you at the reunion this summer." I hugged him tightly so he knew I was genuine in my forgiveness.

But Sam was perplexed. "Did you drive all this way just to talk to me?"

"I did. I just needed to. Thank you. I hope I haven't caused any bad memories to come up."

He shrugged. "Well, it's good to see you. Thanks for coming. You're always welcome."

"I know. You too. See you." We waved goodbye.

I went to my car and immediately dialed Joe. I began to cry before he picked up. When I heard him say, "Hello?" I couldn't reply, and he got worried. "Rachel, are you okay? Was it bad?"

I reassured him, "No, it's okay. I just can't speak yet." My voice was trembling. "Joe, he never said 'sorry,' but he acknowledged what he did, and he says he feels regret that he hurt you. He wishes he could change it. That's good enough for me. I can let it go."

Now it was Joe's turn to be overcome. "That's good enough for me too." His voice cracked. "I didn't think I needed to hear that. But I really did."

"I know you didn't want me to come—you didn't think it would help. But I had to stand up for that little boy and say, 'This wasn't right!' I couldn't protect you then, but I can defend you now. I needed to. I love you."

"I love you, Rachel. Thank you."

"Thanks for trusting me to do it. I know you were worried. It's all good. We're all fine. We hugged." I turned left and drove a block. "Hey, I'm by the cemetery. I'd like to say hello to your mom and dad while I'm here."

"Say hi for me. Call me when you're driving back and give me the play-by-play of what Sam said."

"I will." I pulled into the small cemetery and parked. Even at dusk, it was easy to find the headstone. As I reached it, I felt their presence. I was surprised to find myself doubled over and bawling, tears raining from my face onto the grass, honest words gurgling from my throat.

"Mom! Dad! He broke my heart! He lied to me! For months. For *years*. He hid it well, and I knew, I *probably* knew, but how could I ever guess it was this bad? I don't blame you for sending him to work with Sam. I don't blame you that you didn't know about the sexual abuse when he was a kid—it's no one's fault. It's just part of Joe's journey. I know he didn't mean to, but he could've destroyed our family."

I swatted at something flying around my ear, and I had no choice but to wipe my nose on my sleeve. "Sometimes I still can't wrap my head around the fact that Joseph did this. *This* is my life now? I've tried so hard to stand by him and help him through this like you would want me to. I went to the temple and God said He trusts me, so I've tried to navigate us all through this. I've tried to remind him of what is real. I've tried to help him get himself together. I've defended him and loved him. I've respected him. That's how I'm keeping my covenants. That's all you ever asked of us. I haven't pushed his head under water—I've extended my hand."

I sat cross-legged in the grass, and my crying subsided. I looked at their names etched in the stone, and I realized why I had been drawn here to talk to them. "Dad, Mom, I somehow feel like I let you down. This happened on my watch, you know? You trusted me with him, and I feel like I failed you. I didn't know it was so bad. I didn't know he was falling so far, so fast."

And after I said those words out loud, I knew what they wanted to say to me in return. *This isn't your fault. We love you.* I remembered feeling his mom's presence in the temple, and I knew it was true.

"Oh, how I miss you! I love you! I know you're watching over him—of course you are. You've probably been screaming at him, but he wouldn't hear. He's finally listening, so keep talking. He loves you both. I... I'm trying so hard to do everything right, and I know I can't, so please keep whispering to me too. You sacrificed to bring your twelfth child to earth, and I can sacrifice to bring him back to heaven. I need all the help I can get. Thank you for always loving me."

And then there was no more to say. I knew they had heard every word.

I loved this cabin.

Comfortable, cozy, romantic. And no cell service. Just Joe and me.

Friday night, we got there in time to light a fire in the fireplace. It was a chilly night, so we sat by the fire and waited for the cabin to warm up as we sipped our soup.

We had spent our wedding night in a cabin similar to Aaron's. We liked cabins. We loved the mountains and the solitude. We loved pine trees and the sound of aspens rustling in the breeze. We loved sharing the space with deer and rabbits and moose. The firelight melted away the chill from the stresses of the last few months.

In the morning, we showered and had breakfast. "What do you want to do today?" he asked me over oatmeal. "I thought we'd start out on the four-wheeler."

"Sounds great. We just have to be back to start the Dutch oven around 3:00 so we can eat at 5:00."

"Where do you want to go?"

"Everywhere."

We left at 10:00. The morning haze had burned off to reveal beautiful fall colors in every direction. We only needed our jackets as we rode the four-wheeler along the mountain trails. I loved riding behind Joe. I could whisper in his ear, rub his back, and hug him as tight as I wanted for as long as I wanted. What's not to like?

We bounced over rocks as we climbed to the southernmost lookout. Then we rode east on a familiar path for a while, passing a moose that was standing in the middle of a pond. Then we headed across the hills to the northern lookout, where we had never been.

We stopped the four-wheeler, stood, and stretched. There was so much to be humbled by in the beautiful panorama full of fall colors. The mountaintop breeze whispered a reverent silence. We stood in appreciative awe of rolling hills and hidden valleys nestled within the majestic Wasatch Range. It was breathtaking.

"It's perfect, isn't it?" I said.

"It is," Joe replied. He moved with purpose to stand in front of me. He took my hands. "Rachel Reeve, it has been my honor to be your best friend. You astound me with your kindness, wit, and brilliance. When we got married all those years ago, I thought it would be the best day of my life. But the best ones have been those days that we find our way back to each other. You are my safe place. You are my future. I already covenanted with God to love and honor you, but I want to show you that I understand now what that means."

"Joseph, that was beautiful."

He smiled and winked. "I've been practicing." And then he burst out, "I can't wait another minute! I've gotta do it now. It's burning a hole through my pocket." Joe pulled out a ring box. He opened it to show me two rings, identical except for size. "Titanium, Rachel. This is who we are."

"Joe! They came! You didn't tell me!"

"I wanted it to be a surprise. Are you ready for the switch?"

It was strange how the repaired delicate gold ring with the sparkly diamond on my finger felt antiquated. Memories of that ring were happy, and then incredibly sad. It was time to take it off and put it away—time to finally draw a line in the sand and step across. He handed me my new ring, and I slid it on while he did the same.

"I love them, Joe," I said as we held our hands close to each other to take in the new look. "It feels different. Durable. You're right—this is who we are." He leaned in and kissed me. We smiled and held each other for a long time.

I turned around to take in the view again, to connect this moment to the grandeur of Mother Nature that surrounded us. Joe wrapped his arms around me from behind, leaning forward and resting his chin on my shoulder. "Joe," I said as we looked at the mountains and colors and clouds that stretched for miles, "when we create worlds, they have to look like this."

He started crying. I turned to face him. "What? What did I say?"

He looked into my soul. "For the first time in my life, I actually believe that I'll do that. I will be there. You and me—that's our destiny together.

Rachel, it never applied to me before. I could never see myself in eternity. Now, I see." His breath caught, and his chin quivered under a meek smile. "I know I have been forgiven."

In the morning, we packed up and signed Aaron's Cabin Guest Book (*"Thanks, brother! It was heaven."*). We went to the closest church meeting on the way home. Sacrament meeting happened to be their ward conference. A member of their stake presidency got up to read the general authorities and officers of the Church, stake, and ward for our sustaining vote. He read the name of the President of the Church, and I raised my hand to sustain him.

Joe did not. He would have loved to, but he could not. I marveled at the obedience of this man. No one knew him here. No one knew he couldn't, or shouldn't, raise his arm to the square. But this was the condition set before him, and he was humble and obedient.

They finished the business, we sang the sacrament hymn, and the sacrament was passed. I partook.

Joe did not. He would have loved to. He had been forgiven. He was right with God. But he was not right with the Church. That would take more time, more obedience, more patience. I held his hand and smiled at him. I had always known the grandeur of the soul sitting beside me, and I was witnessing it.

Joseph

I was glad to have told Aaron about my resolve to continue attending church no matter what. I drew on that conversation frequently over the next few months. Pride would have turned me away instantly. I was determined to walk this path with humility and courage. As a result, tender mercies were granted to me over and over.

I had approached the high priests group leader in late August, as I would be attending that class after leaving the Young Men. "So, I can't participate in classes for a while. Can you pass that on to the other instructors?" He was my friend, and he had been a bishop, and the dawn of understanding was in his eye. But no questions, no judgment—just a willingness to help me feel comfortable as I attended the class. There were a few times when it was a bit awkward, as the teacher forgot and asked me a question or asked me to read aloud. The group leader would usually jump in and do it for me, but once in a while, I was left to say, "I'm sorry, I can't." Surely everyone noticed. No one said a thing.

Our home teacher, Brother Richards, was on the high council and knew what was going on, but his companion, Mike, was confused why I was released from the Young Men's presidency after only a year. A couple of times, he stopped us, and with a twinkle in his eye said, "Salt Lake called, didn't they? You just can't say anything yet!" We laughed, but Mike was obviously half-serious. Rach and I decided we should tell him. So one Sunday, in an empty foyer, we told him I had been disfellowshipped. He stared at us forever, finally realizing I was telling him the truth. "I'm so sorry," he kept saying. "I was just joking with you. I'm so sorry." We smiled and assured him everything was fine.

I went to both of the Gospel Doctrine teachers, as they took turns teaching every other week. "I can't participate in classes for a while. I won't be making comments or praying, and I can't read from the scriptures aloud." Both responded with understanding. Once, the teacher forgot and called on our row to read a large section of scripture aloud. Before it was my turn, I had to ask the person sitting next to me to skip over me. Mike noticed what happened, so from that day on, he came and sat next to me to help avoid future awkward possibilities.

I couldn't raise my hand to sustain members of the ward who were getting callings. The first few times, especially being in the front of the chapel, I felt like all eyes were on me—the solitary holdout, the guy not participating in the meeting. Surely our friends who sat around us noticed that I didn't raise my hand or take the sacrament. I guess they expected me to volunteer information. But I didn't, and they didn't ask. And it didn't seem to matter. We greeted each other with warm smiles, eye contact, and handshakes, with genuine well-being questions and conversation. That shocked us.

I had been a member of the choir, a mainstay of the bass section. The choir director told me every week in September that she missed me and needed me at choir. Rachel finally called her and said, "You need to know that they told Joe he can't be in the choir." It took her a minute to understand what Rachel was saying, but she finally got it. She smiled kindly at me after that.

A dear friend in the ward called me late one night to help him administer a priesthood blessing to his child who had become terribly ill. I had to say, "I'm so sorry. I can't come help you for a while." He expressed his love for me and said he would call me again.

In November, a priest—one of *my* priests—asked me to step in and help bless the sacrament. A knife stabbed my heart, but I politely said, "I can't today," and he went on to ask someone else. Once again, I spent the meeting grateful for the maturity of unquestioning Aaronic Priesthood holders.

One of my conditions from the stake presidency was to schedule meetings with the bishop every other week, and with President Patrick monthly. I was constantly leaving messages for executive secretaries, but I did this faithfully. I loved those meetings.

The bishop, my friend, was initially confused at how our meetings would go. "I've heard you teach. There's nothing I can counsel you about. You know it. You just have to figure it out and do it. So, what should we talk about?" I would tell him my conversations with Aaron and Rachel, what I was learning from my counselor, and all my pent-up comments that I would've made during my church classes. But especially, I shared with my bishop my feelings about my Savior. I had frequent confirmations during the week from the Spirit of the truths I had always known, but had never been able to apply to myself until now. It was the highlight of my week.

During one of our visits, I was able to report to Bishop Hanson my experience near Aaron's cabin of knowing I had been forgiven because I could see my place in eternity for the first time. Bishop Hanson celebrated with me, and said, "This is why I love our meetings! I was worried when you were disfellowshipped because some people, especially men, decide, 'Membership is too hard. I can't do what you ask.' I'm constantly chasing people down to come talk to me. You've initiated all your appointments and shown up every time. You've been faithful in what they asked you to do. You've been humble in your commitment to make it right."

"I always look forward to talking to you, Bishop! I love this gospel. There was never a question that I believe the Church is true. I'll do anything to be right with God and right with the Church. If this is what I've been asked to do, I'll do it."

I went to every lesson, every Sunday. Well, I missed a few. Rachel came and found me once in a while on a tough day and would say, "I need to go home now. The lesson is on marriage," or "The lesson is on teaching children about the dangers of pornography," and we would walk home together. We both had our limits.

The tender mercies extended to us by a loving ward was the opening topic of our walk on a crisp October evening, a week before Halloween. Rachel had been worried that any day now, people would start to ask questions. But as time went on, we heard no rumors or speculation of any kind. Rachel asked me, "What if our ward made it harder on you? What if we were surrounded by people, well-meaning or otherwise, who judged you and gossiped about us?"

"Well, it would definitely make it harder. But honestly, I don't think it would change my actions much. I go to church because I believe the gospel is true." But I thought about it more, and realized she had a point. "It is a tender mercy that I can go to church to worship my God among friends—*supported by the Spirit, and surrounded by the spirit of support.*"

"Truly," Rachel said with obvious anxiety in her voice, "it could be a nightmare. It would be horrible to be the topic of conversation—conversation, mind you, dealing with things people have no clue about. This thought keeps me up at night. Our ward could look at you and never trust you again. I mean, look at the struggle Tom is having with you. What if our ward did that? That would devastate me. Absolutely devastate me. That would change how we live, really. I would be in survival mode all the time, trying to protect you, trying to convince people who you really are. I would feel at war in our own neighborhood. It would make peaceful worship almost impossible."

"Well, I know you would defend me, and thanks, but if people don't like me or don't trust me, that's on them. We know the truth. We understand that the Atonement of Jesus Christ changes hearts."

"I know. But I want to defend you, and I also want to defend our marriage. This misrepresents how incredible we are together!"

"That, we are." I squeezed her hand.

Rachel squeezed back. "Joe, I need to address this. It doesn't sit well with me. The Woman was sure that you had a horrible marriage, or why would you be cheating? You know very well that's the common assumption. That's every Hollywood script ever *and* all the songs I now hate—thanks for filling my iPod, by the way. But it's even taking *me* some time to figure out, and I'm standing here on the inside, knowing what's going on. We were happy—things were good. Someone on the outside looking in could very well question why it fell apart, you know?"

"Have you judged people in similar situations?"

"No. Well, yes, I guess I have," she admitted. "It's easy to do. You think you know, right? But you don't. You don't know what happens behind closed doors or in the recesses of someone's heart. You think you know whose weakness is doing what, and you make judgments. People want to know who and why. It's just human nature."

While we waited at the corner for a car to pass, I said, "I think about all the people who are silently grappling with addiction and how hard it is to change. The last thing they need is judgment." We stepped off the curb. "For years, I thought overcoming addiction was only about changing behavior. I white-knuckled my way through it for a long time. But there are so many layers to hack through before you even get to changing the behavior. And then layers after that."

She nodded. "I know it's different for you this time. I have hope."

I agreed with her. "You know, I used to avoid that word. How could I ever hope that I would feel anything but broken? But that's what's different this time—hope because of my Savior."

Rachel

> Joe, I had to text you ASAP. Abby just talked to me. She thinks she and Tom need to wait a while with the whole wedding thing.

Joe texted back immediately:

> Sweetums: Really? Is she okay?
>
> She is. They didn't break up. She said they're young and have some things to work out before they rush into marriage.
>
> Sweetums: Ya think?
>
> Ha ha. Just in time, though. We were going to send announcements out in a few weeks. I'll see you soon. I had another epiphany, but I'll tell you when you get home.

Joe had barely come in the door after work and was taking off his shoes. Sarah was close by doing her homework, and I wanted her to overhear this. I launched into my epiphany. "Of course, we know the story—Enos prayed and wrestled to be forgiven of his own sins. He prayed all day and all night. But Joe, this is electric to me! This is so real! God answered his prayer and said, 'Enos, thy sins are forgiven thee, and thou shalt be blessed.' And, just like that, it was gone! All the guilt and desire for sin were gone, and he knew it was gone. Just gone. He was amazed and he asked, 'Lord, how is it done?' And the Lord said, 'Because of your faith in Christ. Your faith has made you whole.' This is what you were talking about a few weeks ago, about infinite. About being clean. About the desire to sin being gone. All of it. This is the power of Atonement of Jesus Christ right here."

He smiled at me. "It really is like Enos. The guilt is gone, and Rachel, I just can't get over how the desire for that sin is gone. It's only been a few months, but for the first time in my life, I don't feel like I'm on the constant verge of relapse. I truly feel different inside. I don't view myself as fallen, as unredeemable. I feel like a new creature in every way. I've reached out to the Savior, and He grabbed me, and I have been made whole."

I squeezed his hand. "Hey, Abby's upstairs. She could use a hug."

Joseph

"Hey, Abby! Abigail, Lil' Abner, Absalom, Abs of Steel, Abacus, Abbey Road, Absolute, Abracadabra." It took until the last one to get her to smile.

"I love him, Dad. But he's just such a work in progress. And this is a deal breaker. It's more than accepting my family—it's how we view the way the gospel works. Right now, we're pretty far from agreement."

I sat down on her bed next to her. "What if I talked to him man-to-man?"

"No punching, kicking, or biting." She smirked. "No matter how much he deserves it."

"He needs to make peace with his past before he can move on. If there's one thing I understand, it's *that*. Call him and tell him to come over."

I was sitting on the porch when Tom pulled up twenty minutes later. It was a warm enough day to sit outside and chat. I stood, greeted him with a handshake and a smile, and gestured for him to sit in the chair next to me. "Thanks for coming, Tom."

"Sure."

"Is it fair to say that you and I have some things to work out?"

He settled into the chair and crossed his arms. "Joe, you don't owe me anything. But yeah, I have some questions and concerns."

I wasn't sure where to start. I'd spent the last twenty minutes praying, and I had snapshots in my mind of things I wanted to talk about, but now that we were sitting here, it was hazy. So I just jumped in. "Tell me about your dad. Your biological one."

Tom was slow to answer. "He and my mom had been married for fifteen years. They had the four of us—I'm the oldest. I was almost twelve, and he called my mom one day and said he was in love with another woman. He'd been with this other woman for fourteen years. She was pregnant, and he wanted to have a family with her. So he walked out."

I raised my eyebrows. "That's pretty heavy."

He looked at the red and brown leaves on the ground. "Yeah."

"So, what was your dad like?"

"Fine. Just a dad, I guess."

"Did he take you to church? Little League games? The zoo?" I prodded.

"Yeah, I guess so."

"Have you spent all these years feeling basically rejected by someone you trusted?"

"Yep."

"So, do you look at me and see the same possibility? Or maybe even the same *probability*?"

He was very interested in the leaves, his façade of confidence long since dropped. "Yeah."

"I've spent a whole lot of sleepless nights worrying about that very thing. No, not that it's a possibility or probability that I might relapse—that's not going to happen, and we'll cover that in a minute. I've been worrying that if people knew what I did, they would never be able to get past it. If that's all they will ever see when they look at me."

Tom *did* look up. "Joe, I don't even know what it is yet, and I'm pretty sure I can't get past it. Are you sure it's out of your system?"

I had to chuckle a little bit. "I appreciate your honest question. I want to explain my path to you. I need you to separate me from your dad. I don't know him, and I can't speak for his motives, so just try to listen to my experience. Can you do that?"

He nodded.

"I spent years and years going through the motions. People looked at me and thought I was a great person because I was doing all the right things. But I knew the truth. I was so far away from God, I was in hell. And one day I was talking to my brother, and he said, 'If you're in hell, which way are you facing right now? Are you staring straight into hell, heading farther in? Or have you turned around to face God?'"

Tom was searching my face. He was met with tears as I remembered that critical moment of beginning to see myself differently.

"I told my brother that I had turned from my sins and was

facing God. He said, 'Then you are closer to God than you have ever been because you're finally facing the right way.'"

I leaned forward and rested my elbows on my knees as I looked at Tom, who was listening closely. "You know what surprised me? In the midst of sin, I felt God's love. That made me ready to offer up my whole soul to Him. Recently, there was a moment when I saw myself in eternity, and I knew instantly that I had been forgiven. I was washed over," my voice caught, "with a peace I had never known. It *wasn't* a process. I wasn't moving from step to step, inching closer to achieving God's love. It was like..." I had to wipe my nose with my handkerchief, "a divine embrace."

Tom said quietly, "I don't mean to diminish your experience, but I believe repentance *is* a process. You can't just go from being a horrible sinner to," he snapped his fingers, "being welcomed into heaven."

I nodded, but countered, "What about Alma? What about Alma the Younger?" I flipped my mental scriptures to the New Testament. "What about Paul?" As I said the name, a torrent of emotion filled my soul and almost paralyzed me—with joy. I gained control of my voice. "Paul was a vile sinner. He participated in destroying the Church. And then he saw Jesus in a vision, and his life was instantaneously changed. Scales fell from his eyes, and he knew the Savior. He became a great leader. He became the emissary of Christianity."

We were quiet for a while. I let him think about those examples.

Tom straightened his back and said, "But repentance *is* a process. I know it is."

I replied, "Yes, it is. But the word 'repent' means to turn. And it can be a complicated process, or as simple as that."

"So you just turned from your sins, and now you're forgiven and everything's great?"

I matched his posture and looked at him. "I couldn't have been more surprised by the joy I felt at that moment. It was unexpected, but it was undeniable. Wait. You know what? You have a point. It *was* a process. I look back over my life, over each and every painful sin cycle of stops and starts and fixes and relapses, and I can see that each time I tried to turn to God, I was moving closer to that amazing moment that I felt forgiven. And especially this last year, even during the egregious things I did, God's hand was in my life, preparing me for that moment. I don't know why I didn't receive that gift of change thirty-five years ago, or twenty years ago, or all those other times. Except... I do. Tom, the reason I've been traveling this path is so I can understand the Atonement of Jesus Christ. I have those weaknesses that drive me to my knees so I can understand that I need Jesus Christ every minute of every day. I need Him to sanctify me so I can use His power to overcome."

He blinked. He nodded.

"Tom, I know you're invested in providing a safe haven for your future family, one you never had. I admire your forward thinking. So in your preparation, take a lesson about parenthood from our Heavenly Parents. They understand that falling is part of learning to walk. They don't hate you because you fall, or keep falling, or even because your steps are unsteady. When sin and difficulty arise, that's precisely the process They use to teach you to lean on Them to balance. Don't let Satan convince you that you should be ashamed of falling. It's part of your process. It's part of everyone's process. The test comes in using the power and strength of Jesus Christ to get up again."

Abby texted me at work:

> Lil' Abner: Dad, I don't know what you said to Tom the other night, but it triggered some pretty deep conversations. He's looking at a few things differently.
>
> Wow. That's progress.
>
> Lil' Abner: He mentioned that he's starting to wonder if there were things about his dad's situation that he didn't understand.

No kidding? That's huge.

Lil' Abner: Yeah. We'll see. Love you, Dad.

Rachel

"To follow up on a recent walk topic," Joseph said under a waning moon, "I've thought a lot today about how our ward has reacted to this. And I think a lot of it has been because of you."

"What do you mean?"

"You sit by me. You hold my hand. You look at me with those eyes full of love. You don't talk or act differently toward me. They're getting their cues from you."

"Hmm. I hadn't thought about it that way. You know, though, I think a big difference is you. You go to church every Sunday. You don't cower in the back corner. You don't hide. You don't shy away. You hold your head high. You don't carry yourself with shame and misery. You make it easy to accept you and love you. It's not like we're trying to hide what's going on, but if you suddenly started being awkward and all weird, people would really start to wonder. Because you're being completely normal, it makes it easy for everybody else to be normal too."

"There's truth to that as well. But really, it's you and how lovingly you treat me."

"No, it's you, and how you're normal so people can be normal."

"No, it's you, because you're cute," he insisted.

"No, it's you, because you're especially munchable," I insisted.

"We make people sick when we do this, you know."

"That's why we don't do it around other people very much. They get jealous."

In the stillness of our room, Joe whispered, "Rach. Rach? Are you awake?"

"I am now." I heard him sniffle. "Are you okay?"

He was slow to answer. "Rachel, I'm..." He didn't say anything, but from his breathing, I could tell he was crying pretty hard.

I reached for his hand. There was a tissue in it. "What's wrong?"

"Rach, I was thinking about... about people knowing. Not very many people at church know that I've been disfellowshipped, but some do, and

I'm fine with that. And the girls—well, at least Abby and Sarah seem to be okay. It still feels awkward when we see Hannah. And Tom. But none of them even *really know* yet." He took another few breaths and wiped his eyes. "It's unbelievably scary to me to be around family or friends once they find out what I've done. I feel..." he tried to name it. "Fear and dread. I'm worried about the first time I see Mary. She'll look at me differently. What about Josh and Jesse? It can never be the same again."

I sat up and propped myself up against the wall. I reached out and stroked Joe's hair. "Well, first of all, we can help Tom with his issues if he'll let us, or he can go soak his head and marry the daughter of some other fictional 'perfect family.' Secondly, Mary loves you. Remember the care package she sent? That's the Mary who knows and loves you. And third, Josh and Jesse don't know, and they don't ever have to know. And the girls? When we're ready to tell them, it will be an opportunity for them to understand how the Atonement can heal hurts and deepen love."

"But Rachel... what I did... When people think about a creepy cheater, they will immediately associate that with me. I fully expect men to shield their wives and children from me, the hideous monster. I worry about that with the people we love. Will they ever be able to trust me again and not see me as *that guy*?"

"I know it's scary." I kept stroking his hair, hoping it was calming. "Joe, you're a good guy. You're the best guy I know, in fact. That's the guy everyone knows. And now, there's an added human dimension of conquering sin with courage and determination that makes you even more amazing."

"Yeah, or more disgusting."

I paused and prayed for guidance. "Joe, do you remember why I love you?"

He spoke softly. "Yes."

"Do you know why your friends and family love you?"

I felt him shake his head back and forth. His shoulders began to tremble.

He really didn't know. "Joe. *You are worthy.* You are worthy of their love. Trust their ability to see into your heart, who you really are."

Joe sobbed. "I don't feel worthy."

"Joseph, remember who you are. You are a noble son of God."

Joseph

I enjoyed my sessions with my counselor. Rachel had found him. He was the father of one of her childhood friends. In the beginning, he gave me a workbook, and it was tough to read. I did some of it, but I felt like it just didn't apply to me anymore because change had already taken root in my heart. I knew that for others, acknowledging the behavior was an important first step. But I didn't want to dwell in the past, talking about how deviant I had been. I was ready to move forward.

I had come to understand how I had fallen so far, but one thing the counselor helped me understand was how choices-became-be-havior-became-surrendering-my-choices. It was the Parable of the Ketchup Bottle, and it was true. I had made choices early on that pointed me in a distinct direction. The more choices I made toward that end, the more it became habit, the more it became behavior, and the less it became a choice. I had moved straight to the edge and long since jumped off the cliff, so of course I would fall. That made a lot of sense to me.

Rachel's concern was that I needed tools to manage painful memories and stop destructive thoughts before they took root, to direct choices so I could keep my power to act, not be acted upon. The counselor shared good ideas, and in those first critical months, I used a couple of them very successfully.

Besides the tools he shared with me, the things that I found myself relying on heavily were talking to Aaron, talking to Rachel, listening to "The Lamb of God" when I felt sad, daily mindful self-evaluation, and knowing that I was a noble son of God. All of it dovetailed together to direct my thoughts and guide my actions.

My counselor and I went from weekly sessions, to bi-weekly, to monthly, to "I think you're good." It was nice to talk freely and get solid advice about how to change future behavior. I looked at it like follow-up treatment after the cleansing and healing of Jesus's Atonement.

"Joe, I have an idea for your birthday in January. It's actually a done deal." We were walking past illuminated Halloween decorations, and she sounded timid. "I made the reservations today. I got a good deal on airfare and everything."

"Wow! Where are we going?"

"To North Carolina to see Josh and Jesse."

My heart dropped to my feet. "Rach, I'm not sure that's a good idea."

Rachel spoke gently, knowing this was terrifying. "I called and talked to Jesse. I wanted to be sure that our visit wasn't going to interfere with anything they had planned, and she said January would be perfect."

"You called her and talked to her today?" Now *I* was sounding timid.

"Yeah. Joe, I've had this feeling. I really listened to what you said the other night, and I felt like it was time to trust our friends. This experience has changed us, and as our dear friends who care about us, they would want to know about it."

I swallowed hard. "You told her?"

Rachel tried to sound reassuring. "I did. A little bit, anyway."

"What did she say?" My tongue felt heavy.

"Same thing I said—'No, he didn't.' But I explained a few things, and I bore my testimony about the power of the Atonement of Jesus Christ to change hearts. Joe, she said she loves us, misses us, and really wants us to come out and reconnect. It's been a long time since you've been out there." Rachel added, "Plus, they just got a timeshare at the beach. How fun is that?"

I tried to gather my thoughts. Decidedly, this visit might be more than I could do. "Rachel, I gotta say, I'm scared to see them. I've done too much for them to forgive me. They'll never look at me the same way."

"But they will. They love you."

"Rachel, I'm telling you, this makes me feel shame."

She stopped walking and turned to me. She put her cold hands on my warm face. "I hear you. I understand this is frightening. But I talked to her today... I heard her voice... This is safe, Joe. I mean, come on—it's Josh and Jesse. This is important for you to do. We can't hide."

"Rach, I'm not hiding. I just... How should I act around them? It just sounds awkward and humiliating."

"What I meant is, we have to face this. Joe, you've been saved. We have palpably felt that spiritual blessing. But the next hurdle is social—friends and family, right? How do we do that? What does that look like? Together, let's figure out our new normal."

We began walking again. I was silent for quite a while before I said, "I'm glad you made the plans. I really miss Josh. I'm just telling you, I'm scared."

Rachel

Stupid Satan loves using emotional whiplash. It was traditionally one of his best tools for me.

Most people love Christmas, but I loved Thanksgiving, and I celebrated it all month. I had blissfully gone on my weekly temple trip, and I was driving home full of gratitude. I was also happy because it was date night. I saw a billboard for divorce attorneys that said, "Don't be taken for a fool. Let us take him to court."

I went home and sat immobile in the living room. Sadness was a hungry bear and I was slow prey. It feasted on every part of me. When Joe got home from work, I was still in the chair. He was walking toward me, asking, "Rach, how was the temple? You haven't been answering my texts. Do you have your phone on you?"

"I can't do this," was all I could mumble in response.

"What are you talking about?" Joe was now also having emotional whiplash.

"Over and over, it replays in my mind. I can't see anything else but you being with her. I'm such a fool. I can't take it anymore."

"What happened, Rachel?"

"Nothing. I'm not even mad. Just flat-out heartbroken. And it hurts too much to even look at you."

Joe went to the kitchen. I could hear him microwaving something. He brought me a cup of hot cocoa.

"Here. I put in exactly ten marshmallows. I know how you like it."

I didn't reach out to take it from him. He put it on the table next to me and sat down.

I could feel his worry and confusion. I waited for him to talk because I had no words. He finally said, "I can understand how it hurts to look at me. There have been times in the past year when I couldn't even look at myself in the mirror. But you know what gift I've been given since the day I told you what I did? Rachel, I've been seeing myself through your eyes. You've seen me. All of me. You have an ability to see all of it—the good, the bad, and the ugly—and to let love win. You see me as my mother's child. You see me as a child of God. For so many years, I only saw the parts I hated. But I've been seeing myself through your eyes, and that's helping me to know how God sees His children."

Why did he have to say the right things? "Joe... I do see you like that, but..." I tried to shake the bear off my shoulder for even a moment. "I feel stupid. I feel like I'm ignoring what you did. I... It's the dang world that tells me that you're not worth keeping around. The messages I get everywhere I look are to jump ship and save myself, or that I have to hold your feet to the fire because you'll do it again. That I'm weak and a kept woman because I stay with a man who cheats. Anything but staying together... My 'fight' instinct gets weak and turns into a solid desire for 'flight.'"

"Tell me about it. But Rach, we know who we are. We know where we're going. We're loved. We won't let anything take that away from us." He waited until I looked at him, and he whispered, "And we're dang good together."

I knew all that was true. I had heard God's voice telling me to stay. God had shown me the purity of Joe's intentions. I could see the light in Joe's eyes. I needed to recognize this as Satan's blatant attempt to dismantle our hard work.

Logically, that's what I needed to do. But it was too easy to get lost in the sadness. Strength was a choice, albeit a painful one. Stupid whiplash. Stupid Satan. Stupid sadness bear eating me for dinner.

I took my hot cocoa and left Joe to fix dinner alone. Sarah would be home from play practice in an hour. I barricaded myself in my room to call my sister. "Mare, talk this through with me, okay?"

"Sure."

"Could we just talk about why I should stay?" I tried not to sound wounded. "You know me best, and... and I don't have anyone else to ask right now." I realized my toes were ice cold.

"It's okay, Rach. What's on the top of *your* 'Why I Will Stay' list?"

I took a sip of cocoa. It *was* perfect. "That's easy. It's because he's sorry. No, that's a simplistic word. It's more than that. He's contrite. He's different. I haven't told you yet about the experience he had when he was up at Helaman's Camp. He felt like his whole world was crashing down, and he called and talked to his brother. Right after he told Aaron everything, he immediately felt God's love. And then he had a very sacred experience when he built an altar and prayed. He truly felt accepted by the Lord. In that very moment, he felt his heart change. He's got a peace about him that I have never seen. So, I guess that's the top of the list—he's sincerely repentant."

"You'd have nothing if you couldn't absolutely see and feel the sincerity," Mary agreed. "So, what else makes the list?"

I put the phone on speaker so I could interlace my fingers around the warm mug. "I hate to pull this one out because it seems childish, but I love him. I've loved him for thirty years. Well, strike that—I've been with him for thirty years and loved him for *most* of it."

Mary laughed. "True!" She knew our history.

"When we got married, I feel like God gave me the vision of who Joe really is—you know, what he would become. I always knew the reward would be great. I just didn't know the road would be so unbelievably painful... But I *know* him. I'm amazed by his strengths, and I understand his flaws."

"So, love is the second thing?"

"Yeah, but also..." I folded one of my legs under me to try to warm my toes. "We've put a lot of time and effort into our relationship for a lot of years. We have children together. I absolutely don't want to 'stay for the kids' because you and I have both seen situations where that was catastrophic. But there's something to be said for our years together."

Mary agreed. "You were very young when you met him, but as you've grown, you've grown together."

"That's exactly what I'm saying." I took another sip of cocoa. "And I guess this is kind of along the same lines, but he is literally my best friend. He's just so perfect for me... We agree on how to raise kids and how to spend money. We agree on what to see on vacations and which pictures to put on the wall. So I guess that's the third thing on the list—he's my best friend."

"So 'best friend' is number three. So answer this. Could he be your best friend and you *not* be married to him?"

"That's an excellent question." I switched legs so I could warm the other set of toes, and I pictured the hypothetical scenario. "Say we aren't married anymore. I could see asking him to come over to my house so I could talk to him, friend to friend. But then he would instantly understand what I was saying, he'd give great advice, and then I'd want to kiss him.

So... No. I'd better be married to him."

"So, I guess that would be number four on the list?"

I smiled faintly. "Yes."

"Rach, I think this is a good list. I think you should stay with him."

"Thanks... This helps a lot." I took a deep breath. "It's hard to remember sometimes when all I can think about is how he stepped out on me."

Joseph

Our Thanksgiving Day celebration was minimal. We went to Rachel's parents' for dinner, pretended to be happy, and then we came home. For much of the following week, she stayed in bed and read a lot. She kept saying she believed in me and in the miracle of the Atonement, but it was clear she was struggling. By the next Thursday, I told her that getting some crisp night air might be good, and I was surprised that she agreed.

I was wearing my jacket, but Rachel was bundled up with a scarf and mittens. Instead of holding hands, we walked lockstep, arm in arm. Rachel started our talk. "Joe, I don't know how to say this. You'll have to help me." She breathed a warm puff into the cold air. "I know you've been forgiven by God. And I have also fully forgiven you. I've seen your heart; I know your intentions. I'm struggling because I thought I knew those before. Really, we do the same things now that we did then—we love, we laugh, we listen. We're best friends. I've analyzed our relationship from every angle. We evolved from the unhealthy codependence of foolish youth to a beautiful, healthy, mature interdependence."

I couldn't help but interrupt. "I totally agree."

Rachel continued, "So, here's the thing—how can I trust that this is real? I thought it was real *then*. I thought we were heading in the right direction. How do I know you aren't going to go back to porn, or chatting, or lunches with women? How can I trust what we have now when I trusted it then and was so wrong?"

This was a tough question, and I needed to find the right words to answer. I didn't want to sound like the slimy guy who winks and says, "*I've changed, baby. You gotta believe me.*" I asked God to help me share what was genuinely in my heart. "Rachel, I don't want that life. I don't want to hide. I can definitely live without the shame. You know that I value my relationship with my Savior now. That makes all the difference. I didn't understand Jesus's Atonement before."

"But you did. I know you did."

"I really didn't," I confessed.

"So, how can I trust that this change is real? You were pretty good at lying. How can I trust that you are here, with me and with God, with both feet firmly planted, focusing in the right direction, with no desire to look over your shoulder?"

I pulled her closer as we walked because she had started to shiver. "Let me answer that in a different way. As I was driving home from my last appointment with my counselor, I was thinking about what Moroni says in the Book of Mormon. He commends a righteous community for their 'peaceable walk with the children of men.' I love that phrase. So every day, I do a mental evaluation about my peaceable walk, and I go down a list. I think about my relationship with my Savior. Am I in harmony? I think about my relationship with you. Am I in harmony? I think about how I feel toward myself. Am I in harmony? If I'm feeling shame, or anger, or regret, or sadness, I think about what I need to do to regain my peace. I don't wait for the end of the day, or tomorrow, or later, but right then. What do I need to do to reclaim peace?"

"You do that every day?"

"Heck, yeah. Sometimes more than once, if it's a rough day. It's how I know I'm in control of myself. I'm not being acted upon by outside influences. I'm in charge of my own peaceable walk, and I love this feeling of peace. I absolutely love it. I don't want to do anything to make it go away."

Rachel slowed our pace to mull that over. "I have to say, knowing that helps me a lot. But I think about your affair every day. It chases me around sometimes, no matter what I do to try to let it go. Obviously, this last week has been bad. I'm sure time will help, but the pain is still so raw and..." She searched for the word. "Visceral. It slices into the trust I had in you, in our relationship."

"I know. It's okay. I do think it helps you to see my honesty. You have free access to everything I do, and I'm happy to give that to you. You've said that you feel comfort knowing that I'm exactly where I say I'll be."

"Yes, that helps... But the fact that I even have to wonder kinda makes me angry, you know? I'm not used to wondering about you. It's still fresh for me. I've only known about this for four months. You knew about it for a couple of years. I'm still putting pieces together in my mind. And I'm swinging like a circus trapeze from all these conflicting feelings I get. One minute, I feel spiritual and sweet and strong, and then literally the very next, I'm immobilized with mistrust and anger."

I knew her struggle was real. "Rach, I decided a while ago that there's not a grand gesture I can make to prove to you that you can believe me. As time passes and I'm consistent and dependable, you'll have confidence that the change is real and permanent. When I have prayed about what I can do to make this easier on you, this is the answer I get—I can live every day the way I should, in my peaceable walk with God and man."

She thought about that for a few silent minutes. "You know what? That's exactly what I need. I need to see your solid actions, your dependability, your truthfulness over time. That's the only way I'll feel secure in it." She let go of me to pull her coat up around her neck, and then we locked arms again. "I like Aaron's word—metabolize. I need time to heal and metabolize. And although it's painful, I'm glad we can have this conversation."

"It's not so painful. It's healing." I pulled her closer.

The next night, after we watched a movie for date night, we adjourned to our room and commenced the Utah map back-scratching. Rachel was the recipient. I could tell she had a better day because her smile was returning. I rubbed her lower back—St. George to Kanab to the Four Corners—and we talked about getting ready to go to North Carolina. As I was scratching the Wasatch Range, Rachel told me she had found out that The Woman's name was Lila.

I stopped mid-scratch. I was shocked. "How did you find out?"

Rachel explained, "I realized I could find her the same way she found you—I saw her listed as having viewed your profile on LinkedIn."

"I wish you hadn't done that. I'm afraid it will make it worse for you to know things about her."

"When you say that, I feel like you're protecting her, not me."

"I'm not. I'm worried for you. I know how you get, how names and places become painful markers for you."

"Well, you're underestimating me. I feel like this was the last big thing that I needed to know. I saw that her name is Lila, and then I looked her up on Facebook. I understand a little more about her now. What I don't know is why you stayed with her for so long. You guys have nothing in common."

"I know."

"I'm more convinced than ever that I'm exactly what you need." She smiled and winked at me. "Sanpete County, please."

Rachel

My mood had been rebounding. But the seventh of December was an especially bad day, a day that would indeed live in infamy.

The doctor's office called me with the results of my test. For a long time, I had been having severe pain, discomfort, and tissues that were so irritated, they were bleeding. I had avoided seeing a doctor, but I finally went in to get it checked, and an effervescent little nurse called me while I was out Christmas shopping on a sunny but chilly afternoon to announce, "You have trichomoniasis and ureaplasma. We're sending in a prescription for you." I didn't know what those were, and because she sounded twelve, I didn't ask her. I sat in a parking lot and Googled it.

Sexually transmitted diseases.

But... So I Googled the health department STD test. They only test for the big ones. These minor ones slide in under the radar. But really, no STD felt "minor." It was incredibly painful in every way.

I dialed the phone, and when he answered, I exploded. "Joseph! You didn't wear a condom because they, and I quote here, 'made her uncomfortable.' Well, your complete disregard for your wife has just manifested itself in an STD. Why have you made this my life? I was a married woman in a monogamous relationship, and I got an STD. You listened to your selfish desires and had literally no regard for me! You knew she was sleeping with a bunch of guys. Well, thanks for sharing her truck-stop, storm-drain, flypaper, roach motel of a vagina with me! I'm not calling the doctor's office for you. You call them and inform them you are a carrier and need to be treated too. I'm hanging up before I say something I regret."

I breathed deeply. I needed to get control of myself, but my mind was swirling. I decided to give myself twenty minutes to be bitter and angry, and then I would reclaim my peace. After thirty minutes of talking myself down, I was left with this crazy new information still rattling around my head, but now I only felt weak and vulnerable. I was not ready to go home.

I needed a change of pace. I needed something different to think about. I didn't want to be alone. I had a sudden and distinct urge to call Hannah. I tried to sound nonchalant. "I'm out and about. Are you done with classes for the day?"

"Hey, Mom. I just finished a test, so I'm walking home."

"Meet me at the Wilk Circle. Let's go for an early dinner."

"Cool."

I picked her up from campus and we went for Mexican—the comfort food of champions. As we ate, we chatted about our week, about her classes, about the weather. Then she said, "What's up, Mom? You seem like you've had a bad day."

I wanted to be in control of this moment. I had tried to be a mom instead of a wounded soul. I tried to pretend I didn't need to be comforted. I wanted to be the grown-up, the mature adult with all the answers, the voice of reason. But the day had worn me down, and I was weak, and tired, and weak some more, and just tired of being strong. And I sought solace.

"Hannah, I know you haven't wanted to talk about it, but today I need a friend." I wadded the straw wrapper into a ball and looked at her through heavy eyelashes. "This whole situation surrounding Dad being disfellowshipped is just rotten."

The old Hannah surfaced—the reflective, compassionate girl I had come to know through all the years of Rock and Talk—and she reached across the table and touched my hand. "I'm sorry, Mom. I can only imagine how hard this is for you. I've..." She was timid, but she continued quietly, "I've been thinking it had something to do with pornography."

"Yes, it did." And words tumbled from my mouth before I could stop them.

Hannah stared at me. I should've been paying attention, I should've seen it in her eyes, I should've been listening to what wasn't being said. I was too busy being hurt and frustrated. I said the word "affair," and she got up and walked out of the restaurant.

Dang it.

And what was more, I didn't have cash to throw on the table so I could chase after her. I grabbed my purse and our coats, and I went to the hostess at the front of the restaurant. I handed her my debit card. "I've got an emergency. I was sitting at that table over there, party of two. Take this, run my card, and I'll be back in a bit to sign it and get my card back. Is that okay?"

226

The nice lady saw the look of panic in my eyes. She took my card and said, "Uh, sure."

I darted out the door. I looked up and down the street for Hannah. About half a block away, I saw her walking, so I tried to match her pace as I followed after her. I kept mumbling, "God, forgive me. I was weak. Bless Hannah. Forgive me. Bless Hannah." I watched her turn the corner, and I turned the corner about thirty seconds later. I sighed as I saw her sitting on a brick planter box in front of another restaurant.

I approached and stood a few feet away. "Hey," I said quietly.

She didn't look up.

I began crying. "I was so stupid, Hannah. That was incredibly selfish of me. Please forgive my weakness. I shouldn't have told you like that."

She was silent. And visibly angry.

"Can I go get the car?" I offered. "Can we go somewhere?" She still wouldn't look at me, and she had begun to shiver. I knew it wasn't from the cold December air. "Do you want to put on your coat?" I held it out. She didn't respond. This conversation now stopped being about me. I needed to forget myself and focus on this poor child that I just rattled to her very foundation. I wiped my tears and focused. I could see from the look on her face what was going through her head. "Hannah, Dad loves his family very much. Think about it. Think about what you know."

To this, she responded quickly. "He's a freaking hypocrite."

I couldn't totally disagree. "It would seem that way. We have every reason to be mad at him for lying to us. Today, I'm especially weak and angry. But I have spent almost every minute of every day since I found out trying to understand why this happened, and I think I've figured it out. I have tremendous compassion for him. Can I tell you what I think?"

She ignored me and muttered, "I can't believe my own dad is a lying, cheating player."

I couldn't let that go. We didn't call people names in our family. I leaned in closer, and I used my calm Mom Voice. "Hannah, I know you're mad, but that's not fair. You have a right to feel what you're feeling, but you may not call him names."

At this, she looked up at me. Tears welled up, and she bitterly said, "You just finished telling me he lied and cheated on us, so guess what, Mom? He's a player!"

"He made horrible mistakes…"

"And I hate him for it!" she yelled back. "If I can't believe in Dad, then this whole world is going to hell. What's the point of anything?"

I ached for her, but I needed to bring her to a level where she would listen, not just hear. "Have you ever eaten here?" I angled a thumb toward the name on the building.

"What?" She was confused, like she had missed a part of the conversation.

"Have you ever eaten at this restaurant? This planter is sturdy," I kicked it with my toe, "and pretty convenient, so I was wondering if their food was good too."

"What are you talking about?"

"Well, we can either change the subject and talk about things that don't matter, or you can open your heart to the man who has loved you your whole life. You choose."

She looked me in the eye. She was evaluating my statement. I hoped that what she saw in me was love—for her and for her dad.

She folded her arms. "You picked a crappy way to tell me this. In a restaurant? In public? Not your best moment, Mom."

She was right. "I know. Please forgive me. I'm so sorry. I felt so weak today, and I gave in to it." I plopped down on the planter next to her. "I'd like to explain the rest to you. It really will help you understand. Would you like to put your coat on and sit here with me? Or should I go get the car?"

She sat motionless, then suddenly stood and yanked her coat from my arms. "Let's get in the car."

We walked back in silence toward the Mexican restaurant. We neared the car, and I clicked the key fob to unlock it. "Jump in and I'll be right there. I've got to settle the check."

When I got in the driver's seat three minutes later, Hannah was waiting for me with a napkin in her hand that she found in the glove compartment. She had been wiping her cheeks. "Mom, why did you tell me this? Why didn't you call a friend? Why didn't you call Aunt Mary? Why me?"

If I was going to tell her the truth anyway, I may as well say the rest. "Oh, Hannah. I'm so sorry. I needed someone to lean on. Sometimes I feel like I don't have anyone to talk to, and at dinner you were so kind, and you asked me how I was doing, and I cracked. Here's some more painful info, okay? I found out today that I have an STD. I thought we had dodged a bullet, but nope, it showed up all these months later. So I was feeling especially vulnerable and sad."

"What? So you called me? Your *daughter*?"

"Well… yes. I didn't intend to tell you like this. Not now. But I didn't want to go home yet, and for some reason, you came to my mind very first. I guess it was a bad idea." I started the car and backed out.

"It wasn't a bad idea," she whispered toward her window. We drove a few blocks and waited at a stoplight. She dabbed her eyes and looked at me. Her compassion overtook her anger and she said, "I'm sorry you found out you have an STD. That's not fair to you at all."

"Thanks for that." I started driving north on University Avenue. Maybe a drive through the canyon would give us some time to talk. I waited a moment before I asked, "Can I tell you the rest of the story? It would help you to understand. You can ask me any questions, and I'll answer them. But you have to have an open heart."

"Yeah. I guess."

I began with the blond-haired boy who was deeply loved, but deeply lonely. I told her about the teenager who was berated and belittled. I told her about how he was inadvertently taught to seek this particular medication to make himself feel better. And by explaining it, I used his analogy, and I understood his addiction even better. "Think about it like meth. He was so sad, and he needed an escape, a fix." I told her about his battle that raged for years, always under the surface, ready to emerge and destroy him. At this point of the story, I asked, "Does this help you understand the state of his mind at the time?"

"Yeah, but you still don't go out and start sleeping with people," she replied. She was angry, but pragmatic. "No offense, Mom, but that's not how problems are solved."

"Exactly. It's not at all how problems are solved. So follow this logic— you know your problems are pretty messed up, but you're supposed to be strong and fix them, but because you're such a failure, fixing them would be basically impossible, and if anybody found out what you're really like, they won't love you anymore, and you've been taught how to feel better, so… what would you do?"

She wiped her eyes and took a minute to answer. "You've always taught me to face my problems and fix them, so I don't see how Dad can say that to me and then choose to go 'feel better.' That's just disgusting."

Her comment brought me to the crux of my explanation. "Hannah, pain causes people to do things they would never rationally do. And when pain spans years, people become desperate to make it stop. Dad's a logical guy, but it doesn't make any logical sense, does it? When people keep using meth even after it has caused them so much personal damage, it doesn't make any logical sense. You have to stop trying to make sense of it and start listening to the pain."

"So, you're sitting here telling me that you're not mad at him? You understand why he did this, so it's okay with you?"

"Ha ha! Au contraire! I've been pretty ticked off. Today, for example. But I can choose how to react, right? I can yell at him even though he already feels horrible for what he's done. I can choose to say, 'You are a liar and a cheater. I'm done being played.' Or I can choose to believe in the worth of his soul."

Hannah wiped her cheeks with her third napkin from the glove compartment. The Sundance turn-off passed on our left as we continued through the canyon. "So, you just forgave him?"

"I'm gonna pull out an oldie, but a goodie. What would Jesus do?"

"Oh, pul-lease. That's so trite."

"Then listen again. What would the Savior of the world have me to do with the pain-wracked soul of Joseph Reeve?"

Fourth napkin. She handed me one too. "We'd better stop for more napkins because we're about out," she observed.

"There's a McDonald's in Heber. We didn't finish our Diet DPs, you know." We drove across the Deer Creek Dam and along the edge of the cliff in silence. "It's kind of funny that we're right here. This is where it all came crashing down for Dad. He was up here with Helaman's Camp last August, and she called and told him that she had told our bishop. That was the thing that helped him confess and start the process."

"You say stuff like that like it's nothing." Not only was Hannah was jumping into the middle of the story, but this was a pretty surreal conversation for her. I needed to slow down and go at her pace.

"I'm sorry, Hannah. Understand that I was in shock, real shock, for about a month. Probably the same shock you feel right now. But through that experience, I understood that the Atonement of Jesus Christ was also for me. We think it's for people who commit sin, which is definitely true. I understand now that His Atonement helps those who have been hurt by sin. Truly, I felt comforted and loved. And healed."

"I can't believe this is happening," she mumbled.

I could empathize. "Yeah. Same. Dad did cheat on all of us, even though he didn't see it like that at the time. You have every right to feel hurt. But open your heart, and I know you will choose love. It may take time, but the Savior's healing power is there for you."

"Yeah. Maybe." She sounded a million miles away.

"Why 'maybe'? You know the power of God. You've felt it. I've heard your testimony. At times like this, you can choose to remember all those witnesses you've had, or you can be hardened and angry. It's a much easier path to find love and strength from God. You know that."

Hannah looked out of her window and whispered again. "If God would ever help me."

The Spirit said clearly to me, *Don't talk. Just listen.* He knows that's hard for me. *Shutting up,* I replied in my mind. I waited patiently.

"So... I guess I can understand... I'm just lonely." She kept talking to the window. "Everybody likes me, and nobody likes me, you know? And... I don't even know how it started... it was very... intriguing, I guess. I wanted to know more. Man, the internet is a sticky spiderweb... I felt like I should be informed about what's out there. Well, that's what I started to tell myself. Truth is, I just... well, I just do it because I... I know I shouldn't like it... Dang, I waste a lot of time, and I hate that... It's everywhere. Everything reminds me of things I've seen..." Her voice broke. "I do it every day..."

My Hannah? I tried to grasp what she was telling me.

She sobbed into her napkin and used it up. She got the last one from the glove compartment and blew her nose. "I'm the hypocrite!" she yelled. "I know better! I don't have anything to blame! I haven't had a life of pain. My life has been perfect! I'm just lonely, and it makes me feel... less lonely. Except I hate myself! I knew what porn had done to Dad! I knew it! But I can't stop! And now... this is going to be my whole stupid life, isn't it? I'm destined for a life of loneliness and bringing pain to everybody...

I'm weak, I'm stupid, I'm a waste of air, I'm useless…"

I had to jump in. I couldn't let more name-calling go by. "Hannah, you may not talk like that about a person I love!" And now *my* voice broke. "I was there when Heavenly Father transferred your heavenly spirit to your earthly body, and I can promise you, He loves you as much now as He did then."

"Loves me? Then why won't He help me when I ask Him to take this from me? I don't want to keep doing it! It makes me feel horrible!"

My heart was bursting at hearing my daughter—my daughter!—express such agony. She had been suffering alone. I wanted to hug her, but I had to settle for putting my hand on her leg. "Hannah, now that you know my story, you can believe me when I say this—I know you feel like He's not listening to your prayers, but He is. He loves you. He's stretching your faith. Don't give up."

"Some stretching! It's ruining my life. All I want is a relationship with a guy who loves me. I want to find someone who desires me. I want to find someone who sacrifices for me, listens to me, values me. I want someone who shares my goals, laughs with me, reminds me who I am, talks me off the ledge. I want to develop what you and Dad have, and I know it takes a lifetime, but I want that so bad. And I know I'm going about this all wrong. I'm such a…" She stopped and looked at me. "I *feel* like a loser."

We had nine minutes until our McDonald's stop. "You feel bad because porn is porn—it isn't love. Naked people sharing naked things is porn. It's bodies, just bodies, doing biological things. There's no recognition of the soul that resides in that body. And that soul connection is what you're seeking."

"And that's why I hate myself! I know it's an imposter. I know I'm looking in the wrong place for love and acceptance. I know I'm distorting the proper view of relationships. I know, I know, I know! I know all the answers. And I'm just a giant hypocrite. If people knew me and what I was doing, they would hate me."

"Yeah, because you're the only one in the world doing this. You are single-handedly responsible for the multi-billion-dollar porn industry."

"You're not helping, Mom."

"Sorry."

"I was on those apps last year to meet people who weren't stupid.

Yeah, total contradiction, right? These 'brilliant, awesome guys' showed me things and pointed me to websites that are so.... Agh! It's like black magic, Mom. It draws you into a world where nothing is real. It makes you forget about time, responsibility, truth... It makes you forget what you really want. Think about it—if you walked in on someone doing that in a hotel room, you'd slam the door and you'd be like, 'Oh! I'm so sorry!' But on the screen, you're like, 'Oh, this is cool. I'm just gonna pull up a chair and grab some popcorn. Maybe get some nacho cheese and shame stuck in my chest hair.'"

At least she hadn't lost her sense of humor. "Can I just say something here?" I wanted permission.

"Sure. What?"

"My major problem with porn is that no one cares about the souls of the people on the screen. Not even them, I guess. Dad recently talked to a guy who's had a lifetime porn problem. Dad was trying to say, hey, it can get out of hand and turn into this huge mistake, and this path is not where you want to be, so you need to get yourself figured out. His friend said, 'No, I'm fine now. I haven't watched porn for a year. So, hey… this woman you were with… was she hot?' Dad about dropped his gum."

Hannah's jaw dropped. "No, he dit-n't."

"Yes, he did. The guy doesn't even realize what he said. He's so lost, he doesn't know it."

"'Was she hot?' So that's all that matters? Wow."

We stopped at the first traffic light in Heber City. "I know, right? Like she has no soul? It still sticks in my brain, and I want to shake him. Hey, speaking of shake, do you want a drink from McDonald's, or do you need an ice cream from Dairy Keen?"

I knew she rolled her eyes. "That's just what I need, Mom, to substitute a porn problem for an ice cream addiction."

I chose to ignore this. "Exactly. So, which is it?"

She thought about it. "I need to finish a paper tonight. So maybe the drink."

"I'm so sorry I'm taking you away from what you needed to do today." I continued to McDonald's. "Dang, I was pretty selfish. Sorry."

"No, Mom. It's okay. We both needed to talk. Thanks for listening to me." Quietly, she added, "I'm sorry I'm a disappointment."

I chose to let that go by for a moment, and instead I replied, "My favorite part is that we're finally talking." I pulled up to the drive-through and ordered two drinks with extra napkins. "I'm going to call Dad while we're in line, okay? He must be worried. I haven't talked to him since… since I yelled at him today."

I briefly explained to Joe that I would be home by 8:00, I paid for our drinks, and I turned and headed south. Hannah was sipping her drink and seemed calmer, but I knew she was deep in thought. She waited five minutes before she asked, "How could this happen to me?"

I sighed. She was in pain, and I wasn't sure what to say, but she was waiting for me to say something brilliant. "Do you remember when you told us about being on the app? You made a comment about how the guys on there were something like jobless loners who smoke in a dark room by the light of their computer screens. Something like that. Nacho cheese was stuck in their chest hair—that's the part we obviously remember best."

"Yeah. Something like that."

"Let's call that 'Dirty Old Man Syndrome.' Do you really think that's the face of consumers of pornography?"

"Well, yeah, I guess."

"Okay, think of people you pass on campus. And people you sit in church with. And people you pass at the grocery store. I'm not sure of the current percentage, but it's extremely high—most people have viewed pornography at some point in their lives. All people. Not just a high per-centage of dirty old men, but all people. Why do you think we have so many lessons and talks about it? Does it only affect 'disgusting' people? Or even nice, upstanding people like Dad? Or you?"

She didn't respond.

"Is everyone susceptible to desire and temptation?"

"Yes."

"Including you? Even though you know better? Including Dad, even though he's a wonderful man? I think what bothers you is that Dad knew all the right answers too. But it took him a while to fully understand what was going on inside his head. Please understand that the big thing you're doing right, that he didn't do when he was your age, is to talk about it. Don't hide. Don't seek to keep it a secret. Don't begin a pattern of self-hatred."

"Yeah, well, I'm already pretty mad at myself because I'm trying to stop and I can't."

"You have to expect that's how it's going to go. But being frustrated at attempts for self-mastery is different than self-hatred. One can be productive, but the other one is always counterproductive."

"So, now what?"

I thought for a moment. "I know of a kid, not your dad, who went to see a bishop to be counseled about how to fix a chastity issue. The bishop's advice was, 'Stop it.' I'm sure that poor kid's first frustrated, sarcastic thought was, 'Gee! I wish I'd thought of that!' So I'm not going to say, 'Well, stop watching porn.' That doesn't solve the underlying issue. The first thing counselors tell you to figure out is why you do it, more than it's just a curiosity. Everybody has a reason. Lonely? Sad? Bored? Abuse? Attention? Escaping? Rejected? Tired? Answer that question, and then figure out why you feel *that* way. Think about it. It may be the loneliness, but it may be something else. Pray about it. Get honest with yourself. Look at your triggers and then look beneath them."

"Yeah, I can do that."

We drove in companionable silence for a while, and I had another strong impression. "So, here's another thing I'd like you to think about. When it comes to overcoming an addiction, I can't think of anyone better to ask than Dad. I think you'll find that he's incredibly helpful."

She was doubtful. "I don't know. It might be too weird." Silence. "Maybe." Big tears appeared again. "Mom, I'm sorry."

"For what?"

"For Dad. For your STD. For my stupidity."

"Hannah, know this—sex is a gift from God. Intimacy rejoices in the worth of souls. Satan is fantastic at creating imposters." I stopped, but then added, "And antibiotics are also a gift from God."

Joseph

I did Rock and Talk with Sarah and a load of dishes while I waited for Rachel to get home. When she finally walked in the door at 9:30, I followed her into the family room and we sat to face each other. I fully expected a painful conversation. Rachel started. "So, putting our antibiotic extravaganza aside, I've waited to tell you in person about Hannah. I told her."

I was shocked. "I thought you wanted to tell all three of the girls at the same time."

"I know. But it happened."

"How did she take it?" I asked slowly.

"Well, she stormed out of the restaurant, and it took a ride to Heber City to calm her down so she would listen to the rest of the story. She had sort of filled in the blanks herself. Not like she expected *that*, of course, but she knew it was big. I should've found a better time and place. I was totally weak in the moment."

I was exposed. I was scared. I didn't question Rachel's actions, but I wasn't ready for this. "Is she okay?"

"Short answer? Probably. Long answer? She loves you, she knows I love you, and she will eventually understand that this doesn't change any of that. But… it's all wrapped up in this next bit of info that she shared with me. Ready? She feels that she has a pornography problem. Her interest was piqued from the interactions she had with the guys on the dating site, and she started seeking it out."

A rush of bile rose to my mouth, and I swallowed it. "Not Hannah…" I gripped the armrests.

Rachel continued recounting their conversation. "I told her that her first step is to figure out what is driving her, and then we could form a plan of attack. I'm late getting home because I spent the last hour telling her that I think it's a good idea to talk to you about it, even though it might seem weird at first. She said I could tell Abby and Sarah about it, but I think hearing your advice would help the most. She's always talked to me about her life, but she loves the way you explain stuff to her, so…"

My stomach churned. I wasn't going to make it. Without a word to Rachel, I propelled myself out of the chair, ran twenty feet to the bathroom, and threw up. My entire body wanted to turn itself inside out. After five minutes of controlling my impulse to vomit, I washed my hands, swished my mouth, and splashed my face with cold water. I stared at myself in the mirror—this face that had been two-faced. It was time to tell Rachel. I walked out of the bathroom and almost ran into her, standing near the door with a terribly worried look.

"Joe, are you okay? What on earth?"

"Rach, I'm just going to say it. On one of the dating apps, I met a girl named Kyra."

"A girl? Okay."

"Yeah. So, remember when Hannah told us that she was on that app and used a different name?"

In a whisper, she said, "Oh, my gosh. It was 'Kyra.'" She froze. Her mouth hung open.

I couldn't look at Rachel. My mouth tasted like disgust and shame. My skin felt clammy. I looked at the floor and willed it to open up so I could fall into it. "Of all the thousands and thousands of people, why did it have to be her?" I was so horrified, I couldn't even cry. "She said she was young and in college, and so I kept it simple, but it could have..."

Rachel turned and walked away from me. She stopped at the other end of the room and turned around. "Are you *serious*?" She was yelling, and I couldn't blame her. "And when you found out it was her, that wasn't like a huge wake-up call for you? It wasn't enough to make you stop?"

"No!" I remembered the intense hatred I had for Paul when I had read the chat threads on Hannah's phone, and I felt every bit of it return in this moment. "I was in so deep! After I realized what happened, I... I cut Kyra off. I was more careful..."

"More careful?" She was incredulous.

I yelled back, but it was out of anger at myself. "Do you know how many times in the past few months it has occurred to me that every woman I've ever met is somebody's daughter? Every revolting, vile thing I've ever said or done... And it could've been *my* daughter." I cried out with the pain of a damned soul. "I'm responsible for what's happening to Hannah!"

"Ya think?" She was trying to get control of her thoughts, and probably her fists.

"Well, I *didn't* want to think about it then. But I get it! And I'm horrified!"

She sat back down in her chair and held her forehead. She searched for words. "I can't describe how messed up this is. I think we can agree that we never tell her this part." She stared at her knees.

"I can't go back and change what happened," I said plaintively.

"I am now more certain that *you* have to talk to her. *You* need to try to fix what you've done. *This cycle has to stop.*"

It was true. I closed my eyes and raised my chin to the ceiling. I breathed in deeply to gather my thoughts and calm my still-churning stomach. I retraced my steps to my chair and sat in the thick silence. It was clear what needed to happen, but first things first. The thought of it was formidable. "Hannah knows. So it's time to talk to the three of them. We can't ask Hannah to go through Christmas being the only one of her sisters who knows. What about a family council this Sunday?"

Rachel stood and moved away from me to the stairs. She sounded distant. Worn out. "Sunday? I guess that will give me enough time to prepare Abby and Sarah first so it's not a shock."

My head was pounding. Hannah. My daughter. I was filled with anguish and shame for my part in this rocky road she found herself on.

I heard Rachel mumble, "I need to be alone for a while. I'll meet you upstairs when I've calmed down. Text Hannah," and she was gone.

I slowly picked up my phone. I didn't want to, but I couldn't put it off. I was her father and she needed me.

Hey, Hannah. Mom says you're okay. Are you okay?

Ba-Nannah: I guess.

Now what should I say?

> Want to come over for Sunday dinner?
>
> Ba-Nannah: I guess.
>
> I'd like to sit down with you. It's time I tell my children about my experience. What I've learned. Maybe it can help you.
>
> Ba-Nannah: So, Mom told you about my... stuff?
>
> Yes. And Mom told you about me.
>
> Ba-Nannah: Are you mad at me?
>
> Why would I be mad at you?
>
> Ba-Nannah: Because I'm mad at me.
>
> Are you mad at me?
>
> Ba-Nannah: Yes. And that makes me a hypocrite.

At least she was honest.

> Hannah, I really want to talk to you. It helps to talk to someone who loves you, someone who knows the problem and the journey.
>
> Ba-Nannah: I guess. But I don't know how to talk about this with you. This whole thing is freaking me out.

Yeah, me too... But this was about comforting her. A series of one-liner texts as they came to my mind.

> Silence breeds shame.
>
> Shine a light on it.
>
> Honesty takes the sting out.
>
> Light and honesty take away Satan's power.
>
> Let's go through this together.

I waited. Silence.

The most important one-liner:

> I love you, Hannah.

She didn't reply.

I locked the doors, turned off the lights, and went upstairs. I found Rachel sitting on the bed. I sat in the chair. Together, in this sacred sanctuary, we would figure out how to heal from what I had done.

Rachel spoke first. "It doesn't help to rehash it. It's done. Let's fix it."

"I texted her. She will come over on Sunday."

Rachel nodded. But there was more to discuss, and we both knew it. She started. "Here it is—I don't want to minimize that you have claimed your peace. I'm glad you have finally found yourself, and you're unshakeable. I can't tell you how happy that makes me. And I mean that. But I've been sitting here playing the stupid 'What If?' game that nobody wins. What if finding yourself has come at the cost of Hannah's soul? What if this had ruined my life, and our children's lives? What if I had actually left five months ago, or five minutes ago?"

My skin crawled with regret. "That was always what I was scared about. I didn't want to lose you, any of you. I didn't want to hurt you."

"But what if it had gone that way? Are you glad you found yourself, even though you ran the risk of losing your family by doing what you did? Was it worth it to cause us pain?"

"That's a terrible question. I don't know how to answer that. I never wanted to cause you pain, but I needed to heal my own lifetime of issues."

"Exactly, so my issue is… Your soul was saved, but you ran a horrible risk that I would lose mine. I've always put you first. You didn't put me first, and you took it for granted that I would be okay."

"I didn't take it for granted. I hoped you would."

"You didn't put me first. You didn't put our family first."

"No. I didn't." I didn't know what else to say. I didn't know what she needed to hear. There was no satisfactory answer—until I added, "I had to rely wholly on the merits of Christ to save."

Rachel

I prayed to know the right time to tell Sarah and Abby about the affair. As Sarah and I were driving home from the store the next day, the Spirit said to me, *Now is a good time.* At first, I questioned the wisdom of foisting life-changing information on her as we were driving through traffic, but I decided to trust the feeling, so I started out slowly.

"Sarah, I'd like to talk to you about Dad. So... he's been disfellow-shipped for a couple of months now. What do you think? How's it going for you?"

"I don't know how to answer that. It's fine. He goes to church. Not much has changed."

"How does he seem?"

"He seems happier. He laughs more. He talks to us more. He doesn't seem tired and bothered all the time. And I have learned all the words to his 'Lamb of God' CD."

I smiled. "We've always talked to you guys about everything, right? We haven't sugar-coated anything because we don't think that does you any favors. We want you to be prepared so you'll be able to maneuver through your own life with more wisdom and grace than you'd have otherwise. So... I've felt like it's time to tell you the whole story about Dad. Do you want to hear it?"

"No, but I probably should."

"It's actually pretty important. You'll learn a lot from it. Are you afraid you'll see him differently if I tell you the truth?"

"Never."

"That's good because he's still the same ol' lovable guy, just even better. So, let's start here—what do you think he did?"

"Well... I know he had pornography issues as a kid. I've thought that it might have something to do with that. And Uncle Aaron had problems like that too, and I've noticed them talking on the phone a lot more lately, so..."

"You're on the right track. What else have you thought?" I wasn't trying to make her guess so much as prepare her for the worst.

"I... Oh, Mom, it's so awful, I don't even want to say it. It's pretty bad."

"Well, you're actually probably right. It *is* pretty bad."

Sarah gathered her courage and said it quickly. "I was thinking that he probably brought a woman over to our house."

"Wow. That *would* be pretty bad! I can tell you it wasn't *that* bad! I'm grateful he never did that. But your idea is right. He did have…" I didn't pause, but I said it gently, "an affair. That's pretty hard to believe, huh?"

She took a moment. "Yes, but no. I know he was very sad and lonely as a kid, and I know some of those things still make him sad, so I can understand that he made bad decisions." This teenager's tender heart was a gift.

"Wow, Sarah. I wish everyone could be as philosophical as you are! He indeed was very sad, and he made horrible decisions, but you need to understand that he takes full responsibility for what he did. About a year ago, he met a woman online and eventually began an affair with her. He would meet her at her place. He finally realized what he was doing, and he was trying to stop seeing her, but she was just as sad and messed up as he was, and it was tough to get out of the situation."

Sarah nodded. "Mom, I know he loves you. I know he loves us. Dad would never have done this. He must've been totally lost."

"That's why we always want you to talk about stuff that's going on with *you*. When you bottle it up, it can explode into a terrible mess and hurt people you love. The key is talking about what you're going through way before it gets to that point. Dad held on to a lot of stuff, and it's been festering for a long time."

We pulled into our driveway, and I turned off the car. I reached out and held her hand. Tears welled up in her big eyes and began to course down her cheeks. "You know what, Mom? I wish I could've been Dad's friend when he was a kid. I wish I could've helped him."

"Me too," I agreed through my own tears. "I've been trying to fix what happened to that sweet little boy. I've wanted to stand up for him and defend him. I actually went to Uncle Sam's house and talked to him about how he made Dad feel for all those years."

"You did?"

"I did. I'm not blaming Sam. I'm not angry. I was just trying to right a wrong for a little boy. There's one other person I would like to talk to, but it would do no good to approach him now. It was a long, long time ago, and I can only offer peace and hope he fixed his life."

"Wow, Mom. You're not angry. That's amazing. I haven't even seen you angry at Dad."

"Oh, I've been angry at Dad."

"But you love him, and you're trying to help him."

"I do love him. I would do anything to help him. His soul is of great worth." I looked into her eyes and spoke with emphasis. "Sarah, I made covenants with God when I was sealed to my husband. Do you know what a wife does? A wife walks into hell, takes her husband by the hand, stares down the devil, and says, 'You can't have him.'"

Sarah's lip began to quiver. Her dad had always been her hero. "Thank you for saving Dad."

"God and I are working together. That's the power of being a covenant woman."

We went into the house, and Joe happened to be in the living room. He made eye contact with me, and he knew instantly. He stood and began to walk to Sarah, but she ran to him, almost knocking him over. She hugged him fiercely. "I love you, Dad," she said into his shirt. "I'm sorry you were sad."

"I'm so much better now," he said as he held her. "I'm so happy."

And now to tell Abby. I wasn't sure if it was a good time, but I definitely didn't have the strength to pick another day to tell another child. I went upstairs and knocked on her door.

"Enter!" she called.

I walked in. She was sitting at her desk looking at her classes for the winter semester on her computer. "I got a notice saying that my English teacher is taking a leave of absence next semester, and I don't hear great things about the professor they substituted, so now my schedule is all messed up."

"That stinks," I said.

"Sure does. What's up?"

"Can I talk to you?"

She closed her computer. "Sure," and only then did she look up at me and see that I had been crying.

I sat on the edge of her bed, closest to her. "Abby, I want to talk to you about your dad. We're going to have a family council. Hannah's having some problems, and Dad's going to talk about the journey he's been on so it might help her. But I wanted to talk to you first."

"Okay, but you don't have to, Mom."

"I know, but it's the right thing to do."

"Okay."

I blew out a long breath. *Strength.* "Abby, Dad screwed up. He did the last thing I ever thought he would do. He was lost and he forgot himself. He went online and started up relationships, and that turned into meeting people, and that turned into having an affair for six months earlier this year."

"Yeah, I know. I watched your face when Tom said his dad had an affair. You've got a terrible poker face, Mom. But I was just going to let you tell me in your own time. I knew you would."

I bowed my head and cried. I could never hide things from Abby. I finally looked up and said, "You know, Abby, you were amazing that night. I've told you this before, but everything you said, was... wow. You switched into missionary mode so fast. You didn't let the emotion overwhelm you. I was in awe. I want to be like you when I grow up."

"Thanks." She smiled.

"For the first few months, I thought, 'I'll go to the grave with this secret.' But Abby, hiding hurts. It's our truth. I think what Tom's dad did was more damaging because he hid it and lied about it for so long. You've gotta bring it out into the light. Your dad is liberated by finally owning the weakness and allowing God to help him be strong. He's ashamed of what he did, but we're a million times more grateful for the miracle we've received in our lives of witnessing the power of the Atonement of Jesus Christ. And we want to share that with our family."

Abby moved to sit next to me on the bed and held my hand. "I'm glad I was home for this."

"Me too. Honestly, Abby, I was lonely. I am lonely. Dad checks in with the bishop and stake president often, and Aaron calls almost daily. Men don't usually have a support system of friends when they go through tough things, but luckily, through this process, Dad has one built in. Ironically, women normally have their group where they draw strength. I told Mary, and I recently talked to Jesse a little bit. But I've been hiding it too because I'm afraid how people will react to him. No offense, but I'm afraid they'll react like Tom did. It's a shocking thing. It's scary for our sweet little culture that prides itself on decorum and fidelity. So I'm afraid to say anything to my friends. I guess I'm trying to protect him."

Abby put her hand on my knee. "Mom, stop! That's too heavy. Remember what I told Tom that night? You either believe in the Atonement or you don't. People will have to believe that Dad was a great man who, by the way, is now even more of a great man because he's walking the path of redemption without guile or fear. They will believe that, or they won't. But that's on them. We know who Dad is. We know the truth."

It's moments like these that God's love shines through darkness. I actually chuckled. "Have you been reading my journal? Are you using ESP to read Dad's thoughts? We've said these exact words!"

Abby laughed. "Mom, you are the best parents I know."

I kissed her forehead. "Thanks. We're heading for a storm with Hannah. Be available for her, okay?"

Joseph

We prayed all day that Hannah wouldn't back out of Sunday dinner. To her great credit, she showed up. When she first walked in, however, it was awkward. She knew about me, and she saw me differently. I felt vulnerable and embarrassed, which was strange because I didn't feel that way with Sarah or Abby. I recognized this as Satan's way of trying to derail our important day together, so I did my best to assume my peaceable walk with God. I tried to focus on the hundreds of hours we had spent together in better times, doing science homework or tossing a softball in the backyard. I hoped she would also remember those times, and see me as an ally.

We sat down to the chicken I grilled and Rachel's potatoes and veggies. Hannah was reserved. She didn't maintain eye contact with anyone, and she tried to fade into the background. While eating Sarah's lemon crinkle cookies for dessert, she smiled at something Sarah said, but then visibly retreated into her self-imposed emotional exile.

Sarah and Rachel cleaned up the table with Hi-Hi-Ho while Abby and I filled the dishwasher and wiped down the counters, but Hannah disappeared. We found her in the living room. She was curled up on the end of the couch, looking at her phone.

Sarah and Abby sat down next to her on the couch, and Rachel sat in her chair, across the room from mine. I said, "I guess you're all wondering why I've called you here..." They smiled faintly. It was time to tell my children *my* truth with honesty and humility. I had prayed to know how to start this conversation. I had been comforted by the feelings of love for and from Jesus Christ, so I decided that was the best place to start. "Well, we all know why we're here. This is the first time that I..." This was terrifying. "I haven't ever talked to all three of you together like this about my... my experience. Mom explained the first part to you because, well, I felt stupid."

At this admission, Hannah eyed me. Now I knew she was listening.

I took a deep breath. "I want you, my three dear sisters who have been entrusted to my earthly care, to know how deeply I love you. I want you to know how incredibly sorry I am that I have hurt you. My Savior, my Jesus, has saved me from my sins. He has healed my heart. I give thanks every day that my family is still here with me. I could've lost everything."

"Of course we love you, Dad," Sarah said.

Hannah had respectfully put her phone aside, but now she was looking down at her finger that she was nervously picking.

"I believe you're each choosing two very separate things. First, I know you're making a conscious choice to forgive me. Second, I know you're making a conscious choice to continue to extend love and trust to me. Those are very separate things, and I acknowledge that."

Hannah's eyes met mine again. She hadn't considered that. I think she was grateful that I was giving her permission to disconnect those two things. I wasn't sure if she had forgiven me, and I was pretty sure she was shaky on the love and trust as well. But doing one didn't necessarily mean the other. Yet.

"I want to tell you about my journey. Let me start by asking you, what are some of the titles of Jesus Christ?"

Sarah had learned Handel's *Messiah* in choir for her Christmas concert. "Wonderful, Counsellor," she recited. "The mighty God, the everlasting Father, the Prince of Peace."

Rachel had looked up the Topical Guide on her phone, selected a few, and read them reverently. "Advocate. Creator. Firstborn. Good Shepherd. Jehovah. Lamb of God."

Abby had done the same, and she picked up the list. "Light of the World. Lord. Mediator. Messiah. Redeemer. Rock. Savior. Son of God."

Hannah picked at the pillows on the couch.

"I testify to you that I know Jesus Christ is all of those things. There is a lot to say about my personal experience with each of those titles, but I want to start with 'Redeemer.' Picture yourself in a dark, miserable, fallen place. It could be one of your own making, through sin, or maybe you're there because of the sins of others. Or maybe both. Picture Jesus reaching into the darkness for you and saying, 'You don't belong here. You have a divine nature. Come with Me.'" I gestured by reaching out with my own hand.

They seemed to be drawn in by what I was saying, so I continued. "After a lifetime of striving every day to walk in the light with Him, He returns you, a beloved soul with inherent divine nature, to a place of divinity. Where you belong. This whole process is redemption. He is our Redeemer."

Rachel smiled. Abby nodded. Sarah stared into my soul. Hannah mumbled from her corner, "Dad, I understand that you're trying to share your experience with us, and that's all fine and great. But I'm sitting here thinking about all the times you've sat us down for family home evening and for little chats just like this, and I've sat through them all and thought, 'Wow, this is great. Dad's awesome. He's got all the answers.' And you don't. You said those things and went and did the opposite." And then she emphasized mockingly, "You were probably even *doing* them when you were all, 'Be good, children. God loves you!'"

Rachel had told me to expect that Hannah would be emotional. She definitely knew where to aim the arrow and her painful words hit the mark, but I maintained my calm voice. "Hannah, I can't dispute that. It's true."

"See! It's hard for me to understand why you're okay with being a hypocrite."

I am a noble son of God. "That's a valid question, and I'll explain that in a bit. But to understand the answer, I first need you to understand what I'm saying about the power of Jesus Christ."

She would have none of it. She wasn't usually disrespectful, but she spat, "If you lied to me before, why should I believe you now? Why should I ever believe that anything you ever say is true?"

I remembered saying those very words. My simple reply was, "Listen and see if the Holy Ghost bears witness that what I'm testifying to you is true."

She was silent, not sure what to say.

Rachel, Abby, and Sarah were watching us like a tennis match.

My serve. I emphasized each word. "This is what I've learned—His power changes minds and hearts. His power changes habits and souls. He *wants* to save us. We don't have to come unto Him as clean, perfect people. We come in our grime, in our sin, with our weakness, with our imperfections, and as we seek with pure intent, we watch as His miraculous saving power returns our souls to a place of divinity. That's why He's our Redeemer. Turning to Him is called repentance."

Hannah threw down the pillow she had been holding. "Oh, good! I was wondering when you'd get around to that word. So you've repented, said you're sorry, said a couple of prayers, and you're all done. Well, that's nice. What about the rest of us? What about what you did to us?"

I understood her so well at this moment. She was angry, sad, and encapsulated in her own shame. To forgive me meant she could forgive herself, and she couldn't yet. I prayed silently to know what to do, and I immediately saw it. She had been comfortable keeping us all at a safe distance, so I decided to bridge the physical gap. I got up from my chair and knelt directly in front of her. She was mildly alarmed by my nearness. I took her hands in mine and said, "Hannah, what do you want from me? Name it, and I'll give it to you. I just want you back."

She cracked. "I…" She broke. "I want…" She cried. "I just want all this to go away."

She collapsed forward into me, and I held her while she sobbed into my white shirt. Sarah got up and came back with the hand towel from the bathroom and set it next to Hannah. She whispered helpfully, "I didn't think a box of tissues would be enough." It was hard not to laugh.

While Hannah grabbed for the towel and wiped her nose, I said gently, "I know you want it to go away. That's what I'm trying to tell you. I remember up at Strawberry Reservoir at youth conference, you said to me, 'Thank you for living your testimony where I could always see it.' I've learned more about Jesus Christ than I ever knew before, and I'm trying to show you how I'm living it.

I understand your cynicism, but listen. If you won't believe *me*, believe in *Jesus*. Will you listen?"

She shrugged. Then she nodded.

I stayed kneeling. I moved her hair out of her eyes so we could see each other. "Do you understand what it means to reconcile ourselves with God?"

She shook her head.

"Somehow, in the translation of the Bible, 'repent' was given as a word with connotations of pain, sadness, and shame. We've been made to feel that when we have to repent, it's an arduous, embarrassing, horrendous task full of God's wrath and the gall of bitterness. Actually, those things are saved for those who are *un*repentant."

"But I feel like that now, and I'm repentant." She could hardly find voice enough to speak her pain.

I squeezed her hand. "You feel like that now because you're full of shame. I've started to understand repentance as God simply saying, 'Come home. You belong here.' And all it requires from me is an earnest course correction. This is what it means to be reconciled with God." She was still with me. My knees had started to ache, but I didn't want to move from in front of her.

She looked at me, and I saw a very small glimmer of hope in her eyes. "Hey, guys, is it okay if I talk to Dad alone for a while?"

Rachel, Abby, and Sarah didn't need to be asked twice. They headed upstairs together.

I got up and sat next to Hannah on the couch. She leaned against my arm. She finally whispered, "Dad, I'm sorry I was a jerk."

"I'm sorry I was a jerk first."

"Yeah, I'm sorry that you were a jerk first too."

But I was serious. "Hannah, I'm sorry I hurt you." I squeezed her hand again.

"It's hard being mad at you, Dad. I don't like it."

"I can assure you that I don't like it either. That's not like us. We've always gotten along."

"It killed me to find out, Dad," and we leaned on each other for a while before I spoke again.

"Hannah, Mom tells me we have a common problem."

She sat up, but kept her gaze on the towel in her lap. "I'm lonely, Dad. I hate myself. I don't have close friends at the dorm. I go to ward functions, and guys don't talk to me. I really crave human interaction, and it seems like I've tried everything. Going on the apps was easier to meet and talk to people. And now, watching… stuff… fills the need. I don't feel as lonely—just horrible."

"Yeah, I get that." It was hard to hear the trauma of sin that was tormenting my daughter. But I was suddenly so grateful that she was telling me about it, and I was in a place to understand and empathize with her.

"What do I do, Dad?"

"There are a lot of choices. There's no 'right choice' for everyone, and on your journey, you'll probably try just about everything. But first, let's start at the beginning, just to make sure we're in the right space. Sometimes the desire to change is manufactured by peer pressure or guilt, and that generates a change that's fleeting, inadequate, and temporary. A true, lasting change is motivated by *the desire* for true, lasting change. You see that?"

"Yeah, I've seen that in some of my friends' lives. I know that's true." She looked at me. "I think I'm there. I think so…"

"Well, I get that impression. There are a few directions you can go to start. What do you think? Let's do what Mom always did when you were a kid. Show me your fingers. Give me five options."

Hannah held up her thumb first. "I could crawl under a rock and die."

"Good. Make sure that option involves shame and self-hatred. Just power through it alone. Next?"

She added her index finger. "I could ask my roommate to help police my time with technology." Her third finger. "I could meet with someone every week, like my bishop, and be accountable to him." Fourth finger. "I could figure out how to pay for a counselor. Mom said you liked yours." Fifth finger. "Uh… I could pray about it…" The fifth option was always hard to come up with.

"Those are good options. Another one that many people find helpful is a twelve-step program. The Church has addiction recovery groups."

"Do you go to one?"

"No. I chose different options for me. I just finished with the counselor, and I talk to Mom a lot. Actually, I think Aaron is like a sponsor because he's been through something similar. He's a great resource, and talking to him almost every day is truly a godsend. I also meet with my bishop every other week. It was probably intended for accountability, and I guess it is, but mostly I'm glad to talk to a friend."

"I have one or two good friends, but it just seems awkward to talk about this. I could probably talk to Abby or Sarah, but I've been scared."

"I get that. But asking a roommate for help can be good, like, 'Please take my phone and laptop from 10:00 p.m.-6:00 a.m..' That takes care of the source of the temptations, although it doesn't really fix the reason for the temptation."

Hannah nodded.

I asked, "So, which combination of those options that you listed are you comfortable with? Which do you think would work for you?"

"I don't know. I've thought about it. A lot. Right now, I think I'm stuck on the first one, the self-loathing one." She wiggled her thumb. "I'm trying not to be."

"Well, you're asking for help. That's good. In my own experience, and with people I've talked to, it's important to figure out what's driving your behavior. I know lots of people who want to quit drinking, so they go to AA, do the program, get sober, but start smoking like a chimney. People substitute addictions all the time, but the underlying problem is still there. The key is figuring out how you got there and why, and fixing that thing. The behavior modification will follow."

"Mom's trying to get me addicted to ice cream." She smiled fleetingly. "Dad, I can't get over how stupid I feel. This is so dumb. I know better. I just can't…"

"Honey, I get it. Same. You have to move past your shame or you'll get stuck there for a long time."

"Yeah, well, I obviously don't know how to do that. And I know what you're going to say next—pray!—but I feel dumb praying for help."

"Satan wants you to feel dumb. I felt dumb when you got here tonight."

That caught her off guard. "Seriously?"

"Seriously. I had to recognize the feeling and consciously lift it off my path. Satan wants you to stop talking to God, to us. He wants you to feel dumb when you seek help. Then darkness overpowers your light, and he will have you."

"I feel like I'm already there."

"You're not, Hannah. You're here with me, talking about it. The humility you're showing is huge. Plus, you decided to stop being angry with me." She smiled at me, and I smiled back. "Don't give up. Perfection is a lifetime pursuit. Don't get discouraged. If this problem were physical, like diabetes, we would come up with a diet and exercise plan, help you with your food shopping, teach you some different cooking ideas, set you up with regular doctor visits, and expect successes and failures. You wouldn't be embarrassed. Why is an emotional or spiritual problem any different?"

"You're right. But I have to say, because I know that this is wrong and I shouldn't be involved in it, and my path to how I got here was so stupid, I feel like a giant... hypocrite." She felt bad saying that word again.

"Well, you're in good company. Think about it—aren't we all hypocrites to one degree or another? After I talked to Mom about your conversation with her, I got to thinking about Nephi. He was this great guy, but he talks of this huge stumbling block that kept tripping him up. Would you call Nephi a hypocrite?"

"Definitely not."

"Me neither. He's just like you and me, acknowledging that we need help to be reconciled to God."

"I guess that's true. But I don't even know where to start."

I suddenly imagined my mother. "If Grandma were here, she

would tell you to definitely start with Number Five. Always pray. You need Heavenly Father. Prayer can help you figure out and address the source of the problem. Maybe He'll even point out an option we haven't thought of. I have a friend whose answer was, 'Stop focusing on this issue so much.' It worked for him! But for you, as for the things we listed, there are positives and negatives to each. It just depends on what feels right. It will probably be a combination of all of them, especially as you work to get rid of Number One!" I squeezed her thumb.

She smiled weakly at me. "We'll see. I have my doubts. That's the hardest thing right now."

I smiled back encouragingly. "But think about the other options. Study it out. Ask your bishop. Ask other people you trust who have had success what they did. Every twelve-step group has a different personality, so you may have to shop around for a good group, if that's what you choose. Some counselors save lives—some smoked too much weed in grad school."

Hannah laughed. "Okay. I'll keep thinking. I'll read up on it and ask my bishop. I'll keep praying. Maybe your counselor could recommend someone closer to BYU?"

"Sure." I was quiet, and tears sprang to my eyes. "Hannah, I would love to give you a blessing of comfort and strength, but I can't. Can we pray together?"

She nodded and we both dropped to our knees, praying together for wisdom, guidance, peace, strength, knowledge, patience, love, understanding, forgiveness, grace, and mercy. We each prayed, and we both cried.

Rachel

The Christmas break had been lovely. And busy. Hannah and Abby had found an apartment that they could share starting in January, so a big part of our Christmas vacation was spent getting Hannah out of her dorm and the two of them ready to move in together. Sarah had a huge project in history class that she was working on, and I was busy color-coding a timeline of the Civil War for her when Joe called me. There was sadness in his voice. "Hey, Rach."

"Are you okay? You sound stressed."

"I am. I needed to hear your voice. I was remembering what it felt like to talk to the girls a few weeks ago, and I started to feel pretty vulnerable."

He couldn't see me nodding. "That's understandable. Are you ready for our trip to North Carolina next month?"

He blew out a long breath. "That's actually part of my stress. I have a lot to do to get ready to leave. But I think it will be done. Well, mostly done. Enough. The big thing is..." He lowered his voice. "Rachel, even though our conversation with the girls has turned out all right, I still feel a lot of shame when I think about seeing Josh and Jesse. They're the first non-family we've told. I'll be under a microscope because I'll be with them for three solid days. What if they're disgusted with me? Then what?"

"From my own point of view, I feel absolutely confident that things will be normal. They will love you because they have always loved you."

"I'm hyper-self-conscious."

I heard his concern, but I felt certain. "It will be okay, Joe. It really will."

<hr>

We headed to the airport early on a Tuesday morning. We would arrive late, and Josh and Jesse would pick us up from the Raleigh/Durham airport.

Jesse was the first one I saw. It was probably the giant sign she was holding above her head that read, *Joe and Rachel, we have missed your faces!* I walked to her quickly and was scooped up in her embrace.

Joe was close behind and extended his hand to Josh. "That ain't gonna do it, buddy," Josh said, and he pulled Joe in for a bear hug. "And I'm going to hold on extra long to make it uncomfortable." Joe laughed.

I knew instantly that it was going to be okay. And what was more, I knew Joe felt it too.

We chatted about the flight as we walked to their car. We chatted about our kids and how they were doing. We chatted about the weather. We chatted about the busy airport. We chatted about our holiday plans. We chatted about their Church callings.

No sooner had we left the parking garage than Joe acknowledged the elephant in the car. He began to cry.

Joe began immediately to speak his truth to cherished friends who had earned the blessing of hearing it. He bore his witness that God loves His children. He told Josh and Jesse about the shame he had carried for his whole life, and how afraid he was that people might find out what a fraud he was. He was supposed to be a Reeve—valiant! But he was running the race on broken legs, blinded by weakness. He explained how he wasn't raised to stop to fix the problem—just to keep running, keep moving, do more, it'll go away. He unfolded the grief he felt at being a disappointment, which buried him further.

And then he explained about Paul and how he spectacularly crashed. He told them he was sure he had lost everything he loved, including his friends and family, but especially me. He told them about his experience on the mountaintop when he gave his burdens to God, and again on a mountaintop with me when he knew he had been forgiven. He bore testimony that Christ descended below it all, and how He succors each of us according to our distinct and desperate needs. He bore testimony that the Holy Spirit attends us, comforts us, and prompts us. He dispelled the myth that repentance is a burdensome task—it's joyous and full of relief. He concluded by thanking them for inviting us—he had been worried about it, but as soon as he saw them, he understood their love for him.

He had spoken for almost an hour, but we had all listened with rapt attention. Joe finished his story as we pulled into their neighborhood, and I said gratefully, "We feel your love. We were worried that it might be weird."

"Just the long hugs," Josh said.

Jesse responded as I knew she would. "We love you guys too. It means a lot to us to spend this time with you. We've missed you so much!"

Josh said, "We're looking forward to showing you our stomping grounds. Joe, tomorrow you're going on a tour of the plant with me. I can't wait to show you around. Jesse is taking Rachel to a spa downtown. We'll go for lunch and take you to a couple of our favorite places around town. Thursday morning, we'll head to the timeshare at the beach. It's a little cool and windy at the beach this time of year, but there's still plenty of fun stuff to do there, plus just a lot of relaxing and puttering."

When we pulled up to their beautiful house, they told us their story of how they found it when they transferred from Chicago. They took pride in showing it to us, and Josh pointed out things that only Joe could appreciate. They had done amazing things to it, and it was both homey and gorgeous. We oo-ed and ah-ed over their abundant creativity. It was after midnight when we said our exhausted goodnights.

"Joe, are you doing okay?" I asked as we got into bed.

"Yeah. Surprisingly, yeah. I feel… understood."

In the morning, Josh took Joe to work, and Jesse and I headed to the spa for pedicures. We got in the car, and she said, "Spill it."

And this is why I loved her. She knew what I needed. She knew I was alone in my secret. She knew I had been struggling under my gargantuan burden. She knew I needed a safe place to fall. She was a true friend.

So I started from the beginning, but when we got to the spa, I was at the part where he had met women for "just lunch." I said, "This is a terrible place to pause the story, but I don't want to say this in front of other people, so can we pick up the story here after the pedicures?"

Jesse let out a strangled, "Aaauugghh! This is going to be the longest pedicure in America! I know it ends well, but right now I want to kill him."

"That's okay. I did too."

She reached for the door handle. "It's just so hard to believe this happened. I mean, this is Joe! It's still hard to wrap my head around it."

Once our toes were pretty and we were back in the privacy of her car, I picked up the story, ending with my testimony of the saving grace of a merciful Father just as we pulled into her garage.

She turned to face me. Her eyes brimmed with tears. "You… are… full of grace. You are the strongest person I know."

Then I started crying. I knew Jesse's life. It had been full of difficulty. To have her say those words to me was the highest compliment I had ever been paid.

We walked into the house, and Josh and Joe were already back. Joe saw my tears and knew we had been talking. Josh saved the moment by announcing, "And now for the South's best barbeque and a city tour!" We had the best day full of laughing, sharing memories, telling funny stories, and driving around while rocking out to Jesse's "Revving with the Reeves Playlist."

Joseph

After dinner, while Rachel caught up with their girls, Josh took me out to his garage. He had a sweet set-up. He knew how to pick tools. I was a kid in a candy shop.

"Have you ever turned a pen?" Josh asked me.

"No. I don't have the tooling for my lathe."

"You just need this mandrel and live center. You can buy the wood blanks and hardware in bulk." He showed me a box of beautiful wood blocks of different colors. "We gave pens to our neighbors for Christmas presents. It's pretty fun. Want to make one?"

"You know I do."

I chose a cocobolo wood, exotic and rich. He had me center the blank on the drill press and drill through it so we could glue in the sleeves. He showed me how to stack the blanks and spacers in the mandrel and clamp it together with the live center. He set the tool rest, handed me a gouge, turned on the lathe, and loudly said the magic words, "It's all yours."

He watched me as I worked the gouge across the blanks, making them round and giving them shape. Chips peeled off the blanks and flew into the air before falling to the floor. A beautiful pen emerged from the wood. I sanded and polished the pen with finishing oil until it gleamed. Josh gave me the choice of the color for the hardware. I chose gunmetal. We pressed it all together and finally twisted the ink cartridge in place. I triumphantly held up my finished work of art. It felt natural in my fingers.

It said Sawdust Therapy. It said Friendship. It said Unconditional Acceptance. It said Worthy of Love. It said Josh. It said, "Joseph, you're going to be okay."

I tried not to cry as I thanked him. "Man, I've missed doing projects with you."

"It's not the same, is it? Nobody gets me like you do."

We walked to the living room to show Rachel my new pen. I did a good job blinking back the tears. She thought it was beautiful. I would tell her later what it meant to me.

In the morning after we sent their kids off to school, we packed the car for the beach. Adulthood had its perks.

They were right—we loved the timeshare. It was cozy like Aaron's cabin, but with electricity and right on the beach. It was perfect. We dropped our luggage off and spent the afternoon driving around the area, stopping at Jesse's favorite arts-and-crafts shop and Josh's favorite antiques-and-pawn shop.

As the sun was setting, Josh and I grabbed some wood from the side of the cabin and walked fifty yards to the beach. We started a small fire. Jesse brought out a tray of tinfoil dinners and some drinks, and Rachel carried four beach chairs. We waited for coals to set the tinfoil dinners on. We sat in a close circle, all bundled up, and enjoyed the crackling of the fire and the gentle roar of the waves.

As our dinners cooked and Josh stoked the fire, I realized that I felt no shame. They knew the worst thing I had ever done, and they loved me. Where I expected awkwardness, there was only rejoicing for redemption. Our knowledge of the goodness of God was expanded, and our friendship was deepened. And then we began to eat, and we started talking about something else. It was all so… normal.

Rachel

In the morning over breakfast of sausage and French toast, I wanted to make one thing clear. "I don't mean to start the day out serious, but I just have to say this. You've both provided a safe place to be honest and real. Thank you."

Jesse took advantage of the moment. She put down her fork and addressed Joe. "Joe, do you even realize that your vulnerability is your strength? Not many guys have the ability to open up and be honest about all this. You have laid yourself bare for the Lord's reconciling and glory. Your humility and pliability to God's process of shaping you has revealed your lion's heart and your mammoth strength. You are *all strength*."

Joe wrinkled his forehead. "I guess I've never thought about it like that."

Jesse continued, "I absolutely believe that the courage you've confronted this with, and the action you've backed it up with, has a lot to do with the immediate relief you've felt. Many people put their toe or foot into repentance, and in return, they feel that much relief, you know? You have punched the natural man in the face. You punched Satan in the Pop-Tarts."

She was serious in her compliment, but I laughed so hard, orange juice almost came out of my nose.

Josh handed me a napkin and said, "Seriously, we were talking last night when we went to bed. It would've been horrible if you had split up. Thank you for not asking us to choose sides. That would've been like Solomon cutting a baby in half. We couldn't imagine you guys splitting up. How could we ever make a choice like that? You're the strongest couple we know."

"That's what I thought too," I said as I scooped up my last bite of French toast. "So, where are we going today?"

Saturday morning, we drove straight from the beach back to the airport. I hugged Josh first, then Jesse. I quietly said to them both, "Thank you for everything. This was perfect. You'll never know what you did for him. This was the hardest thing he had left to do, and you made it easy. You saved him."

"We love you," was Jesse's simple reply.

Then it was Joe's turn for hugs. To Jesse, he said, "Thanks. We love you guys."

She took him by the shoulders and looked straight into his eyes. "Joseph, you know the Savior. Someday I'll understand Jesus's Atonement like you do today. Thank you for sharing your experience with us."

Josh stepped in and bear-hugged Joe. "It'll be extra long to be uncomfortable."

Joe replied, "That's okay. I love you, brother."

We boarded the plane and found seats together. We sat down and waited for the rest of the plane to board. An idea hit me. "Joe," I said, "I've decided to apply the scriptures to myself."

"You mean, like with wallpaper paste?"

I loved Joe's sense of humor. "Yes. No. I've realized I can't receive forgiveness for my sins unless I extend forgiveness to Lila for her sins. I don't know her. I don't understand where she's coming from. I don't know her backstory. I know she has one. Maybe it explains why she's doing what she's doing—maybe it doesn't. But regardless, I need to extend forgiveness to her."

"I'm sure that will help bring you peace."

"I know it will. Jesus loves her. Jesus loves her as much as He loves me. The worth of her soul is great. I trust Him to work a mighty miracle in her life and bring her happiness. I want that for her. She's doing things that bring tremendous sadness upon herself. I know she loves her children. I hope she can find the path and hold to the rod. That would be good for all of them. But whether or not she fixes her life, I can extend forgiveness for how she chose to affect me. Whether she cares about that or not, whether she understands that or not, I do, and I need to extend forgiveness for it. I'm ready."

"So, no wallpaper paste?"

"Probably not."

Joseph

The second Sunday in April, while the sacrament was being passed, I held up my palm and extended all five fingers. I nudged Rachel and showed her. She narrowed her eyes and leaned her head toward me. "I can count on one hand now," I whispered. "Five more months. I only have five more months to go."

Hannah and Abby both came home from college for the summer. That very first night Hannah was home, I saw the tell-tale signs—nights were hard for her. When she wasn't working as a waitress, she was home, sulking around the house and snapping at us.

Rachel and I decided we wouldn't wait for it to get worse. Two days into her summer vacation, I told her, "When you get home after your shift tonight, I want to Rock and Talk with you."

"Dad, get real. I'm almost twenty. And I won't be home until after 11:30."

"Perfect! See you then!"

I waited at the front door for her. She didn't come in until 11:56. "Hey! Welcome home! How was your shift?"

She shouldn't have been surprised to see me make good on my promise. "Oh. Hi, Dad. It was fine. I had a dine-and-dash. That was fun." She started up the stairs.

"Hey, wait! What about Rock and Talk?"

"What?"

"Rock and Talk. I've got it all ready. Come into the kitchen." I had a deck of cards on the table and the soundtrack from her favorite musical playing on the speaker.

"Dad, I'm tired. What's this?"

"You have time for gin rummy. Have a seat."

She rolled her eyes, knowing there was only one way to get out of it. She pulled out a chair. "Fine. One game. Don't cry when I beat you."

I sat across from her and dealt the cards.

After a week, even on the days she wasn't working, she hung around the kitchen table until I got the cards out. Some days, we would deal and play. Other days, we would deal and hold our cards—I would listen, and she would talk. A few times, she was bold enough to ask how to conquer desire and shame. Occasionally we didn't even get the cards out, but would just sit, talk, sympathize, laugh, snack on chips and salsa, cry, talk about chemistry and balance equations, or count on our fingers ways to solve the world's problems.

One night in mid-June, Hannah asked me, "How can I get over hating myself?"

"Have I ever told you about my peaceable walk?"

"No." She grabbed a tortilla chip.

"Remember that part in the Book of Mormon? Moroni could tell that the people were good because of their peaceable walk with God and man. What does it take to walk peaceably?"

"Um... You tell me."

"No, think about it." I sipped my lemonade.

"Well, to be peaceable with man would be to be honest in your dealings. Kind. Serve others. No gossip over the back fence. The Golden Rule. To have a peaceable walk with God is the same thing, really. But also... Mindful about keeping the commandments. Have more meaningful prayer. Be truthful about your weaknesses. Listen to the Holy Ghost."

"And how's that going?"

"I've been trying hard to do those things. On the days I do them well, I feel closer to God, I guess. But it doesn't always make me feel better, since I know there's still the bad stuff."

"Don't sell your progress short. Can you have peace every day?"

"No, I can't."

"Actually, even on bad days, yes, you can. Every day, sometimes multiple times a day, I talk to Heavenly Father about my peaceable walk. I evaluate myself and how I'm feeling. If there's an attitude or a behavior that needs to change, I ask for help and

I change it. And if I can't change it, I give it over to God. But I don't wait. I used to, but I learned my soul can't afford to wait even one day. This helps me stop negative behavior before it can find a place to take root."

Hannah nodded. "I'll try it. Peaceably pass the salsa."

And that's what we did. Every night. All summer. No amount of sleep was more important than making sure Hannah had the tools to get through the night.

July was a hard month. Rachel does tend to mark anniversaries of sad things, and she marked that this was the month that I was desperately trying to end things with Lila. She marked that this was the month that she was sure our marriage was over, despite all the things she had done to try to get me to open up. It brought back the pain of betrayal, and she spent a few days in bed. She got up to attend the temple for the week, and that did a little to help lift the grief. I never knew what to say—I was afraid of saying the wrong thing. One Friday evening, I took her pizza in bed, and when she smiled weakly at me, I suddenly realized that if it had taken me forty years to metabolize what happened to me, I could give her all the time she needed.

August could have been a hard month because of all the emotional things we did. We marked the day, even the exact time, that we were in the school parking lot when I had changed our lives. We moved Hannah and Abby back into an apartment together for the school year, and we worried and stressed about Hannah's progress. Tom had met with his dad and it didn't go well, so he came over and we had a big heart-to-heart about what it meant to forgive when someone wasn't repentant.

But August wasn't a hard month because we saw it as crossing the finishing line. I had been forgiven by the Lord. I felt like I was right with the Church and hoped that the high council would agree. During our last visit, President Patrick strongly hinted that he felt like my full membership would be restored, so I had high hopes. He scheduled the council for August 23rd.

I asked President Patrick if Aaron could attend the council with me, and he consented. He had been there with me through the whole journey, and I wanted him there at the end. Aaron's reply was, "Brother, I would be honored to come with you. I'll make it a priority to be there." He felt it one of the highest honors of his life to have had the opportunity to travel this road with me.

On the 23rd, the three of us walked to the church together at 6:25. We were ushered into the high council room again where we had an opening song and prayer. President Patrick began by saying, "Brother Reeve, I'm so glad that you're here this day under such different circumstances from a year ago. We welcome your wife and your brother. Bishop Hanson and I have been pleased by your obedience and your progress over this last year. Now is your opportunity to say anything you would like to say on your own behalf."

I cleared my throat. I rose and addressed the council. "I'm grateful to be here tonight. I'm immensely grateful for my journey. I'm grateful for the time that I've been allowed to show my readiness to be welcomed back to full membership. Too often, Church discipline is misunderstood. I didn't 'wait a year to be forgiven'—I knew pretty quickly that I was forgiven. The Holy Ghost hasn't been absent from my life. But I needed the year to be right with the Church and its standards. I know that I am.

"Over this past year, I have come to understand the grace of God that He grants to His children because He loves us. I know... I *know* He loves me. I am a noble son of God. I have seen myself in the scriptures as I read about Peter walking on the water. Jesus immediately reached out to me and saved me from a certain death in troubled waters. I understand Alma the Younger and the seemingly instantaneous, but miraculously permanent change he underwent. I understand more about the Atonement of Jesus Christ than I ever thought possible. My heart has changed. I know that I have been redeemed by the only One who could." I couldn't think of anything else I needed to say. I sat down.

President Patrick turned to Rachel and said, "Sister Reeve, would you like to say a few words?"

Rachel

I pulled out my paper. I had written it down because I didn't want to get flustered and forget anything. I remained seated and began to read.

> *I am an incredibly private person. And yet, one of the most emotionally and spiritually raw things that has ever happened to us has to be shared with the people in this room. It's very humbling for me personally to have you know this, the most uncharacteristic thing Joseph has ever done. However, in the past year, we have both been shown compassion, kindness, and forgiveness by the people here. I express my gratitude and thankfulness to you for your discretion and your ability to see beyond sin to the majesty of his soul.*
>
> *This repentance process has not been a punishment for either of us, but an opportunity to be taught by the Savior how to become clean and whole. Jesus must be sad when the power of His Atonement is looked upon as a punishment as opposed to the very essence and purpose for His mortal existence.*

I paused and looked up. "Joe already said some of this. Sorry. I'd still like to say it."

> *I can testify to you of the following realities:*
> *He is right with God. The sure knowledge of that came very early.*
> *He is right with his wife. He is so very right with his wife.*
> *His children adore him. We have had beautiful and cherished discussions about what he did, and what led him down that road, and how the love of the Savior has brought him from sure destruction to an everlasting joy. Our children love and respect him completely.*
> *He is right with his friends and extended family.*
> *He has made appropriate amends the best he could with those he hurt.*
> *In many ways, nothing about Joe has changed. He is kind to all, warm, genuine, unique, brilliant, and generous. He is*

trustworthy and sensitive. You need to understand that since we were married, we have gone on weekly dates, prayed holding hands, and laughed and joked and talked endlessly. Could there possibly be two people who adore each other more than we do? We seek to spend as much time together as possible. We call and text each other throughout the day because we love to. Our home is a refuge. I trust his counsel—I seek his wisdom.

I turned and smiled at Joe.

This is what has changed—he is full of joy. He does not doubt his worth in the eyes of the Savior. We have likened the Savior to a great heart surgeon who does very precise surgery with a very sharp scalpel, removing only those diseased parts and making a new heart. It is nothing short of a miracle. All the sadness and hopelessness are gone. Because he is happy with himself, and because he understands his relationship with Heavenly Father and Jesus Christ, the desire to sin has been eradicated from his soul. It's just gone. This is the miracle of the infinite Atonement.

The strength of character of this noble son of God has always amazed me, but in the past year, I am stunned. He is brave. He has been able to do things that would make other people stumble or shrink. He has opened his heart and mind to the saving grace of the Lord with a willingness to submit to all things the Lord has seen fit to inflict upon him. He has been born again, redeemed. I testify that he has been washed clean, with his sins no more as scarlet, but his soul is truly as white as snow.

I folded my paper. "Thank you for letting me share that."

"Thank you, Sister Reeve. Does the council have any questions for them?"

One brother asked, "How have you experienced the ennobling power of the Savior?"

I kind of wanted to say, "We just covered that, didn't we?"

But Joe was very gracious in his reply. "The Savior has given me power to rise above a lifetime of burden. He has lifted the burden and taken it from my soul. I can move forward with clean hands and a pure heart, and I intend to walk with the Savior every day."

Another brother spoke directly to me. "Sister Reeve, I appreciate that this is a humbling experience to share with a room full of people. I hope you understand that none of us sit in harsh judgment. We gather here with love and concern, and our similar experiences draw our hearts out to you. You are safe here, and I want to thank you for all you have done to help Brother Reeve be here tonight."

I smiled at him and said, "Thank you."

"Any other questions?" President Patrick asked the group.

Whether it was intended this way or not, the last question made me certain that there would be those who might always raise an eyebrow, always ask if healing was permanent. "How can you be sure that you have changed your behavior?"

Joe was not defensive as he answered simply, "Because of the power of Jesus Christ."

There's no better explanation.

Joseph

We came back into the high council room after a very short wait in the stake president's office to receive the answer.

"Brother Reeve, we are grateful that the Lord has answered our petitions in the affirmative. As of this moment, your full membership is restored to you. Thank you for your obedience to the Lord. We rejoice with you in the Atonement of Jesus Christ. We look forward to working with you in any capacity that the Lord will see fit to call you, now and in the future. Let's close with a word of prayer, then please come to the front of the room so we may each greet you as we leave."

I held on tight to Rachel's hand during the prayer. I was expecting this outcome, but I was not expecting the relief and joy within my soul. I wanted nothing more than to be able to worship and serve Heavenly Father with all the energy of my soul, completely. I wanted to be able to bless others righteously with the gift and power of the priesthood. It was hard to believe that I would actually be able to attend the temple again soon.

Each member of the high council greeted me as they left the room. Many took time to whisper their love and support, noting my humility and sincerity. A few held my gaze and shared that they knew exactly where I was coming from, and they were proud of me.

Aaron, Rachel, and I walked home in the beautiful evening air. We stood by Aaron's car, hugged him, and thanked him for coming. He replied, "Thank you again for asking me to come. This healed my own heart in a lot of ways."

We didn't even get to open the front door—Sarah came running out and threw herself into my arms. We walked inside and told her everything that happened. Rachel went to call Hannah and Abby to tell them the good news, and probably Mary, too, so Sarah and I went into the kitchen for a glass of milk with her freshly baked snickerdoodles.

"These are really good," I said with my mouth full.

"Thanks. I guess I bake cookies when I'm nervous. Or happy. Or bored."

"You can bake me cookies any time you want." I grabbed another. "Sarah, you're amazing. You know that?"

"Why? What are you talking about?"

I tried not to cry while I was eating. "Your love and support for your old dad means more to me than I can say. I'm so glad you've been on this journey with me. I hope you've learned from my mistakes. I know you'll make your own, but I hope this might help you avoid a few of the bigger ones."

"Dad, I love you. Nothing would ever change that. And you're not *that* old."

"You're my favorite daughter. Don't tell the others." We laughed and drank our milk.

Rachel's birthday was at the end of August. I wanted desperately to attend the temple with her for her birthday. She told me that was all she wanted.

The very next evening, I walked into the bishop's office in my suit, white shirt, polished shoes, and tie—I was my mother's son. I extended my hand, but Bishop Hanson ignored it and hugged me. He didn't slap me on the back like guys do—he embraced me like a shepherd who loves his sheep. "I can't tell you how happy I am that you're here tonight," he said to me as he released his grip. We were both tearful.

"I wanted you to be the one to give me my recommend back."

"I'm honored. Have a seat. How did the evening go with the high council?"

"It was a great experience. I felt their love and support. I can say I'm very glad to have gone through this. I've learned a lot."

"I've learned a lot by watching you."

"Thank you."

He clasped his hands and looked into my soul. "Brother Reeve, do you have faith in and a testimony of God, the Eternal Father, His Son, Jesus Christ, and the Holy Ghost?"

It took me a moment to be able to speak. "More than ever." And each subsequent question was a joy to answer. I was right with God. I was right with the Church.

Bishop Hanson cried more tears as he filled out my membership information in the temple recommend book and signed his name. "This is a moment I'm not likely to forget," he said as he passed the book over to me for my signature. He handed me the pen.

"Bishop, I actually have my own pen to use, if you don't mind." I removed my sawdust therapy pen from my pocket. I looked at it and thought of Josh. I looked at it and had flashes of the past year when I'd felt love and acceptance from the people I love. I looked at it and felt redeemed. Reconciled. I wiped away my tears and signed my name on my new temple recommend.

President Patrick was happy to meet us in his office to sign my recommend. He had come in specifically for me. Rachel thanked him repeatedly for his time, and she waited in the foyer for me.

I sat across from him, and he asked me the recommend questions. I couldn't get over the feeling of being renewed in my full church membership. I wasn't proud of myself—I rejoiced in the goodness of Jesus Christ and His boundless love for me.

Two days later, I found myself in the temple with Rachel. She had a family name for me to do. I wanted to take that one person, Dennis Williams, from the baptismal font through the endowment session. Rachel waited for me behind the glass window in the baptistry.

I dressed all in white and walked into the font area. I looked for her and winked. She was beaming. I handed the name to the man at the desk, but he told me they were short on brethren and asked if I could do the baptizing for a small group of people before I got to my family name. I was very happy to say yes. I stepped into the font and helped the first person in. He was a young man, but about my size. I could see why they were anxious for my help. I held out my left forearm, and he held on to it. And then I raised my right arm to the square.

I hadn't done that for a year. A year. My voice cracked as I spoke. "Brother Douglas, having been commissioned of Jesus Christ, I baptize you for and in behalf of…"

I repeated this process a dozen times, and then I was able to be baptized for Rachel's ancestor, Dennis Williams. I personally didn't have the need to be rebaptized, but as I was immersed in the water for Dennis, I hoped he too felt the joy of being entirely cleansed from sin.

Rachel greeted me as I came out of the baptistry. She hugged me and said, "It's been a year since I've seen you put your arm to the square. It made me cry."

We walked upstairs together and then went our separate ways into the dressing rooms. I'd meet her in the chapel after I received the initiatory ordinance for Dennis. There, I heard the same words as never before, and my spirit came alive with thoughts and impressions I hadn't considered. I couldn't wait to tell Rachel.

I got dressed in my white temple clothes quickly so I could join her in the chapel. I had missed my temple clothes. It felt comfortable to be in them again. I walked to the chapel where she was waiting for me, smiling from ear to ear. Purity. My Rachel. The love of my mortal and eternal existence.

During the endowment session, I kept thinking about how much I loved making these covenants on behalf of Dennis Williams. Again, my mind and heart were opened to truths I had known, and I made deeper connections to doctrine and God's plan for His children. For me.

Rachel greeted me in the celestial room. Words could not express how blessed I felt to be there. We sat quietly for a while, and then we began to whisper about the things we had learned during the session. After a few minutes, I said, "You know, I really want to seal Dennis Williams to his parents today. Are you up for that?"

We got in on a sealing session, and there, Dennis was sealed to his parents. We were also able to kneel across from each other as proxies, remembering the covenants we made with God and each other when we were married. It was a beautiful day.

Happy birthday, Rachel. She told me it was her best birthday ever because she had waited for her husband, and she finally received him.

Joseph

Five Years Later

"Hannah Reeve."

We stood and clapped and cheered as she walked across the stage. My job was again to be the photographer. Between camera clicks, I glanced at Rachel and she was crying, but I knew these were tears of fierce pride and gratitude for the road Hannah was walking. We clapped as Hannah shook the hands of the assistant deans, the dean of the College of Physical and Mathematical Sciences, and the other dignitaries. Her beloved high school chemistry teacher was seated with us and was also cheering and crying.

This day was no small miracle. Hannah battled every day. She found a twelve-step group she liked, and I was honored to be her sponsor. We had a code between us, a scale between 1-10 for temptation's power and an A-Z scale for her feelings of self-worth. She would text me a 2D, and I knew she would be okay for the day. Or she would text me a 9T, and I would drop everything and show up at her doorstep, for a drive or talk or blessing. A couple of times, we would stand in the doorway and just hug. A few times she was a 3Z, and it was that letter that always scared me because I knew what it meant, so I brought her home and Rachel slept on her bed with her.

One day, her tear-stained face peeked out from her covers and asked, "Dad, why won't God take this from me? Why is it gone from your heart and not mine? I have begged and pleaded for the desire to go away. I hate it. I don't want to do it. Why is it always there? You've talked about how you white-knuckled your way through life, and how horrible it was. I'm doing that, Dad. It's exhausting. Why won't God take this away? I have faith that He can, but He won't."

I sat on her bed and held her hand. "I don't know. I don't know. Maybe He needs you to be sympathetic to others in this situation, and He's helping you to understand them. Maybe He wants you to learn patience. Maybe He wants you to understand faith before the miracle. I don't know. Some people are never cured. It never goes away. It's like diabetes, and it's just something you end up living with. Maybe you're like the Apostle Paul and it's your thorn in the flesh to keep you humble. I don't know. Most of the time, there is no answer to the question 'why?' But Hannah, this I know—your weaknesses don't have to threaten your peaceable walk. They just make you choose your steps more mindfully. But you can still have peace through your afflictions. In fact, it's an opportunity to access the Savior's power every day."

"I'm sure this is a curse. I'm sure it means He hasn't forgiven me."

"No, Hannah. It very much means that He loves you and trusts you to walk this path. Keep walking. I know it's exhausting. Keep walking."

What I wouldn't do to take this from her. But... I would never take away something that would drive her to her knees and lead her straight to her Savior.

Questions

1. The main characters have biblical names. What does this help you know about them?
2. Why did Joseph have to assume a different name?
3. What do you consider hypocritical behavior?
4. The reactions of Joseph's congregation, Rachel's sister (Mary), Joe's brother (Aaron), and their friends (like Josh and Jesse) were true in the real-life experience. What kind of impact can you personally make in the life of someone who is struggling with temptation or betrayal? How can you support family members who are being affected? What is true friendship?
5. How is trust developed? How is that different from forgiveness?
6. Do you think change can be permanent? Do you believe that Joseph's desire to sin truly went away? Will Hannah's?
7. How do you feel about Joe and Rachel telling their children?
8. The healing process is bumpy for everyone. Joseph and Rachel both made mistakes along the way. What were those mistakes?
9. Joseph and Rachel learned to have constructive painful conversations, meaning they tried to listen without being defensive, and to share their feelings without blame. How can you be better at having painful conversations? How can you develop healthy communication in your relationships? How can that help you endure hardships? Can that prevent future catastrophes?

Frequently Asked Questions, Answered by Randy

Question: Randy, your wife has just written an incredibly personal book based on your life. How do you feel about that? Has writing this book been cathartic for you and your wife?

Answer: The core of this story is not pornography addiction or infidelity. The core of this book is that a life of self-loathing and numbing with a drug of choice (like dopamine) can be turned around by the merciful and infinite atonement of Jesus Christ. Whether your particular drug of choice—or more accurately, the delivery method of your drug of choice—is illegal, immoral, or just unhealthy, it is a weakness given to you by design to help you humble yourself before the Savior of your soul. It is a powerful opportunity He uses to transform you from weakness and turmoil to peace and hope.

The process of metabolizing our pain was a combination of raw and unpolished experiences. Well before the writing of this story, Elin wrote the non-fictional, journal-type version of our story while both of us worked through our thoughts and feelings. Like this story, it detailed how we leaned on the Savior's love to resolve the feelings of pain and betrayal and move forward together. So our healing happened long before this book. This book is about sharing God's love with others who need a positive example.

I have read each revision of this book. We have conferred and agreed on all of it. Much like Joe and Rachel, we discuss everything. Of course I am aware of what is in the book and how raw and vulnerable it is. I feel it is important to be honest to the emotions. This is our experience, and to make it "Pollyanna-ish" to spare embarrassment would be disingenuous to the struggle so many people experience.

Question: This is a fictional book "based on a real-life story." What parts are true?

Answer: The underlying experiences of the book are true. Timelines, names, and dates have been changed to protect those who are involved. We absolutely didn't want to cause harm or injury to anyone else who was involved, so many things have been written in such a way to respect and protect identities. A few fictional characters have been added as a composite of real-life experiences that either happened to us or were expressed to us by others. Beyond that, we have decided not to discuss what specifically is or isn't true (with the exception of the next question).

This story is not intended as a how-to manual for conquering addiction or infidelity, but the principles here are universally applicable. As you seek inspiration for exactly how you should find happiness in Christ, you may be led in a different direction. If anyone goes away from this book saying, "See, his healing was quick. What's wrong with me?" or "I should stay in this bad situation because she stayed," perhaps you should read it again.

Question: Is "Hannah" okay?

Answer: Specifically, Hannah and Tom are fictional characters, and do not correspond to any members of our family. They were created to represent different experiences and reactions.

Question: Why is your story unique?

Answer: Maybe the most unique part of the story is how quickly I jettisoned my pride. Many real-life stories don't have a happy resolution because of an unwillingness to be vulnerable and humble. That compounds the pain and agony for everyone. I have done a lot of work and study about shame and vulnerability, including works by Brene Brown, which I recommend.

Other than that, it's not that unique—I just don't think there are many who are willing to share it. But I know there are *many* who go through it! Both men and women can be victims and/or perpetrators. Satan's destructive voice tells us to hide because perfection is ideal and human frailty is shameful. I strongly believe that hiding and silently fighting for deliverance is spiritually and emotionally damaging. But bringing it into the light, seeking support, and rejoicing in the miracles that God performs every day in the hearts of His children are the tried-and-true ways to combat this insidious, destructive cycle.

Question: Why did you put your names on this?

Answer: Initially, we talked about publishing under a pen name. But this book is about facing the truth and having hard conversations. How could we encourage readers to bring themselves from a place of shame toward the light of God if we hid?

Some of our friends and family have begged us not to use our real names. "If that is part of your past, why do you now want to publicize it and attach your name to the worst thing he's ever done? Doesn't that bring more shame to him and your family?" We don't see it that way. We are done hiding. We are done furthering the idea that this is something to bury. We are stopping the shame cycle. If there is anyone who finds solace and healing in knowing that the miraculous, healing power of the Savior is real and personally applicable, it is worth it.

Question: Many people battle with life-long addictions. How can you say that your change is permanent?

Answer: The key learning of this book is that I'm a noble son of God. The power of the Atonement of Jesus Christ can replace a diseased heart with a new heart. This doesn't eradicate temptation, struggles, or weaknesses, but I have been led to His power to deal with it. There are many instances in the scriptures where people's hearts were changed and they had no more desire to do evil, and those miracles continue today. This I know—my honor was purchased with the blood of my Savior; I'm no longer for sale. But there's no magic about it. I will endure to the end. The daily peaceable walk is real.

Question: Why did you choose therapy instead of a support group?

Answer: Both are valuable. We have friends who have done both of them. The counselor was a personal acquaintance who I felt would be able to help talk me through what I was feeling, and I trusted him to give me mental and emotional tools to deal with my weakness. I knew he would listen to me, help me discuss how choices are surrendered to addiction, and how to regain the ability to choose. I know the Church has various 12-step support programs, and I do recommend them, but choosing this counselor was the right fit for me at the time. But I emphasize that this journey is unique for each person.

I can't overstate how incredibly important it was to talk to my brother who had similar experiences. That year, we talked nearly every day. He was firmly rooted in the gospel and always talked about the healing power of the Atonement. He passed away just as this book was going to press, and I am deeply grateful for his wisdom and compassion.

Question: What were the most important components of your healing? Of your family's healing?

Answer: One of the most important things the Savior taught me that year was that I am not broken. For all my life, I had thought I was a reject, when in reality, the weaknesses were given to me by divine design—purposefully and specifically—to bring me to my knees to come back to Him. Some philosophies are that the addicted person requires extensive external scaffolding to support him and hold him up for the purpose of avoiding the weakness. The amount of power offered by the Atonement of Jesus Christ to change my very nature gives me the strength to stand in His light. But all the components He sent to bless me (an incredible best friend and wife who was dedicated to communicating openly and honestly with me, an in-tune brother, a patient and forgiving family, an understanding bishop, a non-judging ward family and neighborhood, a good counselor, and wonderful friends) were critical to my success.

For Elin and our children, being able to talk about it openly was helpful. Therapy, emotional and spiritual support systems, and medical intervention has been important through the years of healing.

From the beginning of our relationship, we have tried not to react with blame, defensiveness, sarcasm, or vindictiveness. This became essential so that we could communicate and relate on a deeper level.

Question: Did this experience change your relationship with your extended family, your friends, and your ward?

Answer: Initially, it probably did. We told our extended family and there was shock, and probably a lot of disappointment. But they were incredibly supportive. It was a little weird the first time we were together. But the more normal I acted, the more normal it was. I'm sure they followed Elin's lead. There were many who would've picked up pitchforks in her defense. But they could see my sincere desire to change, and see her belief in me, and they were supportive and loving of us both. The examples in the book of my experiences at church are accurate. I didn't ever feel shunned or ostracized, but part of that is because I made a choice not to.

Question: Being disfellowshipped or excommunicated is an emotional subject. (Note: The current terminology is a membership council, which may result in membership restrictions or withdrawal.) What advice do you have for those who have gone through Church membership councils?

Answer: A good place to start is to understand the basic gospel principle upon which all the various Church councils function. From those I have talked to specifically about membership councils, the reactions of those on the membership council and in leadership may vary. Although they seek for God's guidance and inspiration, they are men with their own experiences and emotions. The process is important, but instead of letting others' attitudes determine your direction, focus on turning to the Savior and being reconciled with God. As the book says, you are enrolled in a one-on-one course with the Savior. Let Him teach you. Feel His love and guidance. Be humble. Having my membership obligations removed for a season helped me focus on having the Savior's peace in my life. This period is not meant for seclusion. I searched for and acted on opportunities to love and serve my neighbors and family.

I love this scripture from Micah 7, starting in verse 8:

> Rejoice not against me, O mine enemy: when I fall, I shall arise; when I sit in darkness, the Lord shall be a light unto me. I will bear the indignation of the Lord, because I have sinned against him, until he plead my cause, and execute judgment for me: he will bring me forth to the light, and I shall behold his righteousness. … Who is a God like unto thee, that pardoneth iniquity, and passeth by the transgression of the remnant of his heritage? he retaineth not his anger for ever, because he delighteth in mercy. He will turn again, he will have compassion upon us; he will subdue our iniquities; and thou wilt cast all their sins into the depths of the sea.

Acknowledgements

I feel a little like I'm at the Oscars, pulling out my paper to thank a million people but the music starts playing.

Randy listened to a thousand ideas and was gracious about them all. What an amazing man to let me use his story as a basis for fiction. Thank you, Randy, for walking through all of those feelings again.

Thanks a million to my helpful readers (a few read it multiple times!) in all my drafts: Kayla, Courtney, Tamara and David, Tom and Tamara, Diana, Jean, Gina, Patrice, Brooke and Stephen, Rachael and Ismael, Clark and Debbie, Jon and Lindsey, Dayna, Barb, Jan, Ashley, Mary, Lori, Scott, Kelly, Sacha, the other Kelly, Emma, Jim, and Janey. Thank you to Tristi Pinkston who edited it when I neared the finish line. Thanks to my gals who crossed the finish line with me.

What a pleasure to work with my niece and friend, Brooke Whipple Larson, on her cover design. Alyssa Asplund did the awesome formatting.

Can I say that this experience is both gratifying and terrifying? There is obviously truth in the threads of this story, and going public is a gigantic, planet-sized leap of faith. Please be kind, for you never know the battles that are raging behind smiling eyes.

God is so good. I'm grateful to have eyes to see through the lens of faith.

About the Author

Elin Williams Dastrup grew up in Richfield, Utah, the middle child of wonderful parents. She loves jazz, history, travel, talking with friends, learning new stuff, organizing things, The Book of Mormon, and Diet Dr. Pepper. She and Randy married in 1994 and lived for long stretches in Logan, Utah and Decatur, Illinois before putting down roots in Provo, Utah. Randy and Elin are the parents of two incredible women, and the grandparents of two adorable boys.